A PERSONAL MATTER

KENZABURO OË was born in 1935, in Ose village in Shikoku, Western Japan. His first stories were published in 1957, while he was still a student. In 1958 he won the coveted Akutagawa prize for his novella *The Catch*. His first novel was published in 1958—*Pluck the Flowers, Gun the Kids*. In 1959 the publication of a novel, *Our Age,* brought the critics down on Oë's head: they deplored the dark pessimism of the book at a time supposed to be the new, bright epoch in modern Japanese history. During the anti-security riots in 1960, Oë traveled to Peking, representing young Japanese writers and there met with Mao.

In 1961, he traveled in Russia and Western Europe, meeting with Sartre in Paris and writing a series of essays about youth in the West. In 1962 he published the novel *Screams*; in 1963, *The Perverts*, and a book memorializing Hiroshima called simply, *Hiroshima Notes*. In 1964, Oë published two novels, *Adventures in Daily Life* and *A Personal Matter*, for which he won the Shinchosha Literary Prize. In the summer of 1965 he participated in the Kissinger International Seminar at Harvard. Oë's novel *Football in the First Year of Mannen*, completed in 1967, won the Tanizaki Prize. In 1977, Grove Press published his *Teach Us To Outgrow Our Madness: Four Short Novels.*

Oë lives in Tokyo with his wife and children.

Also by Kenzaburo Oë

Published by Grove Press

Teach Us To Outgrow Our Madness: Four Short Novels

A
PERSONAL
MATTER

by Kenzaburo Oë

Translated from the Japanese by John Nathan

GROVE PRESS, INC., New York

Originally published as *Kojinteki Na Taiken*, copyright Kenzaburo Oë, 1964, by Shinchosa, Tokyo, Japan

First Evergreen Edition 1982
First Printing 1982
ISBN: 0-394-17650-2
Library of Congress Catalog Card Number: 68-22007

Manufactured in the United States of America

GROVE PRESS, INC., 196 West Houston Street, New York, N.Y. 10014

This translation is for "Pooh"

Translator's Note

THERE is a tradition in Japan: no one takes a writer seriously while he is still in school. Perhaps the only exception has been Kenzaburo Oë. In 1958, a student in French Literature at Tokyo University, Oë won the Akutagawa Prize for a novella called *The Catch* (about a ten-year-old Japanese boy who is betrayed by a Negro pilot who has been shot down over his village), and was proclaimed the most promising writer to have appeared since Yukio Mishima.

Last year, to mark his first decade as a writer, Oë's collected works were published—two volumes of essays, primarily political (Oë is an uncompromising spokesman for the New Left of Japan), dozens of short stories, and eight novels, of which the most recent is *A Personal Matter*. Oë's industry is dazzling. But even more remarkable is his popularity, which has continued to climb: to date, the *Complete Works*, in six volumes, has sold nine hundred thousand copies. The key to Oë's popularity is his sensitivity to the very special predicament of the postwar generation; he is as important as he is because he has provided that generation with a hero of its own.

On the day the Emperor announced the Surrender in August 1945, Oë was a ten-year-old boy living in a mountain village. Here is how he recalls the event:

"The adults sat around their radios and cried. The children gathered outside in the dusty road and whispered their bewilderment. We were most confused and disappointed by the fact that the Emperor had spoken in a *human* voice, no different from any adult's. None of us understood what he was saying, but we all had heard his voice. One of my friends could even imitate it cleverly. Laughing, we surrounded him—a twelve-year-old in grimy shorts who spoke with the Emperor's voice. A minute later we felt afraid. We looked at one another; no one spoke. How could we believe that an august presence of such awful power had become an ordinary human being on a designated summer day?"

Small wonder that Oë and his generation were bewildered. Throughout the war, a part of each day in every Japanese school was devoted to a terrible litany. The Ethics teacher would call the boys to the front of the class and demand of them one by one what they would do if the Emperor commanded them to die. Shaking with fright, the child would answer: "I would die, Sir, I would rip open my belly and die." Students passed the Imperial portrait with their eyes to the ground, afraid their eyeballs would explode if they looked His Imperial Majesty in the face. And Kenzaburo Oë had a recurring dream in which the Emperor swooped out of the sky like a bird, his body covered with white feathers.

The emblematic hero of Oë's novels, in each book a little older and more sensible of his distress, has been deprived of his ethical inheritance. The values that regulated life in the world he knew as a child, however fatally, were blown to smithereens at the end of the war. The crater that remained is a gaping crater still, despite imported filler like Democracy. It is the emptiness and enervation of life in such a world, the frightening absence of continuity, which drive Oë's hero beyond the frontiers of respectability into the wilderness of sex and violence and political fanaticism. Like Huckleberry Finn—Oë's favorite book!—he is impelled again and again to "light out for the territory." He is an adventurer in quest of peril, which seems to be the only solution to the deadly void back home. More often than not he finds what he is looking for, and it destroys him.

A word about the language of *A Personal Matter*. Oë's style has been the subject of much controversy in Japan. It treads a thin line between artful rebellion and mere unruliness. That is its excitement and the reason why it is so very difficult to translate. Oë consciously interferes with the tendency to vagueness which is considered inherent in the Japanese language. He violates its natural rhythms; he pushes the meanings of words to their furthest acceptable limits. In short, he is in the process of evolving a language all his own, a language which can accommodate the virulence of his imagination. There are critics in Japan who take offense. They cry that Oë's prose "reeks of butter," which is a way of saying that he has alloyed the purity of Japanese with constructions from Western languages. It is true that Oë's style assaults traditional notions of what the genius of the language is. But that is to be expected: his entire stance is an assault on traditional values. The protagonist of his fiction is seeking his identity in a perilous wilderness, and it is fitting that his language should be just what it is—wild, unresolved, but never less than vital.

March, 1968

1

B IRD, gazing down at the map of Africa that reposed in the showcase with the haughty elegance of a wild deer, stifled a short sigh. The salesgirls paid no attention, their arms and necks goosepimpled where the uniform blouses exposed them. Evening was deepening, and the fever of early summer, like the temperature of a dead giant, had dropped completely from the covering air. People moved as if groping in the dimness of the subconscious for the memory of midday warmth that lingered faintly in the skin: people heaved ambiguous sighs. June —half-past six: by now not a man in the city was sweating. But Bird's wife lay naked on a rubber mat, tightly shutting her eyes like a shot pheasant falling out of the sky, and while she moaned her pain and anxiety and expectation, her body was oozing globes of sweat.

Shuddering, Bird peered at the details of the map. The ocean surrounding Africa was inked in the teary blue of a winter sky at dawn. Longitudes and latitudes were not the mechanical lines of a compass: the bold strokes evoked the artist's unsteadiness and caprice. The continent itself resembled the skull of a man who had hung his head. With doleful, downcast eyes, a man with a huge head was gazing at Australia, land of the koala, the platypus, and the kangaroo. The miniature Africa indicating population distribution in a lower corner of the map was like a dead head beginning to decompose; another, veined with transportation routes, was a skinned head with the capillaries painfully exposed. Both these little Africas suggested unnatural death, raw and violent.

"Shall I take the atlas out of the case?"

"No, don't bother," Bird said. "I'm looking for the Michelin road maps of West Africa and Central and South Africa." The girl bent over

1

a drawer full of Michelin maps and began to rummage busily. "Series number 182 and 185," Bird instructed, evidently an old Africa hand.

The map Bird had been sighing over was a page in a ponderous, leather-bound atlas intended to decorate a coffee table. A few weeks ago he had priced the atlas, and he knew it would cost him five months' salary at the cram-school where he taught. If he included the money he could pick up as a part-time interpreter, he might manage in three months. But Bird had himself and his wife to support, and now the existence on its way into life that minute. Bird was the head of a family!

The salesgirl selected two of the red paperbound maps and placed them on the counter. Her hands were small and soiled, the meagerness of her fingers recalled chameleon legs clinging to a shrub. Bird's eye fell on the Michelin trademark beneath her fingers: the toadlike rubber man rolling a tire down the road made him feel the maps were a silly purchase. But these were maps he would put to an important use.

"Why is the atlas open to the Africa page?" Bird asked wistfully. The salesgirl, somehow wary, didn't answer. Why *was* it always open to the Africa page? Did the manager suppose the map of Africa was the most beautiful page in the book? But Africa was in a process of dizzying change that would quickly outdate any map. And since the corrosion that began with Africa would eat away the entire volume, opening the book to the Africa page amounted to advertising the obsoleteness of the rest. What you needed was a map that could never be outdated because political configurations were settled. Would you choose America, then? North America, that is?

Bird interrupted himself to pay for the maps, then moved down the aisle to the stairs, passing with lowered eyes between a potted tree and a corpulent bronze nude. The nude's bronze belly was smeared with oil from frustrated palms: it glistened wetly like a dog's nose. As a student, Bird himself used to run his fingers across this belly as he passed; today he couldn't find the courage even to look the statue in the face. Bird had glimpsed the doctor and the nurses scrubbing their arms with disinfectant next to the table where his wife had been lying naked. The doctor's arms were matted with hair.

Bird carefully slipped his maps into his jacket pocket and pressed them against his side as he pushed past the crowded magazine counter and headed for the door. These were the first maps he had purchased for actual use in Africa. Uneasily he wondered if the day would ever come when he actually set foot on African soil and gazed through dark sunglasses at the African sky. Or was he losing, this very minute, once and for all, any chance he might have had of setting out for Africa? Was he being forced to say good-by, in spite of himself, to the single and final occasion of dazzling tension in his youth? And what if I am? There's not a thing in hell I can do about it!

Bird angrily pushed through the door and stepped into the early summer evening street. The sidewalk seemed bound in fog: it was the filthiness of the air and the fading evening light. Bird paused to gaze at himself in the wide, darkly shadowed display window. He was aging with the speed of a short-distance runner. Bird, twenty-seven years and four months old. He had been nicknamed "Bird" when he was fifteen, and he had been Bird ever since: the figure awkwardly afloat like a drowned corpse in the inky lake of window glass still resembled a bird. He was small and thin. His friends had begun to put on weight the minute they graduated from college and took a job—even those who stayed lean had fattened up when they got married; but Bird, except for the slight paunch on his belly, remained as skinny as ever. He slouched forward when he walked and bunched his shoulders around his neck; his posture was the same when he was standing still. Like an emaciated old man who once had been an athlete.

It wasn't only that his hunched shoulders were like folded wings, his features in general were birdlike. His tan, sleek nose thrust out of his face like a beak and hooked sharply toward the ground. His eyes gleamed with a hard, dull light the color of glue and almost never displayed emotion, except occasionally to shutter open as though in mild surprise. His thin, hard lips were always stretched tightly across his teeth; the lines from his high cheekbones to his chin described a sharply pointed V. And hair licking at the sky like ruddy tongues of flame. This was a fair description of Bird at fifteen: nothing had changed at twenty. How long would he continue to look like a bird? No choice but living with the same face and posture from fifteen to sixty-five, was he that kind of person? Then the image he was observing in the window glass was a composite of his entire life. Bird shuddered, seized with disgust so palpable it made him want to vomit. What a revelation: exhausted, with a horde of children, old, senile Bird. . . .

Suddenly a woman with a definitely peculiar quality rose out of the dim lake in the window and slowly moved toward Bird. She was a large woman with broad shoulders, so tall that her face topped the reflection of Bird's head in the glass. Feeling as though a monster were stalking him from behind, Bird finally wheeled around. The woman stopped in front of him and peered into his face gravely. Bird stared back. A second later, he saw the hard, pointed urgency in her eyes washing away in the waters of mournful indifference. Though she may not have known its precise nature, the woman had been on the verge of discovering a bond of mutual interest, and had realized abruptly that Bird was not an appropriate partner in the bond. In the same moment, Bird perceived the abnormality in her face which, with its frame of curly, overabundant hair, reminded him of a Fra Angelico angel: he noticed in particular the blond hairs which a razor had missed on her upper lip. The hairs had breached a wall of thick make-up and they were quivering as though distressed.

"Hey!" said the large woman in a resounding male voice. The greeting conveyed consternation at her own rash mistake. It was a charming thing to say.

"Hey!" Bird hurried his face into a smile and returned the greeting in the somewhat hoarse, squawky voice that was another of his birdlike attributes.

The transvestite executed a half-turn on his high heels and walked slowly down the street. For a minute Bird watched him go, then walked away in the other direction He cut through a narrow alley and cautiously, warily started across a wide street fretted with trolley tracks. Even the hysterical caution which now and then seized Bird with the violence of a spasm evoked a puny bird half-crazed with fear—the nickname was a perfect fit.

That queen saw me watching my reflection in the window as if I were waiting for someone, and he mistook me for a pervert. A humiliating mistake, but inasmuch as the queen had recognized her error the minute Bird had turned around, Bird's honor had been redeemed. Now he was enjoying the humor of the confrontation. *Hey!*—no greeting could have been better suited to the occasion; the queen must have had a good head on his shoulders.

Bird felt a surge of affection for the young man masquerading as a large woman. Woud he succeed in turning up a pervert tonight and making him a pigeon? Maybe I should have found the courage to go with him myself.

Bird was still imagining what might have happened had he gone off with the young man to some crazy corner of the city, when he gained the opposite sidewalk and turned into a crowded street of cheap bars and restaurants. We would probably lie around naked, as close as brothers, and talk. I'd be naked too so he wouldn't feel any awkwardness. I might tell him my wife was having a baby tonight, and maybe I'd confess that I've wanted to go to Africa for years, and that my dream of dreams has been to write a chronicle of my adventures when I got back called *Sky Over Africa*. I might even say that going off to Africa alone would become impossible if I got locked up in the cage of a family when the baby came (I've been in the cage ever since my marriage but until now the door has always seemed open; the baby on its way into the world may clang that door shut). I'd talk about all kinds of things, and the queen would take pains to pick up the seeds of everything that's threatening me, one by one he'd gather them in, and certainly he would understand. Because a youth who tries so hard to be faithful to the warp in himself that he ends up searching the street in drag for perverts, a young man like that must have eyes and ears and a heart exquisitely sensitive to the fear that roots in the backlands of the subconscious.

Tomorrow morning we might have shaved together while we listened to the news on the radio, sharing a soap dish. That queen was young but his beard seemed heavy and . . . Bird cut the chain of fantasy and smiled. Spending a night together might be going too far, but at least he should have invited the young man for a drink. Bird was on a street lined with cheap, cozy bars: the crowd sweeping him along was full of drunks. His throat was dry and he wanted a drink, even if he had to have it alone. Pivoting his head swiftly on his long, lean neck, he inspected the bars on both sides of the street. In fact, he had no intention of stopping in any of them. Bird could imagine how his mother-in-law would react if he arrived at the bedside of his wife and newborn child, reeking of whisky. He didn't want his parents-in-law to see him in the grip of alcohol: not again.

Bird's father-in-law lectured at a small private college now, but he had been the chairman of the English department at Bird's university until he had retired. It was thanks not so much to good luck as to his father-in-law's good will that Bird had managed at his age to get a teaching job at a cram-school. He loved the old man, and he was in awe of him. Bird had never encountered an elder with quite his father-in-law's largesse; he didn't want to disappoint him all over again.

Bird married in May when he was twenty-five, and that first summer he stayed drunk for four weeks straight. He suddenly began to drift on a sea of alcohol, a besotted Robinson Crusoe. Neglecting all his obligations as a graduate student, his job, his studies, discarding everything without a thought, Bird sat all day long and until late every night in the darkened kitchen of his apartment, listening to records and drinking whisky. It seemed to him now, looking back on those terrible days, that with the exception of listening to music and drinking and immersing in harsh, drunken sleep, he hadn't engaged in a single living human activity. Four weeks later Bird had revived from an agonizing seven-hundred-hour drunk to discover in himself, wretchedly sober, the desolation of a city ravaged by the fires of war. He was like a mental incompetent with only the slightest chance of recovery, but he had to tame all over again not only the wilderness inside himself, but the wilderness of his relations to the world outside. He withdrew from graduate school and asked his father-in-law to find him a teaching position. Now, two years later, he was waiting for his wife to have their first child. Let him appear at the hospital having sullied his blood with the poisons of alcohol once again and his mother-in-law would flee as if the hounds of hell were at her heels, dragging her daughter and grandchild with her.

Bird himself was wary of the craving, occult but deeply rooted, that he still had for alcohol. Often since those four weeks in whisky hell he had asked himself why he had stayed drunk for seven hundred hours, and never had he arrived at a conclusive answer. So long as his descent into the abyss of whisky remained a riddle, there was a constant danger he might suddenly return.

In one of the books about Africa he read so avidly, Bird had come across this passage: "The drunken revels which explorers invariably remark are still common in the African village today. This suggests that life in this beautiful country is still lacking something fundamental. Basic dissatisfactions are still driving the African villagers to despair and self-abandon." Rereading the passage, which referred to the tiny villages in the Sudan, Bird realized he had been avoiding a consideration of the lacks and dissatisfactions that were lurking in his own life.

But they existed, he was certain, so he was careful to deny himself alcohol.

Bird emerged in the square at the back of the honky-tonk district, where the clamor and motion seemed to focus. The clock of lightbulbs on the theater in the center of the square was flashing SEVEN PM—time to ask about his wife. Bird had been telephoning his mother-in-law at the hospital every hour since three that afternoon. He glanced around the square. Plenty of public telephones, but all were occupied. The thought, not so much of his wife in labor as of his mother-in-law's nerves as she hovered over the telephone reserved for in-patients, irritated him. From the moment she had arrived at the hospital with her daughter, the woman had been obsessed with the idea that the staff was trying to humiliate her. If only some other patient's relative were on the phone. . . . Lugubriously hopeful, Bird retraced his steps, glancing into bars and coffee houses, Chinese noodle shops, cutlet restaurants, and shoestores. He could always step inside somewhere and phone. But he wanted to avoid a bar if he could, and he had eaten dinner already. Why not buy a powder to settle his stomach?

Bird was looking for a drugstore when an outlandish establishment on a corner stopped him short. On a giant billboard suspended above the door, a cowboy crouched with a pistol flaming. Bird read the legend that flowered on the head of the Indian pinned beneath the cowboy's spurs: GUN CORNER. Inside, beneath paper flags of the United Nations and strips of spiraling green and yellow crepe paper, a crowd much younger than Bird was milling around the many-colored, box-shaped games that filled the store from front to back. Bird, ascertaining through the glass doors rimmed with red and indigo tape that a public telephone was installed in a corner at the rear, stepped into the Gun Corner, passed a Coke machine and a juke box howling rock-n-roll already out of vogue, and started across the muddy wooden floor. It was instantly as if skyrockets were bursting in his ears. Bird toiled across the room as though he were walking in a maze, past pinball machines, dart games, and a miniature forest alive with deer and rabbits and monstrous green toads that moved on a conveyor belt; as Bird passed, a high-school boy bagged a frog under the admiring eyes of his girlfriends and five points clicked into the window on the side of the game. He finally reached the telephone. Dropping a coin into the phone, he dialed the hospital number from memory. In one ear he heard the distant ringing of the phone, the blare of rock-n-roll filled the other, and a noise like ten thousand scuttling crabs: the high teens, rapt over their automated toys, were scuffling the wooden floor with the soft-as-glove-leather soles of their Italian shoes. What would his mother-in-law think of this din? Maybe he should say something about the noise when he excused himself for calling late.

The phone rang four times before his mother-in-law's voice, like his wife's made somewhat younger, answered; Bird immediately asked about his wife, without apologizing for anything.

"Nothing yet. It just won't come; that child is suffering to death and the baby just won't come!"

Wordless, Bird stared for an instant at the numberless antholes in the ebonite receiver. The surface, like a night sky vaulted with black stars, clouded and cleared with each breath he took.

"I'll call back at eight," he said a minute later, then hung up the phone, and sighed.

A drive-a-car game was installed beside the phone, and a boy who looked like a Filipino was seated behind the wheel. Beneath a miniature E-type Jaguar mounted on a cylinder in the center of the board, a painted belt of country scenery revolved continuously, making the car appear to speed forever down a marvelous suburban highway. As the road wound on, obstacles constantly materialized to menace the little car: sheep, cows, girls with children in tow. The player's job was to avoid collisions by cutting the wheel and swiveling the car atop its cylinder. The Filipino was hunched over the wheel in a fury of concentration, deep creases in his short, swarthy brow. On and on he drove, biting his thin lips shut with keen eyeteeth and spraying the air with sibilant saliva, as if convinced that finally the belt would cease to revolve and bring the E-type Jaguar to its destination. But the road unfurled obstacles in front of the little car unendingly. Now and then, when the belt began to slow down, the Filipino would plunge a hand into his pants pocket, grope out a coin, and insert it in the metal eye of the machine. Bird paused where he stood obliquely behind the boy, and watched the game for a while. Soon a sensation of unbearable fatigue crept into his feet. Bird hurried toward the back exit, stepping as though the floor were scorching metal plate. At the back of the gallery, he encountered a pair of truly bizarre machines.

The game on the right was surrounded by a gang of youngsters in identical silk jackets embroidered with gold-and-silver brocade drag-ons, the Hong Kong souvenir variety designed for American tourists. They were producing loud, unfamiliar noises that sounded like heavy impacts. Bird approached the game on the left, because for the moment it was unguarded. It was a medieval instrument of torture, an Iron Maiden—twentieth-century model. A beautiful, life-sized maiden of steel with mechanical red-and-black stripes was protecting her bare chest with stoutly crossed arms. The player attempted to pull her arms away from her chest for a glimpse of her hidden metal breasts; his grip and pull appeared as numbers in the windows which were the maiden's eyes. Above her head was a chronological table of average grip and pull.

Bird inserted a coin in the slot between the maiden's lips. Then he set about forcing her arms away from her breasts. The steel arms resisted stubbornly: Bird pulled harder. Gradually his face was drawn in to her iron chest. Since her face was painted in what was unmistakably an expression of anguish, Bird had the feeling he was raping the girl. He strained until every muscle in his body began to ache. Suddenly there was a rumbling in her chest as a gear turned, and numbered plaques, the color of watery blood, clicked into her hollow eyes. Bird went limp, panting, and checked his score against the table of averages. It was unclear what the units represented, but Bird had scored 70 points for grip and 75 points for pull. In the column on the table beneath 27, Bird found GRIP: 110—PULL: 110. He scanned the table in disbelief and discovered that his score was average for a man of forty. *Forty!*—the shock dropped straight to his stomach and he brought up a belch. Twenty-seven years and four months old and no more grip nor pull than a man of forty: Bird! But how could it be? On top of everything, he could tell that the tingling in his shoulders and sides would develop into an obstinate muscle ache. Determined to redeem his honor, Bird approached the game on the right. He realized with surprise that he was now in deadly earnest about this game of testing strength.

With the alertness of wild animals whose territory is being invaded, the boys in dragon jackets froze as Bird moved in, and enveloped him with challenging looks. Rattled, but with a fair semblance of careless-ness, Bird inspected the machine at the center of their circle. In construction it resembled a gallows in a Western movie, except that a kind of Slavic cavalry helmet was suspended from the spot where a hapless outlaw should have hung. The helmet only partly concealed a sandbag covered in black buckskin. When a coin was inserted in the hole that glared like a cyclops' eye from the center of the helmet, the player could lower the sandbag and the indicator needle reset itself at zero. There was a cartoon of Robot Mouse in the center of the indicator: he was screaming, his yellow mouth open wide, *C'mon Killer! Let's Measure Your Punch!*

When Bird merely eyed the game and made no move in its direction, one of the dragon-jackets stepped forward as if to demonstrate, dropped a coin into the helmet, and pulled the sandbag down. Self-consciously but confident, the youth dropped back a step and, hurling his entire body forward as in a dance, walloped the sandbag. A heavy thud: the rattle of the chain as it crashed against the inside of the helmet. The needle leaped past the numbers on the gauge and quivered meaning-lessly. The gang exploded in laughter. The punch had exceeded the capacity of the gauge: the paralyzed mechanism would not reset. The triumphant dragon-jacket aimed a light kick at the sandbag, this time from a karate crouch, and the indicator needle dropped to 500 while the sandbag crawled back into the helmet slowly like an exhausted hermit crab. Again the gang roared.

An unaccountable passion seized Bird. Careful not to wrinkle the maps, he took off his jacket and laid it on a bingo table. Then he dropped into the helmet one of the coins from a pocketful he was carrying for phone calls to the hospital. The boys were watching every move. Bird lowered the sandbag, took one step back, and put up his fists. After he had been expelled from high school, in the days when he was studying for the examination that had qualified him to go to college, Bird had brawled almost every week with other delinquents in his provincial city. He had been feared, and he had been surrounded always be younger admirers. Bird had faith in the power of his punch. And his form would be orthodox, he wouldn't take that kind of ungainly leap. Bird shifted his weight to the balls of his feet, took one light step forward, and smashed the sandbag with a right jab. Had his punch surpassed the limit of 2500 and made a cripple of the gauge? Like hell it had—the needle stood at 300! Doubled over, with his punching fist against his chest, Bird stared for an instant at the gauge in stupefaction. Then hot blood climbed into his face. Behind him the boys in dragon jackets were silent and still. But certainly their attention was concentrated on Bird and on the gauge; the appearance of a man with a punch so numerically meager must have struck them dumb.

Bird, moving as though unaware the gang existed, returned to the helmet, inserted another coin, and pulled the sandbag down. This was no time to worry about correct form: he threw the weight of his entire body behind the punch. His right arm went numb from the elbow to the wrist and the needle stood at a mere 500.

Stooping quickly, Bird picked up his jacket and put it on, facing the bingo table. Then he turned back to the teen-agers, who were observing him in silence. Bird tried for an experienced smile, full of understanding and surprise, for the young champ from the former champion long retired. But the boys merely stared at him with blank, hardened faces, as though they were watching a dog. Bird turned crimson all the way behind his ears, hung his head, and hurried out of the gallery. A great guffawing erupted behind him, full of obviously affected glee.

Dizzy with childish shame, Bird cut across the square and plunged down a dark side street: he had lost the courage to drift with a crowd full of strangers. Whores were positioned along the street, but the rage in Bird's face discouraged them from calling out. Bird turned into an alley where not even whores were lurking, and suddenly he was stopped by a high embankment. He knew by the smell of green leaves in the darkness that summer grass was thick on the slope. On top of the embankment was a train track. Bird peered up and down the track to see whether a train was coming and discovered nothing in the dark. He looked up at the black ink of the sky. The reddish mist hovering above the ground was a reflection of the neon lights in the square. A sudden drop of rain wet Bird's upturned cheek—the grass had been so fragrant because it had been about to rain. Bird lowered his head and, as though for lack of anything else to do, furtively urinated. Before he had finished, he heard chaotic footsteps approaching from behind. By the time he turned around, he was surrounded by the boys in dragon jackets.

With the faint light at their backs, the boys were in heavy shadow, and Bird couldn't make out their expressions. But he remembered their denial of him, thoroughly brutal, that had lurked in their blankness at the Gun Corner. The gang had sighted an existence too feeble, and savage instincts had been roused. Trembling with the need of a violent child to torment a weak playmate, they had raced in pursuit of the pitiful lamb with a punch of 500. Bird was afraid: frantically he searched for a way out. To reach the bright square he would have to rush directly into the gang and break their circle at its strongest point. But with Bird's strength—the grip and pull of a forty-year-old!—that was out of the question: they would easily force him back. To his right was a short alley that dead-ended at a board fence. The narrow alley to his left, between the embankment and a high, wire fence around a factory yard, emerged far on the other side at a busy street. Bird had a chance if he could cover that hundred or so yards without being caught. Resolved, Bird made as if to race for the dead end on his right, wheeled and then charged to the left. But the enemy was expert at this kind of ruse, just as Bird at twenty had been an expert in his own night city. Unfooled, the gang had shifted to the left and regrouped even while Bird was feinting to the right. Bird straightened, and as he hurled himself toward the alley on the left he collided with the black silhouette of a body bent backward like a bow, the same attack the youth had used on the sandbag. No time or room to dodge, Bird took the full force of the worst knock-out punch of his life and fell back onto the embankment. Groaning, he spat saliva and blood. The teen-agers laughed shrilly, as they had laughed when they had paralyzed the punching machine. Then they peered down at Bird silently, enclosing him in an even tighter semicircle. The gang was waiting.

It occurred to Bird that the maps must be getting creased between his body and the ground. And his own child was being born: the thought danced with new poignancy to the frontlines of consciousness. A sudden rage took him, and rough despair. Until now, out of terror and bewilderment, Bird had been contriving only to escape. But he had no intention of running now. If I don't fight now, I'll not only lose the chance to go to Africa forever, my baby will be born into the world solely to lead the worst possible life—it was like the voice of inspiration, and Bird believed.

Raindrops pelted his torn lips. He shook his head, groaned, and slowly rose. The half-circle of teen-agers dropped back invitingly. Then the burliest of the bunch took one confident step forward. Bird let his arms dangle and thrust out his chin, affecting the limp befuddlement of a carnival doll. Taking careful aim, the boy in the jacket lifted one leg high and arched backward like a pitcher going into his windup, then cocked his right arm back as far as it would go and launched forward for the kill. Bird ducked, lowered his head, and drove like a ferocious bull into his attacker's belly. The boy screamed, gagged on vomiting bile, and crumpled silently. Bird jerked his head up and confronted the others. The joy of battle had reawakened in him; it had been years since he had felt it. Bird and the dragon-jackets watched one another without moving, appraising the formidable enemy. Time passed.

Abruptly, one of the boys shouted to the others: "C'mon, let's go! We don't want to fight this guy. He's too fucking old!"

The boys relaxed immediately. Leaving Bird on his guard, they lifted their unconscious comrade and moved away toward the square. Bird was left alone in the rain. A ticklish sense of comedy rose into his throat, and for a minute he laughed silently. There was blood on his jacket, but if he walked in the rain for a while, no one would be able to tell it from water. Bird felt a kind of preliminary peace. Naturally, his chin hurt where the punch had landed, and his arms and back ached; so did his eyes. But he was in high spirits for the first time since his wife's labor had begun. Bird limped down the alley between the embankment and the factory lot. Soon an old-fashioned steam engine spewing fiery cinders came chugging down the track. Passing over Bird's head, the train was a colossal black rhinoceros galloping across an inky sky.

Out on the avenue, as he waited for a cab, Bird probed for a broken tooth with his tongue and spat it into the street.

2

BENEATH the mud- and blood- and bile-streaked map of West Africa thumbtacked to the wall, curled up in a ball like a threatened sow bug, Bird lay sleeping. He was in their bedroom, his and his wife's. The baby's white bassinet, still wrapped in its vinyl hood, crouched like a huge insect between the two beds. Bird was dreaming, groaning in protest against the dawn chill.

He is standing on a plateau on the western bank of Lake Chad, east of Nigeria. What can he be waiting for in such a place? Suddenly he is sighted by a giant phacochoere. The vicious beast charges, churning sand. But that's all right! Bird has come to Africa for adventure, encounters with new tribes and with the perils of death, for a glimpse beyond the horizon of quiescent and chronically frustrated everyday life. But he has no weapon to fight the phacochoere. I've arrived in Africa unequipped and with no training, he thinks, and fear prods him. Meanwhile the phacochoere is bearing down. Bird remembers the switchblade he used to sew inside his pants cuff when he was a delinquent in a provincial city. But he threw those pants away a long time ago. Funny he can't remember the Japanese word for phacochoere. *Phacochoere!* He hears the group that has abandoned him and fled to a safety zone shouting: *Watch out! Run! It's a Phacochoere!* The enraged animal is already at the clump of low brush a few yards away: Bird hasn't a chance of escaping. Then, to the north, he discovers an area protected by an oblique blue line. It must be steel wire; if he can get behind it he may be safe; the people who left him behind are shouting from there. Bird begins to run. Too late! the phacochoere is almost on him. I've come to Africa unequipped and with no training; I cannot escape. Bird despairs, but fear drives him on. Numberless eyes of the *safe people* behind the oblique blue line watch Bird racing toward them.

14

The phacochoere's abominable teeth close sharply, firmly, on Bird's ankle. . . .

The phone was ringing. Bird woke up. Dawn, and raining still. Bird hit the damp floor in his bare feet and hopped to the phone like a rabbit. He lifted the receiver and a man's voice asked his name without a word of greeting and said, "Please come to the hospital right away. The baby is abnormal; the doctor will explain."

Instantly, Bird was stranded. He longed to backtrack to that Nigerian plateau to lick up the dregs of his dream, no matter that it was an evil, sea urchin of a dream, thinly planted with the spines of fear. But he checked himself and, in a voice so objective it might have issued from a stranger with a cast-iron heart, said: "Is the mother all right?" Bird had a feeling he had heard himself asking the same question a thousand times in the same voice.

"Your wife is fine. Please come as quickly as you can."

Bird scuttled back to the bedroom, like a crab making for a ledge. He shut his eyes tight and tried to submerge in the warmth of his bed, as if by denying reality he could instantly banish it. But nothing changed. Bird shook his head in resignation, and picked up his shirt and pants from the side of the bed where he had thrown them. The pain in his body when he bent over recalled the battle the night before. His strength had been equal to the fight, and how proud it had made him! He tried to recapture that feeling of pride, but of course he couldn't. Buttoning his shirt, Bird looked up at the map of West Africa. The plateau in his dream was at a place called Deifa. There was a drawing of a charging wart hog just above it—wart hog! A phacochoere was a wart hog. And the oblique azure line on the map signified a game reserve. So he wouldn't have been safe even if he had reached the slanting fence in his dream.

Bird shook his head again, squirmed into his jacket as he left the bedroom, and tiptoed down the stairs. The old woman who was his landlady lived on the first floor: if she woke up and came into the hall, Bird would have to answer questions honed on the whetstone of her curiosity and good will. But what could he say? So far he had heard only the declaration on the phone: the baby is abnormal! But it was probably as bad as it could be. Bird groped for his shoes on the earth floor in the vestibule, unlocked the front door as quietly as he could, and stepped into the dawn.

The bicycle was lying on its side on the gravel under a hedge. Bird righted it and wiped the tenacious rain off the rotting leather seat with his jacket sleeve. Before the seat was dry, Bird leaped astride and, scattering gravel like an angry horse, pumped past the hedges into the paved street. In an instant his buttocks were chilled and clammy. And it was raining again; the wind drove the rain straight into his face. He kept his eyes wide open, watching for potholes in the street: rain pellets struck his eyeballs. At a broader, brighter street, Bird turned left. Now the wind was whipping the rain into his right side and the going was easier. Bird leaned into the wind to balance the bike. The speeding tires churned the sheet of water on the asphalt street and scattered it like fine mist. As Bird watched the water ripple away from the tires with his body tilted sharply into the wind, he began to feel dizzy. He looked up: no one on the dawn street as far as he could see. The ginkgo trees that hemmed the street were thick and dark with leaves and each of those countless leaves was swollen with the water it had drunk. Black trunks supporting deep oceans of green. If those oceans all at once collapsed, Bird and his bike would be drowned in a raw-green-smelling flood. Bird felt threatened by the trees. High above him, the leaves massed on the topmost branches were moaning in the wind. Bird looked up through the trees at the narrowed eastern sky. Blackish-gray all over, with a faint hint of the sun's pink seeping through at the back. A mean sky that seemed ashamed, roughly violated by clouds like galloping shaggy dogs. A trio of magpies arrowed in front of Bird as brazen as alley cats and nearly toppled him. He saw the silver drops of water bunched like lice on their light-blue tails. Bird noticed that he was startled easily now, and that his eyes and ears and sense of smell had become acutely sensitive. It occurred to him vaguely that this was a bad omen: the same things had happened during those weeks he had stayed drunk.

Lowering his head, Bird raised himself on the pedals and picked up speed. The feeling of futile flight in his dream returned. But he raced on. His shoulder snapped a slender ginkgo branch and the splintered end sprang back and cut his ear. Even so, Bird didn't slow up. Raindrops that whined like bullets grazed his throbbing ear. Bird skidded to a stop at the hospital entrance with a squeal of brakes that might have been his own scream. He was soaking wet: shivering. As he shook the water off, he had the feeling he had sped down a long, unthinkably long, road.

Bird paused in front of the examination room to catch his breath, then peered inside and addressed the indistinct faces waiting for him in the dimness.

"I'm the father," he said hoarsely, wondering why they were sitting in a darkened room. Then he noticed his mother-in-law, her face half-buried in her kimono sleeve as though she were trying not to vomit. Bird sat down in the chair next to her and felt his clothes stick fast to his back and rear. He shivered, not violently as in the driveway, but with the helplessness of a weakened chick. His eyes were adjusting to the darkness in the room: now he discovered a tribunal of three doctors watching in careful silence as he settled himself in the chair. Like the national flag in a courtroom, the colored anatomy chart on the wall behind them was a banner symbolic of their private law.

"I'm the father," Bird repeated irritably. It was clear from his voice that he felt threatened.

"Yes, all right," the doctor in the middle replied somewhat defensively, as if he had detected a note of attack in Bird's voice. (He was the hospital Director; Bird had seen him scrubbing his hands at his wife's side.) Bird looked at the Director, waiting for him to speak. Instead of beginning an explanation, he took a pipe from his wrinkled surgeon's gown and filled it with tobacco. He was a short, barrel of a man, obese to an extreme that gave him an air of dolorous pomposity. The soiled gown was open at his chest, which was as hairy as a camel's back; not only his upper lip and cheeks but even the fatty crop that sagged to his throat was stubbled with beard. The Director had not had time to shave this morning: he had been fighting for the baby's life since yesterday afternoon. Bird was grateful, of course, but something suspicious about this hairy, middle-aged doctor prevented him from letting down his guard. As if, deep beneath that hirsute skin, something potentially lethal was trying to rear its bushy head and was being forcibly restrained.

The Director at last returned the pipe from his thick lips to his bowl of a hand and, abruptly meeting Bird's stare with his own: "Would you like to see the goods first?" His voice was too loud for the small room.

"Is the baby dead?" Bird asked, coughing. For a minute the Director looked suspicious of Bird for having assumed the baby's death, but he erased that impression with an ambiguous smile.

"Certainly not," he said. "The infant's movements are vigorous and its voice strong."

Bird heard his mother-in-law sigh deeply, gravely—it was like a broad hint. Either the woman was exhausted or she was signaling to Bird the approximate depth of the swamp of calamity he and his wife were mired in. One or the other.

"Well then, would you like to see the goods?"

The young doctor on the Director's right stood up. He was a tall man, thin, with eyes that somehow violated the horizontal symmetry of his face. One eye was agitated and timid-looking; the other was serene. Bird had started to rise with the doctor and had slumped back into his chair before he noticed that the beautiful eye was made of glass.

"Could you explain first, please?" Bird sounded increasingly threatened: the revulsion he had felt at the Director's choice of words—the goods!—was still caught in the mesh of his mind.

"That might be better: when you first see it, it's quite a surprise. Even I was surprised when it came out." Unexpectedly, the Director's thick eyelids reddened and he burst into a childish giggle. Bird had sensed a suspicious presence lurking beneath that hairy skin, and now he knew that it was this giggle, this giggle that had revealed itself first in the guise of a vague smile. Bird glared at the giggling doctor in rage before he realized the man was laughing from embarrassment. He had extracted from between the legs of another man's wife a species of monster beyond classification. A monster with a cat's head, maybe, and a body as swollen as a balloon? Whatever the creature was, the Director was ashamed of himself for having delivered it, and so was giggling. His performance, far from befitting the professional dignity of an experienced obstetrician and hospital director, had belonged in a slapstick comedy: a quack doctor routine. The man had been startled and distracted; now he was suffering from shame.

Without moving, Bird waited for the Director to recover from his laughing jag. A monster. But what kind? "The goods," the Director had said, and Bird had heard "monster"; the briars twined around the word had torn the membranes in his thorax. In introducing himself, he had said, "I'm the father," and the doctors had winced. Because something else entirely must have echoed in their ears—*I'm the monster's father*.

The Director quickly mastered himself and regained his mournful dignity. But the pink flush remained on his eyelids and cheeks. Bird looked away, fighting an urgent eddy of anger and fear inside, and said, "What kind of condition is it that it's so surprising?"

"You mean appearance, how it looks? There appear to be two heads! You know a piece by Josef Wagner called 'Under the Double Eagle'? Anyway, it's quite a shock." The Director nearly began to giggle again, but he checked himself just in time.

"Something like the Siamese twins, then?" Bird timidly asked.

"Not at all: there only appear to be two heads. Do you want to see the goods?"

"Medically speaking—" Bird faltered.

"Brain hernia, we call it. The brain is protruding from a fault in the skull. I founded this clinic when I got married, and this is the first case I've seen. Extremely rare. I can tell you I was surprised!"

Brain hernia—Bird groped for an image, anything, and drew a blank. "Is there any hope that this kind of brain-hernia baby will develop normally?" he said in a daze.

"Develop normally!" The Director's voice rose as though in anger. "We're speaking of a brain hernia! You might cut open the skull and force the brain back, but even then you'd be lucky to get some kind of vegetable human being. Precisely what do you mean by 'normally'?" The Director shook his head at the young doctors on either side of him as though dismayed by Bird's lack of common sense. The doctor with the glass eye quickly nodded his agreement, and so did the other, a taciturn man wrapped from his high forehead to his throat in the same expressionless, sallow skin. Both turned stern eyes on Bird—professors disapproving of a student for a poor performance in an oral exam.

"Will the baby die right away?" Bird said.

"Not right away, no. Tomorrow perhaps, or it may hold out even longer. It's an extremely vigorous infant," the Director observed clinically. "Now then, what do you intend to do?"

Disgracefully bewildered, like a punch-drunk pigmy, Bird was silent. What in hell *could* he do? First the man drives you down a blind alley, then he asks what you intend to do. Like a malicious chess player. What *should* he do? Fall to pieces? Wail?

"If you wish, I can have the baby transferred to the hospital at the National University—if you wish!" The offer sounded like a puzzle with a built-in trap. Bird, straining to see beyond the suspicious mist and failing to discover a single clue, was left merely with a futile wariness: "If there are no alternatives—"

"None," the Director said. "But you will have the satisfaction of knowing you have done everything possible."

"Couldn't we just leave the child here?"

Bird as well as the three doctors gawked at the originator of the abrupt question. Bird's mother-in-law sat quite still, the world's most forlorn ventriloquist. The Director inspected her like an appraiser determining a price. When he spoke, it was ugly, he was protecting himself so obviously: "That's impossible! This is a case of brain hernia, don't forget. Quite impossible!" The woman listened without budging, her mouth still buried in her kimono sleeve.

"Then we'll move it to the other hospital," Bird declared. The Director leaped at Bird's decision and he began at once to display a dazzling spectrum of administrative talents. When his two subordinates had left the room under orders to contact the university hospital and make arrangements for an ambulance, the Director filled his pipe again and said with a look of relief, as though he had disposed of a heavy, questionable burden: "I'll have one of our people ride along in the ambulance, so you can be assured we'll get the infant there safely."

"Thank you very much."

"It would be best if our new grandmother stayed here with her daughter. Why don't you go home and change into some dry clothes? The ambulance won't be ready for half an hour."

"I'll do that," Bird said. The Director sidled up to him and whispered, too familiarly, as if he were beginning a dirty joke, "Of course, you can forbid them to operate if you choose to."

Poor wretched little baby! Bird thought.

The first person my baby meets in the real world has to be this hairy porkchops of a little man.

But Bird was still dazed: his feelings of anger and grief, the minute they had crystallized, shattered.

Bird and his mother-in-law and the Director walked in a little group as far as the reception desk, silently, avoiding one another's faces. At the entrance, Bird turned around to say good-by. His mother-in-law returned his gaze with eyes so like his wife's they might have been sisters, and she was trying to say something. Bird waited. But the woman only stared at him in silence, her dark eyes contracting until they were empty of expression. Bird could feel her embarrassment, and it was specific, as though she were standing naked on a public street.

But what could be making her so uncomfortable as to deaden her eyes and even the skin on her face? Bird looked away himself before the woman could lower her gaze, and said to the Director: "Is it a boy or a girl?" The question took the Director off his guard, and he leaked that funny giggle again. Sounding like a young intern: "Let's see now, I can't quite remember, but I have a feeling I saw one, sure I did—a penis!"

Bird went out to the driveway alone. It wasn't raining and the wind had died: the clouds sailing the sky were bright, dry. A brilliant morning had broken from the dawn's cocoon of semidarkness, and the air had a good, first-days-of-summer smell that slackened every muscle in Bird's body. A night softness had lingered in the hospital, and now the morning light, reflecting off the wet pavement and off the leafy trees, stabbed like icicles at Bird's pampered eyes. Laboring into this light on his bike was like being poised on the edge of a diving board; Bird felt severed from the certainty of the ground, isolated. And he was as numb as stone, a weak insect on a scorpion's sting.

You can race this bicycle to a strange land and soak in whisky for a hundred days—Bird heard the voice of a dubious revelation. And as he wobbled down the street, awash in the morning light, he waited for the voice to speak again. But there was only silence. Lethargically, like a sloth on the move, Bird began to pedal. . . .

Bird was bending forward in the breakfast nook for the clean underwear on top of the TV when he saw his arm and realized that he was naked. Swiftly, as though he were pursuing a fleeing mouse with his eyes, he glanced down at his genitals: the heat of shame scorched him. Bird hurried into his underwear and put on his slacks and a shirt. Even now he was a link in the chain of shame that connected his mother-in-law and the Director. Peril-ridden and fragile, the imperfect human body, what a shameful thing it was! Trembling, Bird fled the apartment with his eyes on the floor, fled down the stairs, fled through the hall, straddled his bicycle and fled everything behind him. He woud have liked to flee his own body. Speeding away on a bike, he felt he was escaping himself more effectively than he could on foot, if only a little.

As Bird turned into the hospital driveway, a man in white hurried down the steps with what looked like a hay basket and pushed his way through the crowd to the open tail of an ambulance. The soft, weak part of Bird that wanted to escape tried to apprehend the scene as though it were occurring at a vast remove and had nothing to do with Bird, simply an early morning stroller. But Bird could only advance, struggling like a mole burrowing into an imaginary mud wall through the heavy, viscid resistance that impeded him.

Bird got off his bike and was locking a chain around the front tire when a voice bit into him from behind, terrifying in its disapproval: "You can't leave that bike here!" Bird turned and looked up into the hairy Director's reproving eyes. Hoisting the bike onto his shoulder, he walked into the shrubbery with it. Raindrops clustered on fatsia leaves showered his neck and ran down his back. Ordinarily his temper was quick, but he didn't even click his tongue in irritation. Whatever happened to him now seemed part of an inevitable design which he must accept without protest.

Bird emerged from the bushes with his shoes covered with mud; the Director appeared to regret a little having been so abrupt. Encircling Bird with one short, pudgy arm, he led him toward the ambulance and said emphatically, as though he were disclosing a marvelous secret: "It *was* a boy! I *knew* I'd seen a penis!"

The one-eyed doctor and an anesthetist were sitting in the ambulance with the basket and an oxygen cylinder between them. The anesthetist's back hid the contents of the basket. But the faint hissing noise of oxygen bubbling through water in a flask communicated like a signal from a secret transmitter. Bird lowered himself onto the bench opposite theirs—insecurely perched—there was a canvas stretcher on top of the bench. Shifting his rear uncomfortably, he glanced through the ambulance window and—shuddered. From every window on the second floor and even from the balcony, just out of bed most likely, their freshly washed faces gleaming whitely in the morning sun, pregnant women were peering down at Bird. All of them wore flimsy nylon nightgowns, either red or shades of blue, and those on the balcony in particular, with the nightgowns billowing about their ankles, were like a host of angels dancing on the air. Bird read anxiety in their faces, and expectation, even glee; he lowered his eyes. The siren began to wail, and the ambulance lurched forward. Bird planted his feet on the floor to keep from slipping off the bench and thought: That siren! Until now, a siren had always been a moving object: it approached from a distance, hurtled by, moved away. Now a siren was attached to Bird like a disease he carried in his body: this siren would never recede.

"Everything's fine," said the doctor with the glass eye, turning around to Bird. There was authority in his attitude, mild but evident, and its heat threatened to melt Bird like a piece of candy.

"Thank you," he mumbled. His passivity erased the shadow of hesitation from the doctor's good eye. He took a firm grip on his authority, and thrust it out in front of him: "This is a rare case, all right; it's a first for me, too." The doctor nodded to himself, then nimbly crossed the lurching ambulance and sat down at Bird's side. He didn't seem to notice how uncomfortable the stretcher made the bench.

"Are you a brain specialist?" Bird asked.

"Oh no, I'm an obstetrician." The doctor didn't have to make the correction: his authority was already beyond injury by a misapprehension so minor. "There are no brain men at our hospital. But the symptoms are perfectly clear: it's a brain hernia, all right. Of course, we would know more if we had tapped some spinal fluid from that lump protruding from the skull. The trouble with that is you might just prick the brain itself and then you'd be in trouble. That's why we're taking the baby to the other hospital without touching him. As I said, I'm in obstetrics, but I consider myself fortunate to have run across a case of brain hernia—I hope to be present at the autopsy. You will consent to an autopsy, won't you? It may distress you to talk about autopsies at this point, but, well, look at it this way! Progress in medicine is cumulative, isn't it. I mean, the autopsy we perform on your child may give us just what we need to save the next baby with a brain hernia. Besides, if I may be frank, I think the baby would be better off dead, and so would you and your wife. Some people have a funny way of being optimistic about this kind of case, but it seems to me the quicker the infant dies, the better for all concerned. I don't know, maybe it's the difference in generations. I was born in 1935. How about you?"

"Somewhere around there," Bird said, unable to convert quickly into the Western calendar. "I wonder if it's suffering."

"What, our generation?"

"The baby!"

"That depends on what you mean by suffering. I mean, the baby can't see or hear or smell, right? And I bet the nerves that signal pain aren't functioning, either. It's like the Director said, you remember—a kind of vegetable. In your opinion, does a vegetable suffer?"

Does a vegetable suffer, in my opinion? Bird wondered silently. Have I ever considered that a cabbage being munched by a goat was in pain?

"Do you think a vegetable baby can suffer?" the doctor repeated eagerly, pressing with confidence for an answer.

Bird meekly shook his head: as if to say the problem exceeded his flushed brain's capacity for judgment. And there was a time when he never would have submitted to a person he had just met, at least not without feeling some resistance. . . .

"The oxygen isn't feeding well," the anesthetist reported. The doctor stood up and turned to check the rubber tube; Bird had his first look at his son.

An ugly baby with a pinched, tiny, red face covered with wrinkles and blotchy with fat. Its eyes were clamped shut like the shells of a bivalve, rubber tubes led into its nostrils; its mouth was wrenched open in a soundless scream that exposed the pearly-pink membrane inside. Bird found himself rising half off the bench, stretching for a look at the baby's bandaged head. Beneath the bandage, the skull was buried under a mound of bloody cotton; but there was no hiding the presence there of something large and abnormal.

Bird looked away, and sat down. Pressing his face to the window glass, he watched the city recede. People in the street, alarmed by the siren, stared at the ambulance with curiosity and an unaccountable expectation plainly written on their faces—just as that host of pregnant angels had stared. They gave the impression of unnaturally halted motion, like film caught in a projector. They were glimpsing an infinitesimal crack in the flat surface of everyday life and the sight filled them with innocent awe.

My son has bandages on his head and so did Apollinaire when he was wounded on the field of battle. On a dark and lonely battlefield I have never seen, my son was wounded like Apollinaire and now he is screaming soundlessly. . . .

Bird began to cry. Head in bandages, like Apollinaire: the image simplified his feelings instantly and directed them. He could feel himself turning into a sentimental jelly, yet he felt himself being sanctioned and justified: he even discovered a sweetness in his tears.

Like Apollinaire, my son was wounded on a dark and lonely battlefield that I have never seen, and he has arrived with his head in bandages. I'll have to bury him like a soldier who died at war.

Bird continued to cry.

3

B IRD was sitting on the stairs in front of the intensive care ward, gripping his thighs with grimy hands in a battle with the fatigue that had been hounding him since his tears had dried, when the one-eyed doctor emerged from the ward looking thwarted. Bird stood up and the doctor said: "This hospital is so goddamned bureaucratic, not even the nurses will listen to a word you say." A startling change had come over the man since their ride together in the ambulance: his voice was troubled. "I have a letter of introduction from our Director to a professor of medicine here—they're distant relatives!—and I can't even find out where he is!"

Now Bird understood the doctor's sudden dejection. Here in this ward everyone was treated like an infant: the young man with the glass eye had begun to doubt his own dignity.

"And the baby?" Bird said, surprised at the commiseration in his voice.

"The baby? Oh yes, we'll know just where we stand when the brain surgeon has finished his examination. If the infant lasts that long. If he doesn't last, the autopsy will tell the full story. I doubt that the infant can hold out for more than a day—you might drop in here around three tomorrow afternoon. But let me warn you: this hospital is really bureaucratic—even the nurses!"

As though he were determined to accept no more questions from Bird, the doctor rolled both his eyes toward the ceiling, good and glass alike, and walked away. Bird followed him like a washerwoman, holding the baby's empty basket against his side. At the passageway that led to the main wing, they were joined by the ambulance driver and the anesthetist. These firemen seemed to notice right away that the doctor's earlier joviality had deserted him. Not that they retained any dazzle themselves: while they had been racing their ambulance through the heart of the city as though it were a truck careening across an open field, shrilling the siren pretentiously and jumping traffic lights that bound the law-abiding citizen, a certain dignity had swelled their stoic uniforms. But now even that was gone. From the back, Bird noticed, the two firemen were alike as identical twins. No longer young, they were of medium height and build and both were balding in the same way.

"You need oxygen on the first job of the day, you need it all day long," one said with feeling.

"Yes, you've always said that," the other as feelingly replied.

This little exchange the one-eyed doctor ignored. Bird, though not much moved, understood that the men were nourishing each other's gloom, but when he turned to the fireman in charge of oxygen and nodded sympathetically, the man stiffened as though he had been asked a question, and with a nervous, grunted "huh?" forced Bird to speak. Disconcerted, Bird said: "I was wondering about the ambulance—can you use your siren to run traffic lights on the way back, too?"

"On the way back?" Like the fire department's most talented singing twins, the firemen repeated the question in unison, exchanged a look, their faces flushing drunkenly, and snorted a laugh which dilated the wings of their noses. Bird was both angry at the silliness of his question and at the firemen's response. And his anger was connected by a slender pipe to a tank of huge, dark rage compressed inside him. A rage he had no way of releasing had been building inside him under increasing pressure since dawn.

But the firemen seemed to wither now, as if they regretted having laughed imprudently at an unfortunate young father; their obvious distress closed a valve in the tapline to Bird's fury. He even felt a twinge of remorse. Who had asked that silly, anticlimactic question in the first place? And hadn't the question seeped from a fault which had opened in his own brain, pickled in the vinegar of his grief and lack of sleep?

Bird looked into the baby's hamper under his arm. Now it was like an empty hole which had been dug unnecessarily. Only a folded blanket remained in the hamper, and some absorbent cotton and a roll of gauze. The blood on the cotton and the gauze, though still a vivid red, already failed to evoke an image of the baby lying there with its head in bandages, inhaling oxygen a little at a time from the rubber tubes inside its nose. Bird couldn't even recall accurately the grotesqueness of the baby's head, or the shimmering membrane of fat that gloved its fiery skin. Even now, the baby was receding from him at full speed. Bird felt a mixture of guilty relief and bottomless fear. He thought: Soon I'll forget all about the baby, a life that appeared out of infinite darkness, hovered for nine months in a fetal state, tasted a few hours of cruel discomfort, and descended once again into darkness, final and infinite. I wouldn't be surprised if I forgot about the baby right away. And when it's time for me to die I may remember, and, remembering, if the agony and fear of death increase for me, I will have fulfilled a small part of my obligation as a father.

Bird and the others reached the front entrance of the main wing. The firemen ran for the parking lot. Since theirs was a profession that involved them in emergencies all the time, running around breathlessly must have represented the normal attitude toward life. Off they dashed across the glistening concrete square, arms flailing, as if a hungry devil were snapping at their behinds. Meanwhile, the one-eyed doctor telephoned his hospital from a phone booth and asked for the Director. He explained the situation in a very few words: almost no new developments to report. Bird's mother-in-law came to the phone: "It's your wife's mother," said the doctor, turning. "Do you want to speak?"

Hell no! Bird wanted to shout. Since those frequent telephone conversations the night before, the sound of his mother-in-law's voice reaching him over the telephone line, like the helpless droning of a mosquito, had hounded Bird like an obsession. Bird set the baby's basket on the concrete floor and took the receiver glumly.

"The brain specialist hasn't made his examination yet. I have to come back tomorrow afternoon."

"But what's the point of it all; I mean, what can you hope to accomplish?" Bird's mother-in-law cross-examined him in the tone of voice he had hoped most to be spared, as if she held him directly responsible.

"The *point* is that the baby happens to be alive at the moment," Bird said, and waited with a premonition of disgust for the woman to speak again. But she was silent; from the other end of the line came only a faint sound of troubled breathing.

"I'll be right over and explain," Bird said, and he started to hang up.

"Hello? Please don't come back here," his mother-in-law added hurriedly. "That child thinks you've taken the baby to a heart clinic. If you come now she'll be suspicious. It would be more natural if you came in a day or so, when she's calmer, and said that the baby had died of a weak heart. You can always get in touch with me by telephone."

Bird agreed. "I'll go right over to the college and explain what's happened," he was saying, when he heard the hard click of the connection being broken arbitrarily at the other end of the line. So his own voice had filled the listener with disgust, too. Bird put the receiver back and picked up the baby's basket. The one-eyed doctor was already in the ambulance. Bird, instead of climbing in after him, set the basket on the canvas stretcher.

"Thanks for everything. I think I'll go alone."

"You're going home alone?" the doctor said.

"Yes," Bird replied, meaning "I'm going *out* alone." He had to report the circumstances of the birth to his father-in-law, but after that he would have some free time. And a visit to the professor, compared to returning to his wife and mother-in-law, held a promise of pure therapy.

The doctor closed the door from the inside and the ambulance moved away silently, observing the speed limit, like a *former* monster now powerless and deprived of voice. Through the same window from which, an hour earlier, weeping, he had gazed at pedestrians in the street, Bird saw the doctor and one of the firemen lurch forward toward the driver. He knew they were going to gossip about him and his baby, and it didn't bother him. From the telephone conversation with the old woman had come an unexpected furlough, time to himself to be spent alone and as he liked—the thought pumped strong, fresh blood into his head.

Bird started across the hospital square, wide and long as a soccer field. Halfway, he turned around and looked up at the building where he had just abandoned his first child, a baby on the brink of death. A gigantic building, with an overbearing presence, like a fort. Glistening in the sunlight of early summer, it made the baby who was faintly screaming in one of its obscure corners seem meaner than a grain of sand.

What if I *do* come back tomorrow, I might get lost in the labyrinth of this modern fort and wander in bewilderment; I might never find my dying or maybe already dead baby. The notion carried Bird one step away from his misfortune. He strode through the front gate and hurried down the street.

Forenoon: the most exhilarating hour of an early summer day. And a breeze that recalled elementary school excursions quickened the worms of tingling pleasure on Bird's cheeks and earlobes, flushed from lack of sleep. The nerve cells in his skin, the farther they were from conscious restraint, the more thirstily they drank the sweetness of the season and the hour. Soon a sense of liberation rose to the surface of his consciousness.

Before I go to see my father-in-law, I'll wash up and get a shave! Bird marched into the first barbershop he found. And the middle-aged barber led him to a chair as though he were an ordinary customer. The barber had not discerned any indications of misfortune. Bird, by transforming himself into the person the barber perceived, was able to escape his sadness and his apprehension. He closed his eyes. A hot, heavy towel that smelled of disinfectant steamed his cheeks and jaw. Years ago, he had seen a comic skit about a barbershop: the barber's young apprentice has a hellishly hot towel, too hot to cool in his hands or even hold, so he slaps it down as it is on the customer's face. Ever since, Bird laughed whenever his face was covered with a towel. He could feel himself smiling even now. That was going too far! Bird shuddered, shattering the smile, and began thinking about the baby. In the smile on his face, he had discovered proof of his own guilt.

The death of a vegetable baby—Bird examined his son's calamity from the angle that stabbed deepest. The death of a vegetable baby with only vegetable functions was not accompanied by suffering. Fine, but what did death mean to a baby like that? Or, for that matter, life? The bud of an existence appeared on a plain of nothingness that stretched for zillions of years and there it grew for nine months. Of course, there was no consciousness in a fetus, it simply curled in a ball and existed, filling utterly a warm, dark, mucous world. Then, perilously, into the external world. It was cold there, and hard, scratchy, dry and fiercely bright. The outside world was not so confined that the baby could fill it by himself: he must live with countless strangers. But, for a baby like a vegetable, that stay in the external world would be nothing more than a few hours of occult suffering he couldn't account for. Then the suffocating instant, and once again, on that plain of nothingness zillions of years long, the fine sand of nothingness itself. What if there *was* a last judgment! Under what category of the Dead could you subpoena, prosecute, and sentence a baby with only vegetable functions who died no sooner than he was born? Only a few hours on this earth, and spent in crying, tongue fluttering in his stretched, pearly-red mouth, wouldn't any judge consider that insufficient evidence? Insufficient fucking evidence! Bird gasped in fear that had deepened until now it was profound. I might be called as a witness and I wouldn't be able to identify my own son unless I got a clue from the lump on his head. Bird felt a sharp pain in his upper lip.

"Sit still, please! I nicked you," the barber hissed, resting his razor on the bridge of Bird's nose and peering into his face. Bird touched his upper lip with the tip of his finger. He stared at the blood, and he felt a pang of nausea. Bird's blood was type A and so was his wife's. The quart of blood circulating in the body of his dying baby was probably type A, too. Bird put his hand back under the linen and closed his eyes again. The barber slowly, hesitatingly shaved around the cut on his upper lip, then scythed his cheeks and jaw with rough haste, as if to retrieve lost time.

"You'll want a shampoo?"

"No, that's all right."

"There's lots of dirt and grass in your hair," the barber objected.

"I know, I fell down last night." Stepping out of the barber chair, Bird glanced at his face in a mirror that glistened like a noon beach. His hair was definitely matted, crackly as dry straw, but his face from his high cheekbones to his jaw was as bright and as fresh a pink as the belly of a rainbow trout. If only a strong light were shining in those glue-colored eyes, if the taunt eyelids were relaxed and the thin lips weren't twitching, this would be a conspicuously younger and livelier Bird than the portrait reflected in the store window last night.

Stopping at a barbershop had been a good idea: Bird was satisfied. If nothing else, he had introduced one positive element to a psychological balance which had been tipped to negative since dawn. A glance at the blood that had dried under his nose like a triangular mole, and Bird left the barbershop. By the time he got to the college, the glow the razor had left on his cheeks would probably have faded. But he would have scraped away with his nail the mole of dried blood by then: no danger of impressing his father-in-law as a sad and ludicrous hangdog. Searching the street for a bus stop, Bird remembered the extra money he was carrying in his pocket and hailed a passing cab.

Bird stepped out of the cab into a crowd of students swarming through the main gate on their way to lunch: five minutes past twelve. On the campus, he stopped a big fellow and asked directions to the English department. Surprisingly, the student beamed a smile and singsonged, nostalgically, "It's certainly been a long time, sensei!" Bird was horrified. "I was in your class at the cram-school. None of the government schools worked out, so I had my old man donate some money here and got in, you know, through the back door."

"So you're a student here now," Bird said with relief, remembering who the student was. Though not unhandsome, the boy had saucer eyes and a bulbous nose that recalled the illustrations of German peasants in *Grimm's Fairy Tales*.

"It sounds as if cram-school wasn't much help to you," Bird said.

"Not at all, sensei! Study is never a waste. You may not remember a single thing but, you know, study is study!"

Bird suspected he was being ridiculed and he glowered at the boy. But the student was trying with his whole large body to demonstrate his good will. Even in a class of one hundred, Bird vividly recalled, this one had been a conspicuous dullard. And precisely for that reason he was able to report simply and jovially to Bird that he had entered a second-rate private college through the back door, and to express gratitude for classes that had availed him nothing. Any of the ninety-nine other students would have tried to avoid their cram-school instructor.

"With our tuition as high as it is, it's a relief to hear you say that."

"Oh, it was worth every penny. Will you be teaching here from now on?"

Bird shook his head.

"Oh. . . ." The student tactfully expanded the conversation: "Let me take you to the English department; it's this way. But seriously, sensei, the studying I did at cram-school didn't go to waste. It's all in my head someplace, taking root sort of; and someday it will come in handy. It's just a matter of waiting for the time to come—isn't that pretty much what studying is in the final analysis, sensei?"

Bird, following this optimistic and somehow didactic former student, cut across a walk bordered by trees in full blossom and came to the front of a red-ochre brick building. "The English department is on the third floor at the back. I was so happy to get in here, I explored the campus until I know it like the palm of my hand," the boy said proudly, and flashed a grin so eloquently self-derisive that Bird doubted his own eyes.

"I sound pretty simple, don't I!"

"Not at all; not so simple."

"It's awfully nice of you to say so. Well then, I'll be seeing you around, sensei. And take care of yourself: you're looking a little pale!"

Climbing the stairs, Bird thought: That guy will manage his adult life with a thousand times more cunning than I manage mine; at least he won't go around having babies die on him with brain hernias. But what an oddly unique moralist he had had in his class!

Bird peered around the door into the English department office and located his father-in-law. On a small balcony that extended from a far corner of the room, the professor was slumped in an oak rocking chair, gazing at the partly open skylight. The office had the feeling of a conference room, far larger and brighter than the English offices at the university from which Bird had graduated. Bird's father-in-law often said (he told the story wryly, like a favorite joke on himself) that the treatment he received at this private college, including facilities such as the rocking chair, was incomparably better than what he had been used to at the National University: Bird could see there was more to the story than a joke. If the sun got any stronger, though, the rocking chair would have to be moved back or the balcony shaded with an awning, one or the other.

At a large table near the door, three young teaching assistants, oil gleaming on their ruddy faces, were having a cup of coffee, apparently after lunch. All three of them Bird knew by sight: honor students who had been a class ahead of him at college. But for the incident with the whisky and Bird's withdrawal from graduate school, he certainly would have found himself in pursuit of their careers.

Bird knocked at the open door, stepped into the room, and greeted his three seniors. Then he crossed the room to the balcony; his father-in-law twisted around to watch him as he approached, his head thrown back, balancing himself on the rocking chair. The assistants watched too, with identical smiles of no special significance. It was true that they considered Bird a phenomenon of some rarity, but at the same time he was an outsider and therefore not an object of serious concern. That funny, peculiar character who went on a long binge for no reason in the world and finally dropped out of graduate school—something like that.

"Professor!" Bird said out of habit established before he had married the old man's daughter. His father-in-law swung himself and the chair around to face him, the wooden rockers squeaking on the floor, and waved Bird into a swivel chair with long arm rests.

"Was the baby born?" he asked.

"Yes, the baby was born—" Bird winced to hear his voice shrivel into a timid peep, and he closed his mouth. Then, compelling himself to say it all in one breath: "The baby has a brain hernia and the doctor says he'll die sometime tomorrow or the day after, the mother is fine!"

The taffy-colored skin of the professor's large, leonine face quietly turned vermilion. Even the sagging bags on his lower eyelids colored brightly, as though blood were seeping through. Bird felt the color rising to his own face. He realized all over again how alone and helpless he had been since dawn.

"Brain hernia. Did you see the baby?"

Bird detected a hidden intimation of his wife's voice even in the professor's thin hoarseness, and, if anything, it made him miss her.

"Yes, I did. His head was in bandages, like Apollinaire."

"Like Apollinaire . . . his head in bandages." The professor tried the words on his own tongue as if he were pondering the punch line of a little joke. When he spoke, it was not so much to Bird as to the three assistants: "In this age of ours it's hard to say with certainty that having lived was better than not having been born in the first place." The three young men laughed with restraint, but audibly: Bird turned and stared at them. They stared back, and the composure in their eyes meant they were not the least surprised that a queer fellow like Bird had met with a freak accident. Resentful, Bird looked down at his muddy shoes. "I'll call you when it's all over," he said.

The professor, rocking his chair almost imperceptibly, said nothing. It occurred to Bird that his father-in-law might be feeling a little disgusted with the satisfaction the rocking chair gave him ordinarily.

Bird was silent, too. He felt he had said everything he had to say. Would he be able to conclude on such a clear and simple note when it came time to let his wife in on the secret? Not a chance. There would be tears, questions by the truckload, a sense of the futility of fast talk, an aching throat, and a flushed head: finally a rope of screaming nerves would fetter Mr. and Mrs. Bird.

"I'd better be getting back; there are still papers to be signed at the hospital," Bird said at last.

"It was good of you to come over." The professor showed no sign of getting out of his rocking chair. Bird, feeling lucky not to have been asked to stay longer, stood up. "There's a bottle of whisky in that desk," the professor said. "Take it along."

Bird stiffened, and he could feel the three assistants tense. They must have known as well as his father-in-law about that long, disastrous drunk; now he sensed their eyes beginning to track the development of the incident. Bird, hesitating, recalled a line from the English textbook he was reading with his students; a young American was speaking angrily: *Are you kidding me? Are you looking for a fight?*

Nevertheless, Bird bent forward, opened the top of the professor's desk, and lifted out the bottle of Johnnie Walker with both hands. He was crimson even to his eyeballs, yet he felt a twisted, feverish joy. Ask a man to trample a crucifix and make him prove he's not a Christian: well, they wouldn't see him hesitate.

"Thank you," Bird said. The three assistants relaxed. The professor was working his chair slowly around to its original position, his head erect, his face still slack and scarlet. Bird glanced at the younger men, swiftly bowed, and left the room.

Down the stairs and into the stone courtyard, Bird kept a prudent grip on the whisky bottle, as though it were a hand grenade. The rest of the day was his to spend as he liked by himself—the thought merged in his mind with an image of the Johnnie Walker and foamed into a promise of ecstasy and peril.

Tomorrow, or the day after, or maybe after a week's reprieve, when my wife has learned about the wretched baby's death, the two of us are going to be locked up in a dungeon of cruel neurosis. Accordingly —Bird argued with the bubbly voice of apprehension inside himself—I have a perfect right to today's bottle of whisky and liberating time. Quietly the bubble collapsed. Fine! Let's get down to drinking. First Bird thought of going back to his apartment and drinking in his study, but clearly that was a bad idea. If he returned, the old landlady and his friends might besiege him, by telephone if not in person, with detailed questions about the birth; besides, whenever he looked into the bedroom, the baby's white enamel bassinet would tear his nerves like a gnashing shark. Shaking his head roughly, Bird drove the notion from his mind. Why not hole up in a cheap hotel where only strangers stayed? But Bird pictured himself getting drunk in a locked hotel room and he felt afraid. Bird gazed enviously at the jolly Scotsman in the red cutaway striding across the Johnnie Walker label. Where was he going in such a hurry? All of a sudden, Bird remembered an old girlfriend. Winter and summer alike, during the day she was always sprawled in her darkened bedroom, pondering something extremely metaphysical while she chain-smoked Players until an artificial fog hung over her bed. She never left the house until after dusk.

Bird stopped to wait for a cab just outside the college gates. Through the large window in the coffee shop across the street he could see his former student sitting at a table with some friends. The student noticed Bird at once and began like an affectionate puppy to send sincere, ungainly signals. His friends, too, regarded Bird with vague, blunted curiosity. How would he explain Bird to his friends! As an English instructor who had drunk himself out of graduate school, a man in the grip of an unexplainable passion, or maybe a crazy fear?

The student smiled at him tenaciously until he was in the taxicab. Bird realized as he drove away that he felt as if he had just received charity. And from a boy who in all his time at the cram-school had never learned to distinguish English gerunds from present participles, a former student with a brain no bigger than a cat's!

Bird's friend lived on one of the city's many hills, in a quarter ringed by temples and cemeteries. The girl lived alone in a tiny house at the end of an alley. Bird had met her at a class mixer in October of his freshman year. When it was her turn to stand and introduce herself, she had challenged the class to guess the source of her unusual name: Himiko—fire-sighting-child. Bird had answered, correctly, that the name was taken from the Chronicles of the ancient province of Higo —*The Emperor commanded his oarsmen, saying: There in the distance a signal fire burns; make for it straightaway.* After that, Bird and the girl Himiko from the island of Kyushu had become friends.

There were very few girls at Bird's university, only a handful in the liberal arts who had come to Tokyo from the provinces; and all of those, as far as Bird knew, had undergone a transmutation into peculiar and unclassifiable monsters shortly after they had graduated. A certain percentage of their body cells slowly overdeveloped, clustered and knotted until the girls were moving sluggishly and looking dull and melancholic. In the end, they became fatally unfit for everyday, postgraduate life. If they got married, they were divorced; if they went to work, they were fired; and those who did nothing but travel met with ludicrous and gruesome auto accidents. Himiko, shortly after graduation, had married a graduate student, and she hadn't been divorced. Worse, a year after the marriage, her husband had committed suicide. Himiko's father-in-law had made her a present of the house the couple had been living in, and he still provided her every month with money for living expenses. He hoped that Himiko would remarry, but at present she devoted her days to contemplation and cruised the city in a sports car every night.

Bird had heard open rumors that Himiko was a sexual adventuress who had broken out of conventional orbit. Even rumors that related her husband's suicide to her deviate tastes. Bird had slept with the girl just once, but both of them had been terribly drunk and he wasn't even certain coitus had been achieved. That was long before Himiko's unfortunate marriage, and though she had been driven by keen desire and had pursued her pleasure actively, Himiko had been nothing more in those days than an inexperienced college girl.

Bird got out of the cab at the entrance to the alley where Himiko lived. Quickly, he calculated the money remaining in his wallet; he shouldn't have any trouble getting an advance on this month's salary after class tomorrow.

Bird twisted the bottle of Johnnie Walker into his jacket pocket and hurried down the alley, covering the neck of the bottle with his hand. Since the neighborhood knew all about Himiko's eccentric life, it was impossible not to suspect that visitors were observed discreetly from windows here and there.

Bird pushed the buzzer in the vestibule. There was no response. He rattled the door a few times and softly called Himiko's name. This was just a formality. Bird walked around toward the back of the house and saw that a dusty, secondhand MG was parked beneath Himiko's bedroom window. With its empty seats exposed, the scarlet MG seemed to have been abandoned here for a long time. But it was proof that Himiko was at home. Bird propped a muddy shoe on the badly dented bumper and brought his weight to bear. The MG rocked gently, like a boat. Bird called Himiko's name again, looking up at the curtained bedroom window. Inside the room, the curtains were lifted slightly where they met and a single eye looked down at Bird through the narrow peephole. Bird stopped rocking the MG and smiled: he could always behave freely and naturally in front of this girl.

"Hey! Bird—" Her voice impeded by the curtain and by the window glass, sounded like a feeble, silly sigh.

Bird knew he had discovered the ideal spot for beginning a bottle of Johnnie Walker in the middle of the day. Feeling as though he had entered just one more plus on the psychological balance sheet for the day, he walked back to the front of the house.

4

"I HOPE you weren't asleep," Bird said as Himiko opened the door for him.

"Asleep? At this hour?" the girl teased. Himiko held up one hand against the midday sun but it didn't help; the light at Bird's back descended roughly on her neck and shoulders, bare where her violet terrycloth bathrobe fell away. Himiko's grandfather was a Kyushu fisherman who had taken as a wife, abducted really, a Russian girl from Vladivostok. That explained the whiteness of Himiko's skin; you could see the web of capillary vessels just beneath the surface. In the way she moved, too, was something to suggest the confusion of the immigrant who is never quite at ease in his new country.

Wincing in the rush of light, Himiko stepped back into the shadow of the open door with the ruffled haste of a mother hen. She was in that meager stage of womanhood between the vulnerable beauty of a young girl, which she had lost, and the mature woman's fullness still to come. Himiko was probably the type of woman who would have to spend a particularly long time in this tenuous state.

Quickly, in order to protect his friend from the revealing light, Bird stepped inside and closed the door. For an instant the cramped space of the vestibule felt like the inside of a hooded cage. Bird blinked rapidly while he took off his shoes, trying to accustom his eyes to the dimness. Himiko hovered in the darkness behind him, watching.

"I hate to disturb people when they're sleeping," Bird offered.

"You're so timid today, Bird. Anyway, I wasn't asleep; if I nap during the day I can never get to sleep at night. I was thinking about the pluralistic universe."

Pluralistic universe? Good enough, Bird thought, we can discuss it over whisky. Glancing around him like a hunting dog nosing for a

39

spoor, Bird followed Himiko inside. In the living room it might have been evening, and the gloom was dark and stagnant like a bed of straw for sick livestock. Bird squinted down at the old but sturdy rattan chair he always sat in and carefully lowered himself into it after removing some magazines. Until Himiko had showered and dressed and put on some make-up, she wouldn't turn on the lights, much less open the curtains. Company had to wait patiently in the dark. During his last visit here a year ago, Bird had stepped on a glass and had cut the base of his big toe. Recalling the pain and the panic, he shivered.

It was hard to decide where to put the bottle of whisky: an elaborate confusion of books and magazines, empty boxes and bottles, shells, knives, scissors, withered flowers collected in winter woods, insect specimens, and old and new letters covered not only the entire floor and the table, but even the low bookcase along the window, the record player, and the television set. Bird hesitated, then shuffled a small space on the floor with his feet and wedged the bottle of Johnnie Walker between his ankles. Watching from the door, Himiko said as though in greeting, "I still haven't learned to be neat. Bird, was it like this the last time you were here?"

"Damn right it was; I cut my big toe!"

"Of course, the floor around the chair there was all bloody, wasn't it," Himiko reminisced. "It's been ages, Bird. But everything's the same around here. How about you?"

"As matter of fact, I had a kind of accident."

"Accident?"

Bird hesitated; he hadn't planned to start right in with all his troubles. "We had a child but it died right away," he simplified.

"No! Really? The same thing happened to friends of mine—two friends! That makes three people I know. Don't you think fallout in the rain has something to do with it?"

Bird tried comparing his child who seemed to have two heads with pictures he had seen of mutations caused by radioactivity. But he had only to think to himself about the baby's abnormality and a sense of extremely personal shame hotly rose into his throat. How could he discuss the misfortune with other people; it was inherent in himself! He had the feeling this would never be a problem he could share with the rest of mankind.

"In my son's case, it was apparently just an accident."

"What an awful experience for you, Bird," Himiko said, and she looked at him quietly with an expression in her eyes that seemed to cloud her lids with ink.

Bird didn't trouble himself with the message in Himiko's eyes; instead, he lifted the bottle of Johnnie Walker. "I wanted somewhere to drink and I knew you wouldn't mind even if it was the middle of the day. Have a drink with me?"

Bird sensed himself wheedling the girl, like any brazen young gigolo. But that was the way men whom Himiko knew generally behaved toward her. The man she had married, more openly than Bird or any of her other friends, had played up to her as though he were a younger brother. And suddenly one morning he had hanged himself.

"I can see the baby's death is still close to you, Bird. You haven't recovered yet. Well, I'm not going to ask you anything more about it."

"That would probably be best. There's almost nothing to tell anyway."

"Shall we have a drink?"

"Good."

"I want to take a shower, but you start. Bird! There are glasses and a pitcher in the kitchen."

Himiko disappeared into the bedroom and Bird stood up. The kitchen and the bathroom shared the twisted space at the end of the hall that amounted to the tail of the little house. Bird jumped over a cat crouching on the floor, the bathrobe and underclothes Himiko had just thrown off, and went into the kitchen. On his way back with a pitcher of water, glasses and cups he had washed himself, two in each pocket, he happened to glance past the open glass door and saw Himiko showering at the back of the bathroom, where it was even darker than the hall. With her left hand upheld as if to check the black water pouring out of the darkness above her head and her right hand resting on her belly, Himiko was looking down over her right shoulder at her buttocks and slightly arched right calf. Bird saw back and buttocks and legs, and the sight filled him with a disgust he couldn't repress; his flesh turned to goosepimples. Bird rose on his toes as if to flee a darkness alive with ghosts: and then he was running, trembling, past the bedroom and back to the familiar rattan chair. He had conquered it once, he couldn't say when, and now it had reawakened in him: the juvenile's disgust, anxiety ridden, for the naked body. Bird sensed that the octopus of disgust would extend its tentacles even when he turned to his wife, who now lay in a hospital bed thinking about the baby *who had gone with its father to another hospital because of a defective heart.* But would the feeling last for a long time? Would it grow acute?

Bird broke the seal on the bottle with his fingernail and poured himself a drink. His arm was still shaking: the glass chattered at the bottle like an angry rat. Bird scowled thornily, a hermetic old man, and hurled the whisky down his throat. God, it burned! Coughing shook him and his eyes teared. But the arrow of red-hot pleasure pierced his belly instantly, and the shuddering stopped. Bird brought up a child's belch redolent of wild strawberries, wiped his wet lips with the back of his hand, and filled his glass again, this time with a steady hand. How many thousands of hours had he been avoiding this stuff? Harboring something like a grudge against no one he could name, Bird emptied his second glass busily, like a titmouse pecking at millet seeds. His throat didn't burn this time, he didn't cough, and tears didn't come to his eyes. Bird lifted the bottle of Johnnie Walker and studied the picture on the label. He sighed rapturously, and drank a third glass.

By the time Himiko came back, Bird was beginning to get drunk. As Himiko's body entered the room disgust lifted its head, but its function was impaired by the poisons in the alcohol. Besides, the black, one-piece dress Himiko had put on diminished the threat of the flesh it covered: like a mass of shaggy hair, it made her look like a laughable cartoon bear. When Himiko had combed her hair she turned on the lights. Bird cleared a space on the table, set up a glass and a cup for Himiko and poured her whisky and a glass of water. Himiko sat down in a large, carved, wooden chair, managing her skirt with extreme care so that no more than necessary of her freshly washed skin was exposed. Bird was grateful. He was gradually overcoming his disgust, but that didn't mean he had uprooted it.

"Here we are," Bird said, and drained his glass.

"Here we are!" Himiko pouted her lower lip like an orangutan sampling a flavor, and took a tiny sip of whisky.

They sat there, quietly lacing the air with hot, whisky breath, and for the first time looked each other in the eye. Fresh from her shower, Himiko wasn't ugly; the woman who had shrunk from the sunlight might have been this girl's mother. Bird was pleased. Moments of regeneration as striking as this could still occur at Himiko's age. "I thought of a poem when I was in the shower. Do you remember this?" Himiko whispered one line of an English poem as though it were a spell. Bird listened, and asked her to recite it again.

" 'Sooner murder an infant in its cradle than nurse unacted desires.' "

"But you can't murder all the babies in their cradles," Bird said. "Who is the poet?"

"William Blake. You remember, I wrote my thesis on him."

"Of course, you were working on Blake." Bird turned his head and discovered the Blake reproduction hanging on the wall that adjoined the bedroom. He had seen the painting often but he had never looked at it carefully. Now he noticed how bizarre it was. A public square walled in by buildings in the style of the Middle East. In the distance rose a pair of stylized pyramids: it must have been Egypt. The thin light of dawn suffused the scene—or was it dusk? Sprawled in the square like a fish with a ripped belly was the dead body of a young man. Next to him his distraught mother, surrounded by a group of old men with lanterns and women cradling infants. But the scene was dominated by the giant presence overhead, swooping across the square with arms outspread. Was it human? The beautifully muscled body was covered with scales. The eyes were full of an ominous dolor and were fanatically bitter; the mouth was a hollow in the face so deep it swallowed up the nose—a salamander's mouth. Was it a devil? a god? The creature appeared to be soaring upward, reaching for the turbulence of the night sky even while it burned in the flames of its own scales.

"What's he doing? Are those supposed to be scales or is he wearing a coat of mail like the knights in the Middle Ages?"

"I think they're scales," Himiko said. "In the color plate they were green and they looked much scalier. He's the Plague! Doing his best to destroy the oldest sons of Egypt!"

Bird didn't know much about the Bible; perhaps it was a scene from Exodus. Whatever, the creature's eyes and mouth were virulently grotesque. Grief, fear, astonishment, fatigue, loneliness—even a hint of laughter boiled limitlessly from its coal-black eyes and salamander mouth.

"Isn't he a groove!" Himiko said.

"You like the man with the scales?"

"Sure I do. And I like to imagine how I'd feel if I were the spirit of the Plague myself."

"Probably so badly your eyes and mouth would start looking like his." Bird glanced at Himiko's mouth.

"It's frightening, isn't it? Whenever I have a frightening experience, I think how much worse it would be if I were frightening someone else —that way I get psychological compensation. Do you think you've made anyone else as afraid as you've ever been in your life?"

"I wonder. I'd have to think about it."

"It's probably not the sort of thing you can think about; you have to know."

"Then I guess I've never really frightened another person."

"I'm sure you haven't—not yet. But don't you suppose it's an experience you'll have sooner or later?" Himiko's tone was reserved, nonetheless prophetic.

"I suppose murdering a baby in its cradle would terrify yourself and everyone else, too." Bird poured himself and Himiko a drink, emptied his own glass in a swallow and filled it again. Himiko wasn't drinking at such a fast clip.

"Are you holding back?" Bird said.

"Because I'll be driving later. Have I ever given you a ride, Bird?"

"I don't think so. We'll have to go one of these days."

"Come over any night and I'll take you. It's dangerous in the day because there's too much traffic; my reflexes are much faster when it's dark."

"Is that why you shut yourself up all day long and think? You lead a real philosopher's life—a philosopher who races around in a red MG after dark—not bad. What's this pluralistic universe?"

Bird watched with mild satisfaction as delight tightened Himiko's face. This was restitution for the rudeness of his sudden visit and for all the drinking he planned to do: not that many people besides himself would lend an attentive ear to Himiko's reveries.

"Right now you and I are sitting and talking together in a room that's a part of what we call the real world," Himiko began. Bird settled down to listen, carefully balancing a fresh drink on his palm. "Well it just so happens that you and I exist in altogether different forms in countless other universes, too. Now! We can both remember times in the past when the chances of living or dying were fifty-fifty. For example, when I was a child, I got typhoid fever and almost died. And I still remember perfectly well the moment when I reached a crossroads; I could have descended into death or climbed the slope to recovery. Naturally, the Himiko sitting with you in this room chose the road to recovery. But in that same instant, another Himiko chose death! And a universe of people with brief memories of the Himiko who died went into motion around my young corpse all inflamed with typhoid rash. Do you see, Bird? Every time you stand at a crossroads of life and death, you have two universes in front of you; one loses all relation to you because you die, the other maintains its relation to you because you survive in it. Just as you would take off your clothes, you abandon the universe in which you only exist as a corpse and move on to the universe in which you are still alive. In other words, various universes emerge around each of us the way tree limbs and leaves branch away from the trunk.

"This kind of universal cell division occurred when my husband committed suicide, too. I was left behind in the universe where he died, but in another universe on the other side, where he continues to live without committing suicide, another Himiko is living with him. The world a man leaves behind him when he dies, say at a very young age, and the world in which he escapes death, continue to live—the worlds that contain us are constantly multiplying. That's all I mean by the pluralistic universe.

"And you know something, Bird? You don't have to feel so sad about your baby's death. Because another universe has diverged from the baby, and in the world developing in that universe the baby is growing healthy and strong this very minute. In that world you're a young father drunk on happiness and I'm feeling groovy because I've just heard the good news and we're drinking a toast together. Bird? Do you understand?"

The smile on Bird's face was peaceful. The alcohol had spread to the remotest capillary in his body and it was taking its full effect: pressure had been equalized between the pink darkness inside him and the world outside. Not that the feeling would last long, as Bird well knew.

"Bird, you may not understand fully but do you get at least the general idea? There must have been moments in your twenty-seven years when you stood at a dubious junction of life and death. Well, at each of those moments you survived in one universe and left your own corpse behind in another. Bird? You must remember a few of those moments."

"I do, as a matter of fact. Are you saying I left my own corpse behind on each of those occasions and escaped alive into this universe?"

"Exactly."

Could she be right? Bird wondered sleepily. Had another Bird remained behind as a corpse at each of those critical moments? And was there an assortment of dead Birds in myriad other universes, a frail and timid schoolboy, and a high-school student with a simple mind but a much stronger body than his own? Then which of those many dead was the most desirable Bird? One thing was certain: not himself, not the Bird in this universe.

"Then is there a final death when your death in this world is your death in all the others, too?"

"There must be: otherwise, you'd have to live to infinity in at least one universe. I'd say you probably die your final death of old age when you're over ninety. So we all live on in one universe or another until we die of old age in our final universe—that sounds fair, doesn't it, Bird?"

Sudden comprehension forced Bird to interrupt: "You're still tormenting yourself about your husband's suicide, aren't you? And you've conceived this whole philosophical swindle in order to rob death of its finality."

"Say what you want, my role since he left me behind in this universe has been to wonder constantly why he died. . . ." The gray skin around Himiko's weakening eyes colored with ugly swiftness. ". . . now that's an unpleasant role but I've stepped into it, I'm not shirking my responsibilities, at least not in this universe."

"Please don't think I'm criticizing you, Himiko, because I'm not. I just don't like to see you fooling yourself. . . ." Bird smiled, trying to dilute the poison in his words, yet he persisted. "You're trying to make something relative out of the irrevocability of your husband's death by assuming another universe where he is still alive. But you can't make the absoluteness of death relative, no matter what psychological tricks you use."

"Maybe you're right, Bird . . . can I have another glass of whisky, please." Himiko's voice was dry, empty of interest. Bird filled both their glasses and prayed that Himiko would drink away her memory of his spontaneous criticism and continue again tomorrow to dream about her pluralistic universe. Like a time-traveler visiting a world ten thousand years in the past, Bird was terrified of being responsible for any mishap in the world of present time. The feeling had been growing in him slowly since he had learned that his baby was a freak. Now he wanted to drop out of this world for a while, as a man drops out of a poker game when he has a bad run of cards.

In silence Bird and Himiko exchanged magnanimous smiles and drank their whisky purposefully, like beetles sucking sap. The noises from the summer afternoon street sounded to Bird like signals from a vast distance, unheeded signals. Bird shifted in his chair and yawned, shedding one tear as meaningless as saliva. He filled his glass again and drank down the whisky in a swallow—to ensure that his descent from the world would be smooth. . . .

"Bird?"

Bird started, spilling whisky on his lap, and opened his eyes; he could feel himself in the second stage of drunkenness.

"What?"

"That buckskin coat you got from your uncle—whatever happened to it?" Himiko moved her tongue slowly, working at accuarate pronunciation. Her face, like a large tomato, was round and very red.

"That's a good question; I used to wear it in my first year at school."

"Bird! You still had it in the winter of your sophomore year—"

Winter—the word splashed into the pool of Bird's whisky-weakened memory.

"That's right—I spread it on the wet ground in that lumberyard the night we made it together. The next morning it was caked with mud and wood shavings. I could never wear it again: the cleaners wouldn't take buckskin coats in those days. I think I rolled it up in a closet and later I must have thrown it away."

As he spoke, Bird remembered that dark night in the middle of winter and the incident that seemed already in the distant past. It was their sophomore year at college. Bird and Himiko had been drinking together, and they were very drunk. Bird walked Himiko home; he grabbed her in the darkness in the lumberyard behind her boarding house. They faced each other in the cold, shivering, and their caresses were simple until Bird's hand, as though by accident, touched Himiko's vagina. Agitated, Bird pressed Himiko against some lumber that was stacked against a board fence and labored to insert himself in her. Himiko did her best to help but she gave up at last and softly laughed. Though both of them were in a frenzy, the embrace was still in the domain of play. Nonetheless, when he realized he would not be able to insert his penis as long as they were standing, Bird felt himiliated by circumstance, which made him dogged. He spread his buckskin coat on the ground and lay Himiko down on top of it—laughing still. Himiko was a tall girl: her head and her legs below the knee rested on the bare ground. After a while the laughing stopped and Bird supposed she was approaching orgasm. But a little later he inquired, and Himiko replied that she was merely cold. Bird interrupted their lovemaking.

"I was a real savage in those days," Bird said reflectively, like an octogenarian.

"I was a savage, too."

"I wonder why we never tried again somewhere else."

"What happened in the lumberyard seemed so accidental, I had a feeling the next morning that it could never be repeated."

"It was extraordinary, all right. An incident. Almost a rape," Bird said uncomfortably.

"Almost? It *was* rape," Himiko corrected.

"But was there really no pleasure at all for you? I mean, you were nowhere near coming?" Bird sounded resentful.

"What did you expect—after all, that was my first time."

Bird stared at Himiko in amazement. She wasn't, he knew, a person to tell that variety of lie or joke. He was dumbfounded, and then a sense of ridiculousness a hair's breadth away from fear drove a short laugh past his lips. The laughter infected Himiko, too.

"Life is full of wonder," Bird said, turning a fierce red that wasn't entirely the whisky's fault.

"Bird, don't sound so crushed. The fact that I had never had sex before can only have been significant for me, if it had any meaning at all —it had nothing to do with you."

Bird filled a cup instead of a glass and drank the whisky down in a single breath. He wanted to remember the incident in the lumberyard more accurately. It was true that his penis had been repelled again and again by something hard and stretched like a drawn lip. But he had assumed that the cold had simply shriveled Himiko. Then what about the bloodstains on the bottom of his shirt the next morning? Why hadn't that made him suspect? he wondered: and like a whim, desire seized him. Bird bit his lips closed as if he were fighting pain, and gripped his whisky cup. At the very center of his body a tumor of knotted pain and apprehension was engendered, unmistakably desire itself. Desire that resembled the pain and anxiety that seize a patient behind the ribs in a cardiac attack. What Bird felt now was not that meek desire, hardly a mole on the slack face of daily life, the polar opposite of the African dream that glinted high in the skies of his mind, that was demeaned once or twice a week even while it was eliminated when he dug into his wife, not that homey desire which sank in the mud of lugubrious fatigue with one lewd, listless grunt. This was desire that could not be assuaged by a thousand repetitions of the act, not a ticket you relinquished after one trip around on the toy train. Desire you could satisfy once and never again, perilous desire that made you wonder uneasily when the sating moment came if Death weren't stealing up behind your naked, sweating back. This was desire Bird might have satisfied late one winter night in a lumberyard if he had known for certain that he was raping a virgin.

Bird willed his throbbing, whisky-heated eyes to dart a weasel glance at Himiko. His brain ballooned, pulsing with blood. Cigarette smoke circled the room like a school of trapped sardines: Himiko seemed adrift on a sea of mist. She was watching Bird, her face in a funny, rapt, too simple smile, but her eyes were perceiving nothing. Himiko was lost in a whisky dream and her body seemed softer and rounder all over, particularly her red, fervid face. If only, Bird thought ruefully, I could repeat that winter night rape scene with Himiko. But he knew there wasn't a chance. What if they *did* make it again sometime, their intercourse would evoke the ravaged sparrow of a penis Bird had glimpsed this morning when he dressed and would evoke his wife's distended genitals sluggishly contracting after the agony of childbirth. Sex for Bird and Himiko would be linked to the dying baby, linked to all of mankind's miseries, to the wretchedness so loathsome that people unafflicted pretended not to see it, an attitude they called humanism. The sublimation of desire? This was scrapping it entirely. Bird gulped his whisky and his tepid insides shuddered. If he wanted to re-create in all its marvelous tension the sexual moment he had ruined that winter night, he would probably have no choice but to strangle the girl to death. The voice flapped out of the nest of desire inside him: *Butcher her and fuck the corpse!* But Bird knew he would never undertake that kind of adventure in his present state. I'm just feeling wistful and deprived because I learned Himiko was a virgin. Bird was disdainful of his own confusion and he tried to repudiate that part of himself. But the sea urchin of disquiet and black-hot desire would not swim away. If you can't slaughter her and rape the corpse, find something that can evoke a situation just as taut and volatile! But Bird was helpless; he could only stand in wonderment before his ignorance of peril and perversion. Bird drained his cup like a basketball player taking a drink of water after he has been ordered off the court for too many errors: peevishly, with self-disdain and evident distaste. The whisky had lost its bite now, and its bouquet; it wasn't even bitter anymore.

"Bird—do you always gulp your whisky by the glassful? As if it were tea? I can't even drink tea that fast if it's still hot."

"Always, it's always this way, when I drink," Bird mumbled.

"Even when you're with your wife?"

"Why?"

"You couldn't possibly satisfy a woman when you've been drinking that way. What's more important, I doubt that you could bring it off yourself, no matter how hard you tried. You'd end up with a whacky heart like a prostrate distance swimmer—and leave an alcohol slick like a rainbow next to the woman's head!"

"Are you thinking of going to bed with me now?"

"I wouldn't sleep with you when you've had this much to drink; it would be meaningless for both of us."

Bird worked a finger through a hole inside his pocket and explored something warm and soft: a silly, drowsing mouse. And withered, in perfect opposition to the sea urchin flaming in his chest.

"Nothing doing there, is there, Bird!" Confidently, Himiko challenged the slight movement.

"I may not be able to come myself but I can certainly carry on like a Chinese Monkey and boost you over the wall!"

"It's not that simple, you know—for me to have an orgasm. Bird, you don't seem to remember very clearly what happened when we lay on the ground in that lumberyard. There's no reason why you should. But for me, that was an initiation rite. It was a cold, squalid rite, ridiculous and pathetic, too. Since then I've been running a long-distance race and it's been a battle all the way, Bird!"

"Did I make you frigid?"

"If you mean the ordinary orgasm, I discovered that for myself right away. I had help from some of the guys in my class, almost before the mud under my nails from the lumberyard had dried. But ever since then

I've been chasing a better orgasm, and then one better still—like climbing a flight of stairs!"

"And that's all you've done since you graduated from college?"

"Since *before* I graduated. I can see now that's been my real work since I was a student."

"You must be plenty sick of it."

"No, that's not true, Bird. One of these days I'll prove it to you —unless you want your only sexual memory of me to be that incident in the lumberyard. Bird?"

"And I'll teach you what I've picked up during my own long-distance race," Bird said. "Let's stop pecking at each other with our beaks like a pair of frustrated chicks; let's go to bed!"

"You've had too much to drink, Bird."

"You think a penis is the only organ that has anything to do with sex? I'd say that's pretty crude for an explorer in search of the supreme orgasm."

"Would you use fingers, then? Or lips? Or maybe some organ too freaky to believe, like an appendix? Sorry, that's not for me; it's too much like masturbation."

"You're certainly frank," Bird winced.

"Besides, Bird, you're not really looking for anything sexual today. You look to me as if sex would disgust you. Let's say we did go to bed together, you'd have all you could do to crumple between my legs and vomit. Your disgust would overwhelm you, and you'd smear my belly with brown whisky and yellow bile. You would, Bird! That happened to me once and it was awful."

"I guess we do learn from experience sometimes; your observations are correct," Bird said dejectedly.

"There's no hurry," Himiko consoled.

"No. No hurry. Seems like a hell of a long time since I was in a situation where I had to hurry. I was always in a hurry when I was a kid. I wonder why."

"Maybe because one has so little time as a child. I mean, you grow up so fast."

"I grew up fast, all right. And now I'm old enough to be a father. Only I wasn't adequately prepared as a father so I couldn't come up with a proper child. You think I'll ever become the father of a normal child? I have no confidence."

"No one is confident about that kind of thing, Bird. When your next baby has turned out to be perfectly healthy then you'll know for certain that you're a normal father. And you'll feel confident in retrospect."

"You've really become wise about life." Bird was heartened. "Himiko, I'd like to ask you—" The sleep anemone was engulfing him in waves and Bird knew he wouldn't be able to resist for more than a minute. He peered at the empty glass wavering in his field of vision and shook his head, wondering whether to have another drink; finally he conceded that his body could not accept another drop of whisky. The glass slipped through his fingers, struck his lap, and rolled onto the floor.

"Himiko, I'd like to ask you one more thing," Bird said, trying a little weight on his legs to see if he could stand, "—what kind of world after death do you go to when you die as an infant?"

"If there is such a world, it must be very simple, Bird. But can't you believe in my pluralistic universe? Your baby will live to the ripe old age of ninety in his final universe!"

"Ah yes," Bird said. "Well. I'm going to sleep. Himiko! Is it night yet? Would you take a peek through the curtains, please."

"It's the middle of the day, Bird. If you want to sleep, you can use my bed; I'll be going out as soon as it's dark."

"You'd abandon a pitiful friend for a red sports car?"

"When a pitiful friend is drunk, the best thing to do is to leave him alone. Otherwise we might both regret it later."

"Absolutely right! You have a hold on all the best of mankind's wisdom. So you drive around in that MG all night? Until dawn?"

"Sometimes, Bird. I have rounds to make—like a sandman looking for children who can't sleep!"

When Bird finally hoisted himself out of the rattan chair, limp and heavy as another man's body, he wrapped an arm around Himiko's sturdy shoulders and headed for the bedroom. A funny dwarf was dancing around inside the fiery sun that was his head, scattering powdered light like the fairy he had seen in Peter Pan. Bird laughed, tickled by the hallucination. As he collapsed on the bed, he managed one grateful exclamation: "Himiko! You're like a kind great-aunt!"

Bird slept. Across the twilight square in his dream a scaly man moved with dark, sad eyes and a terrifying gash of a salamander mouth: but soon he was enfolded in the eddying, reddish-black dusk. The sound of a sports car pulling away; deep, comprehensive sleep.

Twice during the night Bird woke up, and neither time was Himiko there. He was awakened by restrained but persistent voices calling from outside the window: "Himiko! Himiko!"

In the first voice there was still an adolescent ring. The next time Bird opened his eyes, he heard the voice of a middle-aged man. He got out of bed, lifted the curtains where they met just as Himiko had done to look at him, and peered down at the night visitor. In the pale moonlight Bird saw a small gentleman in a linen tuxedo that looked too tight, as though it had shrunk; his round, eggish head lifted to the window, the little man was calling Himiko's name with a clouded expression that seemed to be a compound of embarrassment and mild self-disgust. Bird dropped the curtains and went into the next room to get the whisky bottle. In one swallow he drank what remained, burrowed back into his girlfriend's bed, and instantly fell asleep.

5

A GAIN and again the moaning invaded his sleep until, reluctantly, Bird woke up. At first he thought he was moaning himself; indeed, as he opened his eyes, the numberless devils spawning in his belly pierced his innards with their tiny arrows and forced a moan from his own lips. But now he heard again a moan that wasn't coming from himself. Gingerly, without disturbing the position of his body, Bird lifted his head only and looked down at the side of the bed. Himiko was asleep on the bare floor, wedged between the bed and the television set. And she was moaning like a strong animal, transmitting moans as if they were signals from the world of her dream. The signals indicated fear.

Through the dim mesh of air in the room Bird watched Himiko's young, round, ashen face stiffen as though in pain and go stupidly slack. The blanket had slipped to her waist; Bird scrutinized her chest and sides. Her breasts were perfect hemispheres but they drooped unnaturally to either side, avoiding one another. The region between her breasts was broad and flat and somehow stolid. Bird sensed a familiarity with this immature chest: he must have seen it in the lumberyard that winter night. But Himiko's sides and the swell of her belly, almost hidden under the blanket, did not evoke nostalgia. There was a suggestion there of the fat which age was beginning to plant in her body. And that hint of flabbiness was a part of Himiko's new life; it had nothing to do with Bird. The fatty roots beneath her skin would probably spread like fire and transform completely the shape of her body. Her breasts, too, would lose the little youth and freshness they retained.

Himiko again moaned and her eyes shuttered open as though she had been startled. Bird pretended to be asleep. When a minute later he

54

opened his eyes, Himiko was asleep again. Now she lay still as a mummy, wrapped to her throat in the blankets, sleeping a silent, expressionless insect's sleep. She must have managed to reach an agreement with the ogres in her dream. Bird closed his eyes in relief and turned back to his threatening blackmailer of a stomach. Suddenly his stomach inflated until it filled his body and crowded the entire world of his consciousness. Fragments of thought tried to penetrate to the center of his mind: when did Himiko get back?—had the baby been carried to the dissection table with its head in bandages like Apollinaire?—would he make it through class today without accident?—but one by one they were repulsed by the pressure his stomach applied. Bird knew he would vomit any minute and fear chilled the skin on his face.

What will she think of me if I filthy this bed with vomit? When I was good and drunk I took her virginity in what amounted to a rape, outdoors, in the middle of winter, and I didn't even realize what I was doing! Years later, when I spend the night in her room, I get drunk all over and wake up ready to spill my guts. How lousy can you be! Bird brought up in quick succession ten reeking burps and sat upright in bed, groaning with the pain in his head. The first step away from the bed was fraught with difficulty but finally Bird was on his way to the bathroom. He discovered to his surprise that he was wearing only his underwear.

When Bird closed the ill-fitting glass door and found himself secluded in the bathroom, he tasted the joy of an unanticipated possibility: he might just succeed in emptying his stomach without being caught by Himiko. If he could vomit as delicately as a grasshopper . . .

Kneeling, Bird rested his elbows on the modern toilet bowl, lowered his head, and waited in an attitude of pious prayer for the tension in his stomach to explode. His face had been thoroughly chilled, but now it was flushed with an unnatural heat, and then abruptly numb and icy again. Peering into it from this position, the toilet was like a large, white throat, the more so because of the clear water in the narrowed bottom of the bowl.

The first wave of nausea hit. Bird barked, his neck stiffened, and his belly heaved. Smarting water filled his nose and tears dribbled down his cheeks to the bits of vomited food that stuck to his upper lip. Again Bird gagged and weakly vomited up what remained in his esophagus. Yellow sparks whirled in his head—time for a short reprieve. Straightening like a plumber who has just finished up a job, Bird wiped his face with toilet paper and loudly blew his nose. Ah, he sighed. But it wasn't over yet; not a chance. Once Bird was sick to his stomach he threw up at least twice; it was always the same. And he couldn't rely the second time on the muscles in his stomach; the second time he had to force the spasm by twisting a finger in the slime of his throat. Bird sighed again in anticipation of the agony, and lowered his head. The inside of the toilet bowl, filthy now, was desolating. Bird closed his eyes in an excess of disgust, groped above his head, and pulled the chain. A flood of water roared and a small whirlwind coolly grazed his forehead. When he opened his eyes, the large white throat gaped at him again pristinely. Bird thrust a finger into his own red and paltry throat, and forced himself to vomit. Groans and meaningless tears, the yellow sparks inside his head, membranes smarting in his nose. Finishing, he wiped his soiled fingers and mouth and his tear-streaked cheeks and slumped against the toilet bowl. Would this amount at least to partial restitution for the baby's suffering? Bird wondered, and then he blushed at his own impudence. If any suffering was fruitless it was the agony of a hangover; what he suffered now could not expiate suffering of any other kind.

You can't let yourself feel consoled by this phony restitution, not even for as long as a flickering in your brain—Bird admonished himself in the manner of a moralist. Yet his relief after the vomiting and the relative silence of the demons in his belly, albeit that could not last long, made for the first tolerable minutes Bird had spent since opening his eyes. He had a class to teach today, and there would be forms to complete at the hospital for the baby who was probably dead by now. Bird would contact his mother-in-law about the baby's death and he would have to discuss with her when to inform his wife. It was a hell of a schedule. And here I am in my girlfriend's bathroom, slumped against the toilet in a daze with my strength all puked away. It was preposterous! And yet Bird was not afraid; in fact, the present half-hour of helplessness and utter irresponsibility tasted sweetly of self-salvation. Crumpled on the floor as he was, aware only of the smarting in his nose and throat, Bird was a kind of brother to the baby on the verge of death. My only saving grace is that I don't bawl the way a baby does. Not that my behavior isn't ten times as disgraceful. . . .

Had it been possible, Bird would have elected to hurl himself into the toilet as he pulled the chain and thus be flushed with a roar of water down into a sewery hell. Instead he spat once, moved away from the toilet reluctantly, and opened the glass door. At that moment he had forgotten about Himiko somehow, but as soon as he placed one bare foot in the bedroom he knew that she was wide awake and had pictured to herself the little drama in the toilet and the peculiar silence that had followed. The girl lay on the floor as before, but Bird could see in the fine powder of light sifting through a crack where the curtains met that her eyes, while darkly shadowed from corner to corner, were open wide. He had no choice but to scurry around her feet like a mouse, heading for his shirt and pants at the foot of the bed. Meanwhile, Himiko would probably stare with eyes opaque as open camera lenses at his flaccid belly and sinewy thighs.

"Did you hear me vomiting like a dog in there?" Bird asked in a timid voice.

"Like a dog? You don't often hear a dog with such terrific volume," Himiko said in a voice still fogged with sleep, gazing at Bird as if to inspect him, her quiet eyes wide.

"This was a St. Bernard as big as a cow," Bird said in disappointment.

"It sounded bad—are you through?"

"Yes, for now." Bird wobbled toward the bed, trampling Himiko's legs so badly on the way that she cried out in protest, and finally managed to reach his pants. "But I'm sure I'll be sick again sometime this morning; it always happens that way. I haven't been drinking for a while, and hangovers have stayed away from me, so this may be the worst one of my life. Now that I think about it, it was trying to polish off a hangover with a little hair of the dog that started me circling in endless alcoholic orbit." Bird tried for a droll effect by exaggerating the mournfulness in his voice, but he ended on a bitter, introspective note.

"Why not try the same again?"

"I can't afford to be drunk today."

"Lemon juice will perk you up; there are some lemons in the kitchen."

Bird peered into the kitchen obediently. In the sink, stabbed by a ray of light right out of the Flemish school that cut into the kitchen through a pane of frosted glass, a dozen pell-mell lemons glistened with such rawness that the nerves of Bird's weakened stomach quaked at the sight of them.

"Do you always buy so many lemons?" Having struggled frantically into his pants and buttoned his shirt up to the neck, Bird was in possession of himself again.

"It depends, Bird," Himiko replied with terrific indifference, as if she were trying to impress on Bird the boredom of his question. Bird, rattled again, "When did you get back, anyway? Did you drive around in that MG until dawn?" Instead of answering, Himiko merely stared at him mockingly, so Bird hurried to add, as if the report were crucial: "Two friends of yours came around in the middle of the night. One seemed to be just a boy and the other was a middle-aged gentleman with a head like an egg; I got a look at him from behind the curtain. But I didn't say hello."

"Say hello? Naturally, you didn't have to," said Himiko, unmoved. Bird took his wristwatch out of his jacket pocket and checked the time —nine o'clock. His class began at ten. A cram-school instructor brave enough to stay home without notifying the office or to show up late for a class would have to be quite a man. Bird was neither so dauntless nor so dim of wit. He tied his necktie by feel.

"I've been to bed with each of them a few times and they think that gives them the right to come over here in the middle of the night. The young one is a freaky type; he's not specially interested in just the two of us sleeping together; his dream is to be around when I'm in bed with someone else so that he can help out. He always waits until somebody is with me here and then he comes around. Even though he's fantastically jealous!"

"Have you given him the chance he's looking for?"

"Certainly not!" Himiko snapped. "That boy has a thing for adults like you; if you ever got together he'd do everything he could to please you. Bird, I bet you've had that kind of service lots of times before. Weren't there boys below you in college who worshiped you? And there must be students in your classes who are particularly devoted. I've always thought of you as a hero figure for kids in that kind of sub-culture."

Bird shook his head in denial and went into the kitchen. He realized as the soles of his feet touched the chilly wooden floor that he had not put on his socks, and wasn't that going to be a chore! If he put pressure on his stomach when he bent over to look for his socks he might throw up again. Bird winced. But it felt good to tread the floor in bare feet, and grasping a lemon with wet fingers while water from the tap pummeled his hands was pleasurable too, if only mildly. Bird selected a large lemon, cut it in half, and squeezed the juice into his mouth. A sensation of recovery he remembered well dropped cold and tingly with lemon juice from his throat toward his tyrannized stomach. Bird returned to the bedroom and began looking for his socks, carefully holding himself straight up.

"That lemon really seems to have done the job," he said to Himiko gratefully.

"You may vomit again but this time it'll taste of lemon; it might be nice."

"Thanks a lot for the encouragement." Bird watched the contentment the juice had brought him scatter like mist before a wind.

"What are you looking for? You look like a bear hunting a crab."

"My socks," Bird murmured; his bare feet struck him as ridiculous.

"In your shoes, so you can put them on together when you leave."

Bird looked down at Himiko doubtfully as she lay on the floor in her blanket and supposed this was the custom here whenever one of her lovers bundled into bed. She probably took the precaution so that her friends could flee the house in their bare feet with their shoes in hand if a bigger and wilder lover should appear.

"I'd better be going," Bird said. "I have two classes this morning. Thanks a lot for last night and this morning."

"Will you come again? Bird, it's possible we may need each other."

If suddenly a mute had screamed, Bird would not have been more astonished. Himiko was looking up at him with her thick eyelids lowered and her brow creased.

"Maybe you're right. Maybe we do need each other."

Like an explorer tramping marsh country, Bird made his way in trepidation over thorny stems and scratchy bits of wire through the darkness of the living room; and when finally he bent forward in the vestibule, he hurried into his socks and shoes, afraid that nausea might set in.

"So long," Bird called. "Sleep well!" Himiko was silent as a stone.

Bird stepped outside. A summer morning filled with light as sharp as vinegar. As Bird passed the scarlet MG, he noticed the key in the ignition switch. One of these days a thief would make off with the car with no trouble at all. The thought saddened him. Himiko! How could such a diligent, careful, and astute co-ed have been transformed into this flawed personality? The girl had married only to have her young husband kill himself, and now, after the catharsis of racing her car far into the night, she saw dreams that made her moan in terror.

Bird started to take the key out of the switch. But if he returned to the room where his friend lay in the darkness, frowning in silence with her eyes shut tight, getting back outside again promised to be difficult. Bird let go of the key, and looked around; there were no car thieves lurking in the vicinity, he consoled himself, at least not at the moment. On the ground next to one of the spoke wheels was a cigar butt. That little man with an egg for a head must have dropped it there last night. The group looking after Himiko on more intimate terms than Bird was certain to be large in number.

Bird shook his head roughly and took a few deep breaths, trying to defend himself against the crawfish of his hangover, armored in a host of threats. But he was unable to rid himself of a bludgeoned feeling, and he stepped out of the glistening alley with his head bowed.

Nonetheless, Bird cunningly managed to hold up all the way to and through the school gate. There was the street, the platform, then the train. Worst was the train, but Bird survived the vibrations and the odor of other bodies despite his parched throat. Of all the passengers in the car, Bird alone was sweating, as if full summer had rushed in to occupy the square yard around him only. People who brushed bodies with him all turned back to stare suspiciously. Bird could only cringe and, like a pig that had glutted a crate of lemons, exhale citric breath. His eyes restlessly roamed the car, searching for a spot to which he could dash in case of an urgent need to vomit.

When he finally arrived at the school gate without having been sick to his stomach, Bird felt like an old soldier exhausted by a long retreat from battle. But the worst was still to come. The enemy had circled and lay in wait ahead.

Bird took a reader and a chalk box out of his locker. He glanced at the Concise Oxford Dictionary on top of the shelf, but today it looked too heavy to carry all the way to class. And there were several students in his class whose knowledge of idioms and rules of grammar far exceeded his own. If he encountered a word he had never seen, or a difficult phrase, he would only have to call on one of them. The heads of Bird's students were so crammed with knowledge of details they were as complicated as hyper-evolved clams: the minute they tried to perceive a problem integrally, the mechanism tangled in itself and stalled. It was accordingly Bird's job to integrate and summarize the entire meaning of a passage. Yet he was in constant doubt close to an incombustible fixation about whether his classes were of any use when it came to college entrance examinations.

Hoping to avoid his department chairman, a personable, keen-eyed University of Michigan graduate who had risen, it was clear, from the foreign student elite, Bird stepped outside through a rear exit, avoiding the elevator in the teachers' lounge, and started up the spiral stairs that clung like ivy to the outside wall. Not daring to look down at the prospect unfolding below him gradually, barely enduring the swaying of the stairs like the motion of a rolling ship produced by students pounding past him: pale, panting, belching with a groan every step or two of the way. So slowly did Bird climb that students overtaking him, dismayed for an instant by their own speed, stopped short and peered into his face, hesitated, then raced on again, shaking the iron stairs. Bird sighed, his head swimming, and clung to the iron railing. . . .

What a relief to reach the top of the stairs! and then someone called his name and Bird's uneasiness returned. It was a friend who was helping sponsor a Slavic languages study group that Bird had formed with some other interpreters. But since Bird had all he could do at the moment playing cat-and-mouse with his hangover, meeting someone he had not expected struck him as a terrific nuisance. He closed himself like a shellfish under attack.

"Hey—Bird!" his friend called: the nickname was still valid in any situation, for all categories of friend. "I've been calling since last night but I couldn't get you. So I thought I'd come over—"

"Oh?" said Bird, unsociably.

"Have you heard the news about Mr. Delchef?"

"News?" Bird repeated, feeling vaguely apprehensive. Mr. Delchef was an attaché in the legation from a small socialist state in the Balkans and the study group's instructor.

"Apparently he's moved in with a Japanese girl and won't go back to the legation. They say it's been a week. The legation wants to keep things in the family and bring Mr. Delchef back themselves, but they've only been here a little while and, well, they're short of people. The girl lives in the slummiest part of Shinjuku, it's like a maze in there; there just isn't anyone at the legation who gets around well enough to search for strays in a neighborhood like that. That's where we come in: the legation has asked the study group to help out. Of course, we're partly responsible for the whole thing anyway—"

"Responsible?"

"Mr. Delchef met her at that bar we took him to after a meeting, you know, the Pullman Car." Bird's friend snickered. "Don't you remember that small, peculiar, pasty-faced girl?"

Bird recalled her right away, a small, peculiar, pasty-faced girl. "But she didn't speak English or any Slavic language and Mr. Delchef's Japanese is no good at all—how do they get along?"

"That's the hell of it; how do you suppose they spent a whole week, clammed up, or what?" The friend seemed embarrassed by his own innuendo.

"What will happen if Mr. Delchef doesn't go back to the legation? Will that make him a defector or something?"

"You can bet it will!"

"He's really asking for trouble, Mr. Delchef—" Bird said glumly.

"We'd like to call a meeting of the study group and think it over. Are you free tonight?"

"Tonight?—" Bird was nonplused. "—I—can't make it tonight."

"But you were closer than any of us to Mr. Delchef. If we decide to send an envoy from the study group, we were hoping you'd agree to go—"

"An envoy—anyway, I couldn't possibly make it tonight," Bird said. Then he forced himself to add: "We had a child but there was something wrong and he's either dead already or dying right now."

"God!" Bird's friend exclamed, wincing. Above their heads the bell began to ring.

"That's awful, really awful. Listen, we'll manage without you tonight. And try not to let it get the best of you—is your wife all right?"

"Fine, thank you."

"When we decide what to do about Mr. Delchef, I'll get in touch. God, you look run down—take care of yourself—"

"Thank you."

Bird, watching his friend flounce down the spiral stairs in reckless haste, as though he were running away, was angry with himself for having kept silent about his hangover. Bird went into his classroom. And just for a second he was confronting one hundred fly-head faces. Then he lowered his gaze as though reflexively; wary of lifting his head again and looking his students in the face, and holding the reader and the chalk box in front of his chest like weapons of self-defense, he stepped up to the lectern.

Classtime! Bird opened the reader at the bookmark to the passage at which he had stopped the week before, without any notion of what it was. He began to read aloud, and he realized right away that it was a paragraph from Hemingway. The reader was a large collection of short passages from modern American literature, chosen by the department chairman because he happened to like them and because each was mined with grammatical traps. Hemingway! Bird was encouraged. He liked Hemingway, especially *The Green Hills of Africa*. The passage in the reader was from *The Sun Also Rises*, a scene near the end when the hero goes for a swim in the ocean. The narrator swims out beyond the breakers, taking a dunking now and then, and when he reaches the offing where the water is calm, he turns over on his back and floats. All he can see is sky, and beneath him he feels the rise of the swell and the fall. . . .

In the depths of his body, Bird felt the beginning of an irrepressible and certain crisis. His throat went utterly dry; his tongue swelled in his mouth like a foreign body. Bird submerged in the amniotic fluid of fear. But he continued to read aloud, glancing like a sick weasel, craftily and feebly, at the door. Could he make it in time if he charged in that direction? But how much better to ride the crisis out without having to make a run for it. Hoping to take his mind off his stomach, Bird tried to place the paragraph he was reading in context. The hero lay around on the beach and went in for another swim. When he returned to the hotel, a telegram was waiting from his mistress, who had run off with a young bullfighter. Bird tried to remember the telegram: COULD YOU COME HOTEL MONTANA MADRID AM RATHER IN TROUBLE BRETT.

Yes, that sounded right: and he had remembered it easily. It's a good omen, of all the telegrams I've ever read, this was the most appealing. I should be able to overcome the nausea—more a prayer than a thought. Bird continued to reconstruct: the hero dives into the ocean with his eyes open and sees something green oozing along the bottom. If that appears in this passage, I'll make it through without throwing up. It's a magic spell. Bird went on: "I" came out of the water, returned to the hotel, and picked up his telegram. It was just as Bird had remembered it: COULD YOU COME HOTEL MONTANA MADRID AM RATHER IN TROUBLE BRETT.

But the hero had left the beach, and not a word about swimming underwater with his eyes open. Bird was surprised; had he been thinking of another Hemingway novel? Or was the scene from an altogether different writer? Doubt broke the spell and Bird lost his voice. A web of bone-dry cracks opened in his throat and his tongue swelled until it tried to burst from his lips. Facing one hundred fly-heads, Bird lifted his eyes and smiled. Five seconds of ridiculous, desperate silence. Then Bird crumpled to his knees, spread his fingers like a toad on the muddy wooden floor, and with a groan began to vomit. Bird vomited like a retching cat, his neck thrust stiffly from his shoulders. And his guts were being twisted and wrung dry: he looked like a puny demon writhing beneath the foot of an enormous Deva king. Bird had hoped at least to achieve a little humor in his vomiting style, but his actual performance was anything but funny. One thing, as the vomit submerged the base of his tongue and ran back down his throat, just as Himiko had predicted, it had a definite taste of lemons. The violet that blooms from the dungeon wall, Bird told himself, trying to regain his composure. But such psychological wiles crumbled like pie crust in the face of spasms that now struck with the force of a full gale: a thundrous groan wrenched Bird's mouth open and his body stiffened. From both sides of his head a blackness swiftly grew like blinders on a horse and darkly narrowed his field of vision. Bird longed to burrow into a still darker, still deeper place, and from there to leap away into another universe!

A second later, Bird found himself in the same universe. With tears wetting both sides of his nose, he gazed mournfully down into the puddle of his own vomit. A pale, red-ochre puddle, scattered with vivid yellow lemon lees. Seen from a low-flying plane at a desolate and withered time of year, the plains of Africa might hue to these same colors: lurking in the shadow of those lemon dregs were hippo and anteaters and wild mountain goats. Strap on a parachute, grip your rifle, and leap out and down in grasshopper haste.

The nausea had subsided. Bird brushed at his mouth with a muddy, bile-fouled hand and then stood up.

"Due to circumstances, I'd like to dismiss class early today," he said in a voice like a dying gasp. The class appeared convinced; Bird moved to pick up his reader and the box of chalk. All of a sudden, one of the fly-heads leaped up and began to shout. The boy's pink lips fluttered, and his round, effeminate, peasant's face turned a vibrant red, but as he muffled his words inside his mouth and tended to stutter besides, it wasn't easy to understand what he was asserting. Gradually, all became quite clear. From the beginning, the boy had been criticizing the unsuitability of Bird's attitude as an instructor, but when he saw that Bird's only response was to display an air of perplexity, he had become a hostile devil of attack. Endlessly he harangued about the high cost of the tuition, the briefness of the time remaining until college entrance exams, the students' faith in the cram-school, and their sense of outrage now that their expectations had been betrayed. Gradually, as wine turns to vinegar, Bird's consternation turned to fear, aureoles of fear spread around his eyes like deep rings: he felt himself turning into a frightened monocle monkey. Before long, his attacker's indignation would infect the other ninety-nine fly-heads: Bird would be surrounded by one hundred furious college rejects and not a chance of breaking free. It was brought home to him again how little he understood the students he had been instructing week after week. An inscrutable enemy one hundred strong had brought him to bay, and he discovered that successive waves of nausea had washed his strength onto the beach.

The accuser's agitation mounted until he was on the verge of tears. But Bird couldn't have answered the young man even if he tried: after the vomiting his throat was as dry as straw, secreting not one drop of saliva. The most he felt he could manage was one eminently birdlike cry. Ah, he moaned, soundlessly, what should I do? This kind of awful pitfall is always lurking in my life, waiting for me to tumble in. And this is different from the kind of crisis I was supposed to encounter in my life as an adventurer in Africa. Even if I did fall into this pit I couldn't pass out or die a violent death. I could only stare blankly at the walls of the trap forever. I'm the one who'd like to send a telegram, AM RATHER IN TROUBLE—but addressed to whom?

It was then a youth with a quick-witted look stood up from his seat in a middle row and said quietly, untheatrically, "Knock it off, will you —stop complaining!"

The mirage of hard, thorny feeling that was beginning to mount throughout the classroom instantly disappeared. Amused excitement welled in its place and the class raised its voice in laughter. Time to act! Bird put the reader on top of the chalk box and walked over to the door. He was stepping out of the room when he heard shouting again and turned around; the student who had persisted in attacking him was down on all fours, just as Bird had been when he was sick, and he was sniffing the pool of Bird's vomit. "This stinks of whisky!" the boy screamed. "You've got a hangover, you bastard! I'm going to the Principal with a darektapeel and getting your ass fired!"

A darektapeel? Bird wondered, and as he comprehended—Ah!—a direct appeal!—that delightful young man stood up again and said in gloomy tones that brought new laughter from the class, "You shouldn't lap that stuff up; it'll make you puke."

Liberated from his sprawling prosecutor, Bird climbed down the spiral stairs. Maybe, just as Himiko said, there really was a band of young vigilantes ready to ride to his assistance when he blundered into trouble. For the two or three minutes it took him to climb down the spiral stairs, though from time to time he scowled at the sourness of vomit lingering on his tongue or at the back of his throat—for those few minutes, Bird was happy.

6

A T the junction of corridors that led to the pediatrics office and the intensive care ward, Bird halted in indecision. A young patient approaching in a wheelchair swerved, glowering, to let him pass. Where his two feet should have been, the patient rested a large, old-fashioned radio. Nor were his feet to be seen in any other place. Abashed, Bird pressed himself against the wall. Once again the patient looked at him threateningly, as if Bird represented all men who carried their bodies through life on two feet; then he shot down the corridor at amazing speed. Watching him go, Bird sighed. Assuming his baby was still alive, he should proceed straight to the ward. But if the baby was dead, he would have to present himself at the pediatrics office to make arrangements for an autopsy and cremation. It was a gamble. Bird began to walk toward the office. He had placed his bet on the baby's death, he installed the fact prominently in his consciousness. Now he was the baby's true enemy, the first enemy in its life, the worst. If life was eternal and if there was a god who judged, Bird thought, then he would be found guilty. But his guilt now, like the grief that had assailed him in the ambulance when he had compared the baby to Apollinaire with his head in bandages, tasted primarily of honey.

His step quickening steadily, as if he were on his way to meet a lover, Bird hurried in quest of a voice that would announce his baby's death. When he received the news, he would make the necessary arrangements (arranging for the autopsy would be easy because the hospital would be eager to cooperate; probably the cremation would be a nuisance). Today I'll mourn the baby alone, tomorrow I'll report our misfortune to my wife. The baby died of a head wound and now he has become a bond of flesh between us—I'll say something like that. We'll manage to restore our family life to normal. And then, all over again, the same

67

dissatisfactions, the same desires unrealized, Africa the same vast distance away. . . .

With his head atilt, Bird peered into the low reception window, gave his name to the nurse who stared back at him from behind the glass, and explained the situation as it had stood a day ago when the baby had been brought in.

"Oh yes, you want to see that baby with the brain hernia," the nurse said cheerfully, her face relaxing into a smile. She was a woman in her forties, with a scattering of black hairs growing around her lips. "You should go directly to the intensive care ward. Do you know where it is?"

"Yes, I do," Bird said in a hoarse, wasted voice. "Does that mean the baby is still alive?"

"Why of course he's alive! He's taking his milk very nicely and his arms and legs are good and strong. Congratulations!"

"But it *is* a brain hernia—"

"That's right, brain hernia," the nurse smiled, ignoring Bird's hesitation. "Is this your first child?"

Bird merely nodded, then hurried back down the corridor toward the intensive care ward. So he had lost the bet. How much would he have to pay? Bird encountered the patient in the wheelchair again at a turn in the corridor, but this time he marched straight ahead without so much as a sidelong glance and the cripple had to wheel himself frantically out of the way just before the collision. Far from being intimidated by the other, Bird wasn't even conscious of the patient's affliction. What if the man had no feet: Bird was as empty inside as an unloaded warehouse. At the pit of his stomach and deep inside his head, the hangover still sang a lingering, venomous song. Breathing raggedly, his breath fetid, Bird hurried down the corridor. The passageway that connected the main wing and the wards arched upward like a suspension bridge, aggravating Bird's sense of unbalance. And the corridor through the wards, hemmed on both sides by sickroom doors, was like a dark culvert extending toward a feeble, distant light. His face the color of ash, Bird gradually quickened his step until he was almost running.

The door to the intensive care ward, like the entrance to a freezer, was of rugged tin sheeting. Bird gave his name to the nurse standing just inside the door as if he were whispering something shameful. He was in the grip again of the embarrassment he had felt about himself for having a body and flesh when he had first learned yesterday of the baby's abnormality. The nurse ushered Bird inside officiously. While she was closing the door behind him, Bird glanced into an oval mirror that was hanging on a pillar just inside the room and saw oil and sweat glistening from forehead to nose, lips parted with ragged breathing, clouded eyes that clearly were turned in upon themselves: it was the face of a pervert. Jolted by sudden disgust, Bird looked away quickly, but already his face had engraved its impression behind his eyes. A presentiment like a solemn promise grazed his flushed head: from now on I'll suffer often from the memory of this face.

"Can you tell me which is yours?" Standing at Bird's side, the nurse spoke as if she were addressing the father of the hospital's healthiest and most beautiful baby. But she wasn't smiling, she didn't even seem sympathetic; Bird decided this must be the standard intensive care ward quiz. Not only the nurse who had asked the question but two young nurses who were rinsing baby bottles beneath a huge water heater on the far wall, and the older nurse measuring powdered milk next to them, and the doctor studying file cards at a cramped desk against the smudgy poster-cluttered wall, and the doctor on this side of him, conversing with a stubby little man who seemed, like Bird, to be the father of one of the seeds of calamity gathered here—everybody in the room stopped what he was doing and turned in expectant silence to look at Bird.

Bird's eye swept the babies' room on the other side of the wide, plated-glass partition. His conscious sense of the doctors' and nurses' presence in the ward instantly dropped away. Like a puma with fierce, dry eyes searching the plain for feeble prey from the top of a termite mound, Bird surveyed the babies behind the glass.

The ward was flooded with light that was harsh in its opulence. Here it was no longer the beginning of summer, it was summer itself: the reflection of the light was scorching Bird's brow. Twenty infant beds and five incubators that recalled electric organs. The incubator babies appeared only as blurred shapes, as though mist enshrouded them. But the babies in the beds were too naked and exposed. The poison of the glaring light had withered all of them; they were like a herd of the world's most docile cattle. Some were moving their arms and legs slightly, but even on these the diapers and white cotton nightshirts looked as heavy as lead diving suits. They gave the impression, all of them, of shackled people. There were a few whose wrists were even secured to the bed *(what if it was* to prevent them from scratching their own tender skins) or whose ankles were lashed down with strips of gauze (*what if it was* to protect the wounds made during a blood transfusion), and these infants were the more like wee, feeble prisoners. The babies' silence was uniform. Was the plate glass shutting out their voices? Bird wondered. No, like doleful turtles with no appetite, they all had their mouths closed. Bird's eyes raced over the babies' heads. He had already forgotten his son's face, but his baby was marked unmistakably. How had the hospital director put it, "Appearance? there seem to be two heads! I once heard a thing by Wagner called 'Under the Double Eagle'—" The bastard must have been a classical music buff.

But Bird couldn't find a baby with the proper head. Again and again he glanced irritably up and down the row of beds. Suddenly, without any cue, the infants all opened their calf's liver mouths and began to bawl and squirm. Bird flinched. Then he turned back to the nurse as if to ask "what happened?" But the nurse wasn't paying any attention to the screaming babies and neither was anyone else in the room; they were all watching Bird, silently and with deep interest, still playing the game: "Have you guessed? He's in an incubator. Now, which incubator do you suppose is your baby's home?"

Obediently, as if he were peering into an aquarium tank that was murky with plankton and slime, Bird bent his knees and squinted into the nearest incubator. What he discovered inside was a baby as small as a plucked chicken, with queerly chapped, blotchy skin. The infant was naked, a vinyl bag enclosed his pupa of a penis, and his umbilical cord was wrapped in gauze. Like the dwarfs in illustrated books of fairy tales, he returned Bird's gaze with a look of ancient prudence on his face, as if he, too, were participating in the nurses' game. Though obviously he was not Bird's baby, this quiet, old-mannish preemie, unprotestingly wasting away, inspired Bird with a feeling akin to friendship for a fellow adult. Bird straightened up, looking away with effort from the baby's moist, placid eyes, and turned back to the nurses resolutely, as if to say that he would play no more games. The angles and the play of light made it impossible to see into the other incubators.

"Haven't you figured it out yet? It's the incubator way at the back, against the window. I'll wheel it over so you can see the baby from here."

For an instant, Bird was furious. Then he understood that the game had been a kind of initiation into the intensive care ward, for at this final cue from the nurse, the other doctors and nurses had shifted their concern back to their own work and conversations.

Bird gazed forbearingly at the incubator the nurse had indicated. He had been under her influence ever since he had entered the ward, gradually losing his resentment and his need to resist. He was now feeble and unprotesting himself; he might have been bound with strips of gauze even like the infants who had begun to cry in a baffling demonstration of accord. Bird exhaled a long, hot breath, wiped his damp hands on the seat of his pants, then with his hand wiped the sweat from his brow and eyes and cheeks. He turned his fists in his eyes and blackish flames leaped; the sensation was of falling headlong into an abyss: Bird reeled. . . .

When Bird opened his eyes, the nurse, like someone walking in a mirror, was already on the other side of the glass partition and wheeling the incubator toward him. Bird braced himself, stiffening, and clenched his fists. Then he saw his baby. Its head was no longer in bandages like the wounded Apollinaire. Unlike any of the other infants in the ward, the baby's complexion was as red as a boiled shrimp and abnormally lustrous; his face glistened as if it were covered with scar tissue from a newly healed burn. The way its eyes were shut, Bird thought, the baby seemed to be enduring a fierce discomfort. And certainly that discomfort was due to the lump that jutted, there was no denying it, like another red head from the back of his skull. It must have felt heavy, bothersome, like an anchor lashed to the baby's head. That long, tapered head! It sledge-hammered the stakes of shock into Bird more brutally than the lump itself and induced a nausea altogether different from the queasiness of a hangover, a terrific nausea that affected Bird's existence fundamentally. To the nurse observing his reactions from behind the incubator, Bird nodded. As if to say "I've had enough!" or to acknowledge submission to a thing he could not understand. Wouldn't the baby grow up with its lump and continue to grow? The baby was no longer on the verge of death; no longer would the sweet, easy tears of mourning melt it away as if it were a simple jelly. The baby continued to live, and it was oppressing Bird, even beginning to attack him. Swaddled in skin as red as shrimp which gleamed with the luster of scar tissue, the baby was beginning ferociously to live, dragging its anchor of a heavy lump. A vegetable existence? Maybe so; a deadly cactus.

The nurse nodded as though satisfied by what she saw in Bird's face, and wheeled the incubator back to the window. A squall of infant screaming again blew up, shaking the room beyond the glass partition where light boiled as in a furnace. Bird slumped and hung his head. The screaming loaded his drooping head as gunpowder loads a flintlock. He wished there were a tiny bed or an incubator for himself: an incubator would be best, filled with water vapor that hung like mist, and Bird would lie there breathing through gills like a silly amphibian.

"You should complete the hospitalization forms right away," the nurse said, returning to his side. "We ask you to leave thirty thousand yen security."

Bird nodded.

"The baby takes his milk nicely and his arms and legs are lively."

Why the hell should he drink milk and why exercise? Bird almost asked reproachfully—and checked himself. The querulousness that was becoming a new habit disgusted him.

"If you'll just wait here I'll get the pediatrician in charge."

Bird was left alone, and ignored. Nurses carrying diapers and trays of bottles jostled him with their extended elbows but no one so much as glanced at his face. And it was Bird who whispered the apologies. Meanwhile, the ward on this side of the glass partition was dominated by the loud voice of the little man who seemed to be challenging one of the doctors.

"How can you be sure there's no liver? And how could a thing like that happen? I've heard the explanation about a hundred times but it still doesn't make sense. I mean, is that stuff about the baby not having any liver true? Is it, doctor?"

Bird managed to wedge himself into a spot where he wasn't in the way of the bustling nurses and stood there drooping like a willow and looking down at his sweaty hands. They were like wet leather gloves. Bird recalled the hands his baby had been holding up behind its ears. They were large hands like his own, with long fingers. Bird hid his hands in his pants pockets. Then he looked at the little man in his late fifties who was developing a pertinacious logic in conversation with the doctor. He was wearing a pair of brown knickers and a sport shirt with the top button open and the sleeves rolled up. The shirt was too large for his slight frame, which was meagerly fleshed with something like dried meat. His bare arms and neck were burned as black as leather, appallingly sinewed; it was a quality of skin and muscle found in manual laborers who suffer from chronic fatigue because they are not robust. The man's kinky hair clung to the saucer-top of his large head like a lewd, oily cap, his forehead was too broad and his eyes were dull, the smallness of his lips and jaw upset the balance of his face. He evidently worked with his hands, but he was not a mere laborer. More likely he had to help out with the heavy work while abrading his power of thought and his nerves with the responsibility of a small business. The man's leather belt was as wide as an obi, but it was easily counterpoised by the exaggerated alligator watchband armoring the wrist he was waving in the doctor's face, a good eight inches above his own. The doctor's language and manner were precisely those of a minor official, and the little man appeared to be trying frantically to turn the argument to his advantage by blowing down the other's suspect authority with the wind of sheer bravado. But from time to time he turned to glance behind him at the nurses and Bird, and in his eyes was a kind of defeatism, as though he acknowledged a decline from which he would never manage to recover. A strange little man.

"We don't know how it happened, you'd have to call it an accident, I suppose. But the fact is that your child has no liver. The stool is white, isn't it! Pure white! Have you ever seen another baby with a stool like that?" the doctor said loftily, trying to move the little man's challenge out of the way with the toe of one shoe.

"I've seen baby chicks leave white droppings. And most chickens have livers, right? Like fried chicken liver and eggs? Most chickens have livers but there are still baby chicks whose droppings are white sometimes!"

"I'm aware of that, but we're not talking about baby chickens—this is a human baby."

"But is that really so unusual, a baby with a white stole?"

"A white stole?" the doctor interrupted angrily. "A baby with a white stole would be very unusual, yes. Do you suppose you mean a white stool?"

"That's right, a white stool. All babies without livers have white stools. I understand that, but does that mean automatically that all babies with white stools have no liver, does it, doctor?"

"I've already explained that at least a hundred times!" The doctor's outraged voice sounded like a scream of grief. He meant to laugh at the little man, but the large face behind his thick, horn-rimmed glasses was contorted in spite of himself and his lips were trembling.

"Could I hear it just once more, doctor?" The little man's voice was calm now, and gentle. "Him not having any liver is no laughing matter for my son or me either. I mean, it's a serious problem, right, doctor?"

In the end the doctor gave in, sat the little man down next to his desk, took out a medical card, and began to explain. Now the doctor's voice and occasionally the voice of the little man edged with a note of doubt ferried between the two men with an intentness that excluded Bird. He was trying to eavesdrop, head cocked in their direction, when a doctor about his own age bucked through the door and moved briskly into the ward to a spot directly behind him.

"Is the relative of the baby with the brain hernia here?" the doctor called in a high thin voice like the piping of a tin flute.

"Yes," Bird said, turning around. "I'm the father—"

The doctor inspected Bird with eyes that made him think of a turtle. And it didn't stop with the eyes; his boxy chin and sagging, wrinkled throat recalled a turtle too—a brutal snapping turtle. But in his eyes, which had a whitish cast because the pupils were hardly more than expressionless dots, there was also a hint of something uncomplicated and benign.

"Is this your first child?" the doctor said, continuing to examine Bird suspiciously. "You must have been wild."

"Yes—"

"No developments worth mentioning so far today. We'll have somebody from brain surgery examine the child in the next four or five days; our Assistant Director is tops in the field, you know. Of course, the baby will have to get stronger before they can operate or there wouldn't be any point to it. We're terribly crowded at brain surgery here so naturally the surgeons try to avoid pointless wastes of time."

"Then—there will be an operation?"

"If the infant gets strong enough to withstand surgery, yes," the doctor said, misinterpreting Bird's hesitation.

"Is there any possibility that the baby will grow up normally if he's operated on? At the hospital where he was born yesterday they said the most we could hope for even with surgery was a kind of vegetable existence."

"A vegetable—I don't know if I'd put it that way. . . ." The doctor, without a direct reply to Bird's question, lapsed into silence. Bird watched his face, waiting for him to speak again. And suddenly he felt himself being seized by a disgraceful desire. It had quickened in the darkness of his mind like a clot of black slugs when he had learned at the reception window that his baby was still alive, and gradually had made clear to him its meaning as it propagated with horrid vigor. Bird again dredged the question up to the surface of his conscious mind: how can we spend the rest of our lives, my wife and I, with a monster baby riding on our backs? Somehow I must get away from the monster baby. If I don't, ah, what will become of my trip to Africa? In a fervor of self-defense, as if he were being stalked through the glass partition by the monster baby in an incubator, Bird braced himself for battle. At the same time he blushed and began to sweat, ashamed of the tapeworm of egotism that had attached itself to him. One ear was deafened by the roar of blood hurtling through it and his eyes gradually reddened as though walloped by a massive, invisible fist. The sensation of shame fanned the red fire in his face and tears seeped into his eyes—ah, Bird longed, if only I could spare myself the burden of a monstrous vegetable baby. But voice his thoughts in an appeal to the doctor he could not do, the burden of his shame was too heavy. Despairing, his face as red as a tomato, Bird hung his head.

"You don't want the baby to have an operation and recover, partially recover anyway?"

Bird shivered: he felt as if a knowing finger had just stroked the ugliest part of his body and the most sensitive to pleasure, like the fleshy pleats in his scrotum. His face turning scarlet, Bird made his appeal in a voice so mean he couldn't bear to hear it himself:

"Even with surgery, if the chances are very slight . . . that he'll grow up a normal baby. . . ."

Bird sensed that he had taken the first step down the slope of contemptibility. The chances were he would run down the slope at full tilt, his contemptibility would snowball even as he watched it. Bird shuddered again, aware of the ineluctability of it. Yet now, as before, his feverish, misted eyes were imploring the doctor.

"I suppose you realize I can't take any direct steps to end the baby's life!" The doctor haughtily returned Bird's gaze, a glint of disgust in his eyes.

"Of course not—" Bird said hurriedly, very much as if he had heard

something highly irregular. Then he realized that the doctor had not
been taken in by his deviousness. That made it a double humiliation,
and Bird, in his resentment, didn't try to vindicate himself.

"It's true that you're a young father—what, about my age?" Slowly
turning his turtle head, the doctor glanced at the other members of the
staff on this side of the glass partition. Bird suspected the doctor was
trying to mock him, and he was terror-stricken. If he tries to make a
game of me, he whispered at the back of his throat with empty bravado,
his head swimming, I'll *kill* him! But the doctor intended to conspire in
Bird's disgraceful plot. In a hushed voice that no one else in the ward
could hear, he said:

"Let's try regulating the baby's milk. We can even give him a
sugar-water substitute. We'll see how he does on that for a while, but if
he still doesn't seem to be weakening, we'll have no choice but to
operate."

"Thank you," Bird said with a dubious sigh.

"Don't mention it." The doctor's tone of voice made Bird wonder
again if he wasn't being ridiculed. Soothingly then, as at a bedside,
"Drop around in four or five days. You can't expect a significant change
right away and there's no point getting all worked up and rushing
things," he declared, and, like a frog gulping down a fly, snapped his
mouth shut.

Bird averted his eyes from the doctor and, bowing, headed for the
door. The nurse's voice caught up with him before he could get out:

"As soon as possible, please, the hospitalization forms!"

Bird hurried down the gloomy corridor as if he were fleeing the scene
of a crime. It was hot. He realized now for the first time that the ward
had been air conditioned, his first air conditioning of the summer. Bird
wiped furtively at tears that were hot with shame. But the inside of his
head was hotter than the air around him and hotter than his tears;
shivering, he moved down the corridor with the uncertain step of a
convalescent. As he passed the open window of the sick ward, crying
still, patients like soiled animals supine or sitting up in bed watched him
go with wooden faces. The fit of tears had subsided when he reached an
area where the corridor was lined with private rooms, but the sensation
of shame had become a kernel lodged like glaucoma behind his eyes.
And not only behind his eyes, it was hardening in all the many depths of
his body. The sensation of shame: a cancer. Bird was aware of the

foreign body, but he could not consider it; his brain was burned out, extinguished. One of the sickrooms was open. A slight, young, completely naked girl was standing just inside as if to bar the door. In bluish shadow, her body seemed less then fully developed. Hugging the meager protuberances that were her breasts with her left hand, as though in pity, the girl dropped her right hand to stroke her flat belly and pluck her pubic hair; then, challenging Bird with eyes that glittered, she inched her feet apart until her legs were spread and sank a gentle and once again pitying finger into the golden cilia around her vagina, sharply silhouetted for an instant in the light from the window behind her. Bird, though he was moved to compassion not unlike love for the girl, walked past the open door without giving the nymphomaniac time to reach her lonely climax. The sensation of shame was too intense for him to sustain concern for any existence but his own.

As Bird emerged at the passageway that led to the main wing of the hospital, the little logician with the leather belt and the alligator watchband caught up with him. He fell into step alongside Bird with the same overbearing defiance he had demonstrated in the ward, bouncing off the balls of his feet in an attempt to cover the difference in their heights. When he began to talk, looking up into Bird's face, it was in the booming voice of a man who has made up his mind. Bird listened in silence.

"You've got to give them a battle, you know, fight! fight! fight!" he said. "It's a fight with the hospital, especially the doctors! Well, I really let them have it today, you must have heard me."

Bird nodded, remembering the little man's "white stole." Bluffing wildly to gain the advantage in his fight with the hospital, he had lost a round to Mrs. Malaprop.

"My boy hasn't got a liver, you see, so I've got to fight and keep fighting or they might just cut him up alive. No, that's the God's truth! You want things to go right in a big hospital, you've got to get in a mood to fight first thing! It doesn't do any good to behave nice and quiet and try to get them to like you. I mean, you take a patient that's dying, he's quieter than a year-old corpse. But us relatives of the patient can't afford to be so nice. Fight! let me tell you, it's a fight. Like a few days ago I told them right out, if the baby hasn't got a liver then you go ahead and make him one! You've got to know some tactics if you want to fight, so I've been reading up. And I told them, I said babies with no rectum have been fitted out with artificial rectums so you ought to be able to figure out an artificial liver. Besides, I said, you take a liver, it's got a lot more class than an ordinary asshole!"

They were at the main entrance to the hospital. Bird sensed that the little man was trying to make him laugh, but of course he wasn't in a laughing mood. "Will the baby recover by the fall?" he asked in place of an apology for his long face.

"Recover? Fat chance: my son has no liver! I'm just fighting all two thousand employees in this great big hospital."

The hint of unique grief and of the dignity of the weak in the little man's reply was enough to shock Bird. Refusing an offer of a lift to the station in his three-wheel truck, Bird walked out to the bus stop alone. He thought about the thirty thousand yen he would have to pay the hospital. He had already decided where he would get the money; and for just the instant needed for the decision, the sensation of shame was displaced by a despairing rage at no one in particular, that made Bird tremble. He had just slightly more than thirty thousand yen in the bank, but it was money he had deposited as the beginning of a reserve fund for his trip to Africa. For the present, that thirty thousand odd yen was hardly more than a marker indicating a frame of mind. But even the marker was now about to be removed. Now, except for two road maps. Bird was left with nothing that related directly to a trip to Africa. Sweat gushed from all the skin on his body, and Bird felt a damp, ugly chill on his lips and ears and fingertips. He took his place at the end of the line at the bus stop, and, in a voice like the droning of a mosquito, swore: "Africa? What a fucking laugh!" The old man directly in front of Bird started to turn around, decided against it, and slowly straightened his large, bald head. Everyone had been beaten senseless by the summer that had consumed the city prematurely.

Bird, too, closed his eyes feebly and, shivering with a chill, sweated. Soon he could smell his body beginning to exude an unpleasant odor. The bus didn't come; it was hot. Folding in the shame and all the rage eddying in Bird's head, a reddish darkness spread. And then a sprout of sexual desire pushed up through the darkness and grew before Bird's eyes like a young rubber tree. His eyes closed still, Bird groped for his trousers and felt his erected penis through the cloth. He felt wretched, base, rueful; he longed for the ultimate in antisocial sex. The kind of coitus that would strip and hold up to the light the shame that was worming into him. Bird left the line and looked for a taxi with eyes brutalized by the light, seeing the square as though in a negative, with blacks and whites reversed. He intended to return to Himiko's room, where the light of day was shut out. If she turns me down, he thought irritably, as if to whip himself, I'll beat her unconscious and fuck her then.

7

Y OU know, Bird, you're always in the worst *condition* when you try to get me into bed with you." Himiko sighed. "Right now you're about the least attractive Bird I've ever seen."

Bird was obstinately silent.

"But I'll sleep with you just the same. I haven't been fastidious about morality since my husband committed suicide; besides, even if you intend to have the most disgusting kind of sex with me, I'm sure I'll discover something *genuine* in no matter what we do."

Genuine—*authentic, true, real, pure, natural, sincere, earnest;* the English instructor at a cram-school arranged the translation words inside his head. And in his present state, Bird thought, none of those meanings came even near to applying to him.

"Bird, you get into bed first; I want to wash."

Slowly Bird took off his sweaty clothes and lay back on top of the worn blanket. Propping his head on both fists he squinted down at the paunch around his belly and at his whitish, insufficiently erected penis. Himiko, with the glass door to the bathroom wide open, lowered herself backwards onto the toilet, opened her thighs wide and doused her genitals with water from a large pitcher which she held in one hand. Bird watched her from the bed for a while and supposed that this was wisdom obtained from sexual relations with foreign men. Then he returned to gazing quietly down at his own belly and penis, and waited.

"Bird . . ." Himiko called as she vigorously rubbed herself dry with a large towel; the water had splashed all the way to her chest. ". . . there's a danger of pregnancy today; have you come prepared?"

"No, I haven't."

Pregnancy! The flaming thorns on the word pierced Bird to the softest quick and a low, grieved moan escaped him. The thorns burrowed all the way into his vital organs and continued to burn there.

"Then we'll have to think of something, Bird." Himiko lowered the pitcher to the floor with a noise like a pistol report, and came back to Bird's side rubbing her body with the bath towel. With one hand, Bird clenched his wilted penis in embarrassment.

"I lost it all of a sudden," he said. "Himiko! I'm no good at all now." Breathing strongly, healthily, Himiko peered down at Bird and continued to dry her sides and her chest between her breasts. She appeared to be speculating on the meaning hidden in Bird's words. The smell of her body roused acute memories of college summers and Bird caught his breath: skin toasting in the sun. Himiko wrinkled her nose like a spaniel puppy and laughed a simple, dry laugh. Bird went scarlet.

"You just think you're no good," Himiko said carelessly and dropping the towel around her feet, she moved to cover Bird's body with her own, her small breasts thrusting like fangs. Bird, like a child, fell captive to the self-defense instinct; still clutching his penis with one hand, he drove his other arm straight at Himiko's belly. His hand sinking into her soft flesh made his skin crawl.

"It was your shouting 'pregnancy' just now that did it," he said in hurried justification.

"I did not shout," Himiko objected with a look of outrage.

"It hit me awfully hard. Pregnancy is the one word I just can't take!"

Himiko covered her breasts and abdomen with her arms, probably because Bird was doggedly concealing his penis. Like the wrestlers of antiquity who wrestled in the nude, they first defended their most vulnerable parts with their bare hands and then stood their ground, eyeing each other warily.

"What's wrong, Bird?" Himiko said without anger. Gradually she had realized the gravity of the situation.

"I thought about pregnancy and—fell apart."

Himiko brought her legs together and sat down next to Bird's thigh. Bird twisted away on the narrow bed to make more room for her. Himiko, lowering the arm that still covered her breasts, gently touched the hand that Bird still clenched around his penis.

"Bird, I can make you hard enough," she said quietly but with conviction. "A lot of time has passed since that lumberyard."

Bird submerged in a feeling of dark, clammy helplessness, and endured the ticklish play of Himiko's fingers on his hand. Would he be able to present his own case convincingly? He had his doubts. But he had to explain, to leap the wall of his predicament.

"It's not a question of technique," he said, turning his eyes away from the earnest, sorrowful aspect of Himiko's breasts. "The problem is fear."

"Fear?" Himiko appeared to be turning over the word in her mind in hope of discovering the bud of a joke.

"I'm afraid of the dark recesses where that grotesque baby was created," Bird said in an attempt at explanation in a joking vein, which, failing, sank him even deeper into gloom. "When I saw the baby with his head wrapped in bandages, I thought of Apollinaire. It sounds sentimental, but I felt as if the baby had been wounded in the head on a battlefield, like Apollinaire. My baby got hit in solitary battle inside a dark, sealed hole I've never seen. . . ." As he spoke, Bird recalled the sweet, redeemable tears he had shed in the ambulance—but the tears of shame I wept in the hospital corridor today are already beyond redemption. ". . . I can't send my weakling penis onto that battle-ground!"

"But isn't that confined to you and your wife? I mean, isn't it a fear you ought to experience when she first approaches you about sex after she's recovered?"

"Assuming we ever make it again—" Bird faltered, already oppressed by a moment of consternation still weeks away, "—I know I'll feel as if I'm having incest with my baby son on top of this fear of mine. Now wouldn't that make even a steel penis go limp?"

"Poor Bird! If I gave you enough time, you'd count off a hundred and one *complexes* in defense of your own *impotence.*"

Satisfied with her little joke, Himiko lay face down in the narrow space alongside Bird's body. Bird, trying to make himself even smaller on the bed as it sagged like a hammock under the added weight, listened in mortal terror to the sound of Himiko's restrained breathing next to his ear. If she had already plugged in the coil of desire he would be obliged to do something for her. But burrow his baby mole of a fragile penis into the dark, closed culvert beyond those dank and unaccountable folds —that he could not do. Himiko's earlobe brushed Bird's temple hotly. Though she lay in limp silence, her body seemed to be under attack by a million gadflies of desire. Bird considered easing her need a little at a time with his fingers, or lips, or tongue. But she had gone on record the night before as having the same distaste for that as masturbation. If he brought it up again and was refused in the same words, both of them would feel as if they had cruelly spurned each other. It occurred to Bird that something might be managed if Himiko only had a little of the sadist in her. He would try anything, so long as it didn't involve the hole from which calamity had welled. She could beat or kick or stomp him and he would bear it quietly; he wouldn't even hesitate to drink her urine. For the first time in his life, Bird now discovered the masochist in himself. And since this was *after* he had mired in a bottomless swamp of shame, he even felt attracted in a self-abusive way to these new, and trifling, disgraces. It was just in this fashion, he supposed, that one inclined toward masochism. But why not say *himself* and be frank about it! Not so many years from now, as a forty-year-old masochist, Bird might remember this day as the anniversary of his conversion to the cult. Bird pursued a fixation: that his degeneracy was self, and no place other, centered.

"Bird?"

"Yes?" Bird said in resignation; so the attack had begun at last!

"You've got to destroy the sexual taboos that you've created for yourself. Otherwise, your sexual world will warp terribly!"

"I know. I was just thinking about masochism," Bird said. Contempt-ibly enough, he expected Himiko to leap at the fly he had cast and to extend a base probe of her own with a wistful reply that she, on her part, had thought often about sadism. Bird lacked even the reckless honesty of the aspiring pervert. Clearly the poisons of shame had brought him to a debased extreme.

But when Himiko spoke after what seemed a puzzled silence, it was not to pursue Bird's riddle:

"If you're going to conquer your fear, Bird, you'll have to isolate it by defining its object precisely."

Uncertain for the moment of what Himiko intended, Bird was silent.

"Is your fear limited to the vagina and the womb? Or are you afraid of everything female, of my entire existence as a woman, for example?"

Bird thought for a minute. "Of the vagina and the womb, I suppose. Since you personally have nothing to do with my misfortune, the only reason I can't face you when you're naked has to be that you're armed with a vagina and a womb!"

"In that case, wouldn't you simply have to eliminate the vagina and the womb?" Himiko said with careful impartiality. "If you can confine your fear to the vagina and the womb, then the enemy you have to fight lives only in that realm. Bird! What are the attributes of the vagina and the womb that frighten you?"

"It's the kind of thing I was talking about. I have this feeling there's what you'd call another universe back in there. It's dark, it's infinite, it's teeming with everything antihuman: a grotesque universe. And I'm afraid that if I entered it, I'd get trapped in the time system of another dimension and wouldn't be able to return—my fear has certain resemblances to an astronaut's fantastic acrophobia!"

Bird had sensed that Himiko's logic was leading to something that would aggravate his sense of shame, and he was hiding behind a screen of language because he wanted to avoid whatever it might be. But Himiko wasn't to be put off: "Do you suppose you wouldn't be particularly afraid of the female body if the vagina and womb were excluded from it?"

Bird hesitated. Then he said, blushing, "It's not terribly important but, well, the breasts—"

"What you're saying is that you wouldn't have to be afraid if you approached me from behind."

"But—"

"Bird!" Himiko would accept no more protests. "I always think of you as the type of man younger men tend to idolize. Haven't you ever been to bed with one of those younger brothers?"

The plan Himiko outlined was more than sufficient to overcome Bird's own fastidiousness about sexual morality. Bird was stunned. Never mind how it would be for me, he thought, released for just an instant from preoccupation with himself. Himiko would have to endure considerable pain, probably her body would tear and she would bleed: we both might be smeared in filth! But suddenly, twisted into his disgust like a length of rope, Bird felt a new desire welling.

"Won't you feel humiliated afterward?" Bird whispered in a voice hoarse with desire: this was a final demonstration of reluctance.

"I didn't feel humiliated even when I got covered in blood and mud and wood shavings in the middle of a winter night in that lumberyard."

"But I wonder," Bird said, "will there be any pleasure in it for you?"

"At the moment I'm only interested in doing something for you,

Bird," Himiko said. Then she added with unbounded gentleness, as if to make certain Bird wouldn't have to feel awkward, "Besides, as I said before, I can discover what I'd call something *genuine* in any imaginable brand of sex."

Bird was silent. Without moving on the bed, he watched Himiko select something from the city of little jars on her dresser, walk into the bathroom, take out of a drawer a large clean towel. The tides of anxiety rose slowly, trying to submerge him. Bird sat up abruptly, lifted the whisky bottle from the side of the bed where it had rolled, and swigged from the bottle. He recalled how, at the bus stop in front of the hospital under the noonday sun, he had longed for the most malefic sex, a fuck rife with ignominy. And now it was possible. Bird took another swallow of the whisky and fell back on the bed. Now his penis was keen and hard, pulsing hotly. Himiko avoided his eyes as she returned to the bed, a mournful, leaden expression on her face. Was she also in the grip of some extraordinary desire? With satisfaction Bird felt a smile spread from his lips to his cheeks. I've leaped the highest wall first, I should be able to clear all the hurdles of shame now, like a track man in infinite time.

"Bird, there's nothing to be so uneasy about," Himiko said, detecting indications contrary to Bird's perception of himself. "Chances are it'll be nothing at all."

. . . in the beginning he was solicitous of Himiko. But as failure followed on failure he began to feel that the small ludicrous noises and the peculiar odor were a kind of mockery, and his resentment gradually deprived him of all feeling but an egotistical engrossment in himself. Before long, Bird had forgotten Himiko, and the moment he felt himself succeed he grew hectically intent. Fragments of thought—hate floppy breasts and harsh animal genitals, desire lonely orgasm all to myself, avoid woman's eyes peering up into your face—burst like shining shrapnel across Bird's mind: this was the prelude to pleasure. To worry about the woman's orgasm as you screwed, registering in your mind the responsibility for her after she was pregnant, was to do battle with your shuddering rear in order to put shackles around your own neck. Bird raised a war-cry at the back of his flaming head: I'm trampling a woman now in the most ignominious way! I'm capable of all that's meanest and most vile, I'm shame itself, the hot mass my penis is rending now is really me, he raged, and was smitten by an orgasm of such intensity that it made his head swim.

Bird convulsed with pleasure, and each convulsion drove a cry of agony from Himiko. Only half conscious, Bird listened to her screams. Abruptly, as if hatred had grown too much for him, he bit into Himiko's neck where it joined her shoulder. Again she screamed. Opening his eyes, Bird saw a drop of blood trickling past her ashen earlobe toward her cheek. He groaned once more.

Bird sensed the horror of what he had done only after the orgasm had passed, and he felt turned to stone. He wondered if the humanity could be restored to their relationship after coition this inhuman. He lay on his stomach like a rock, breathing raggedly, and wished he could extinguish himself. But Himiko was good enough to whisper in a gentle voice rich with everyday peace:

"Come into the bathroom without touching yourself; I'll finish up for you."

With amazement came succor and liberation. Himiko handled him as if he were a paralyzed invalid while he looked away with a flaming face. Surprise gradually sank into Bird and settled. There was no doubting that he was in the hands of a sexual expert. In what fashion had his girlfriend traversed the long road since that night in the middle of winter? Bird requited Himiko's attentions only by bathing with disinfectant the wounds his own teeth had inflicted on her shoulder. He bathed the three scattered bites clumsily, like a timid child. Relieved, he watched the color quietly returning to Himiko's cheeks and eyelids.

The sheets freshly changed, Bird and his friend again lay side by side on the bed. Their breathing now was regular. Himiko's silence distressed Bird, but he was reassured by her quiet breathing and by the calmness of her eyes as she stared up into the dimness. Besides, Bird was immersed himself in a deep feeling of peace, far from any inclination to psychological excavation. He was savoring gratefulness. Not so much confined to Himiko alone as gratefulness for the peace he had discovered, though certainly it could not last long, at the vortex of the maelstrom whirling around him with its vicious traps. Of course the ring of shame enclosing him was expanding even now: a symbol of his shame was already enshrined in a distant hospital ward. But Bird was reclining in a warm tub of peace. He noticed then that an internal obstacle, overcome, had passed away.

"Shall we try again, the regular way?" Bird said. "I don't think I'm afraid anymore."

"Thank you, Bird. Why don't you take some sleeping pills if you need them, and then let's sleep until tonight. If you're still free of your fear when you wake up—"

Bird agreed; he felt he wouldn't need sleeping pills in his present state.

"You're a comfort to me," he said simply.

"I mean to be. I bet you haven't been comforted once since all this began. And that's not good, Bird. At a time like this you must be careful to have someone comfort you almost more than you need at least once. Otherwise you'll find yourself helpless when the time comes to summon up your courage and break away from chaos."

"Courage?" Bird said without considering what Himiko might mean. "When am I going to have to call on courage?"

"Oh you will, Bird, lots of times from now on," Himiko said carelessly, yet with unsmiling authority in her voice.

Bird found himself looking at Himiko as an old and tested warrior in the campaigns of daily life, with incomparably more experience than himself. Not only was she a sexual expert, her competence extended to a myriad other aspects of life in this real world. Bird acknowledged to himself that he was coming under Himiko's influence: it was thanks to help from her that he had just overcome one of his fears. Had he ever felt so uncomplicated talking with a woman after intercourse? He didn't think so. After sex, even sex with his wife, Bird had always fallen captive to feelings of self-pity and disgust. He mentioned this to Himiko, without mentioning his wife.

"Self-pity? disgust? Bird, then you couldn't have been sexually mature. And the women you slept with probably felt self-pity and disgust, too. I bet it was never completely satisfying, was it, Bird?"

Bird was envious; jealous, too. That youth and the little dandy like an egg ogre who had called Himiko from outside her window in the middle of the night must both have had, he felt certain, completely satisfying intercourse with her. As Bird lay in petulant silence, Himiko said, carelessly again, though clearly she was displeased: "There's nothing as arrogant and shitty as having sex with somebody and then feeling sorry for yourself. Bird, even disgust is better than that!"

"You're right. But the kind of people who feel sorry for themselves after sex don't ordinarily have help from an expert like you, and they've lost all their confidence."

Bird felt as if he were reclining on a psychiatrist's couch, and when he had emptied himself of unabashed and self-indulgent talk, he began drifting off to sleep, wondering how a young man married to this woman of gold could have committed suicide. Into the dulled emptiness the sleep virus had created in his head, a notion climbed: might Himiko not be making her amends to her dead husband by tolerating Bird and those other two? He had hanged himself in this very room, stepping off this bed, precisely as naked as Bird was now. Summoned that day by a phone call from Himiko, Bird had freed the dead boy's neck from the noose thrown over the rafters and had helped lower him to the floor, like a butcher in a freezer lowering a side of slaughtered beef from a frosted hook. In the pale dream just below the surface of sleep, Bird saw himself and the dead youth as one. With the part of himself that was awake he could feel Himiko's hands sponging him dry, while in his dream he apprehended the movement of her trembling hands on his own body as she purified the dead boy. I *am* the dead boy, Bird thought, and the summer about to get under way will be easy to endure, because a dead boy's body is icy as a winter tree! Trembling then as he struggled toward the surface of his dream, Bird whispered *but I won't commit suicide!* and sank into the darkness of a deeper sleep.

. . . Bird's waking dream was harsh, the reverse face of the innocent dream that had ushered him into sleep, a thing armored in burrs that inspired anguish. Sleep for Bird was a funnel which he entered through the wide and easy entrance and had to leave by the narrow exit. Inflating like a blimp, his body was slowly traversing the dimness of infinite space. He has been subpoenaed by the tribunal beyond the darkness, and he is pondering a means of blinding them to his responsibility for the baby's death. Ultimately, he knows he will not be able to dupe the jurors, but he feels at the same time that he would like to make an appeal—those people in the hospital did it! Is there nothing I can do to escape punishment? But his suffering grows only more ignoble as he continues to drift, a puny zeppelin.

Bird woke up. Not a muscle that wasn't stiff and aching, as though he had been lying in the lair of a creature whose body was constructed differently from his own. He felt as though his body were wrapped in layers of plaster cast. Where the hell could I be—at a crucial time like this! he whispered, thrusting only the antlers of wariness through a vague fog. At a crucial time like this, when he was fighting hand to hand with a baby like a monster! Bird recalled his conversation with the doctor in the ward, and the sensations of peril gave way to those of shame. Not that peril had vanished; it was encysted behind the sensations of shame. Where the hell am I—at a crucial time like this!

Bird raised his voice a little and could hear that it was pickled in the vinegars of fear. He shook his head as though in spasm and—groping for a clue to the nature of the trap of darkness he was caught in —shuddered.

He was naked as a baby, defenseless, and, to make it worse, someone just as naked was curled against him asleep. His wife? Was he sleeping naked with his wife and hadn't told her yet the secret of the grotesque baby she had just borne? Ah, it couldn't be! Fearfully Bird put out his hand and touched the naked woman's head. As he slid his other hand down her naked shoulder to her side (the body was large, opulent, with animal softness, qualities opposite to those of his wife's body), the naked woman slowly but steadily twined her body around him. Awareness sharpened to clarity, and Bird, as he discovered his lover Himiko, discovered desire as well, desire which no longer stigmatized the attributes of womanhood. Ignoring the pain in his arms and shoulders, Bird embraced Himiko like a bear hugging an enemy. Her body, still fast asleep, was large and heavy. Bird slowly tightened his grip until the girl was pressed against his chest and belly with her head hanging limply backward above his shoulders. Bird peered into her upturned face; rising whitely out of the darkness, it seemed painfully young. Suddenly Himiko woke up, smiled at Bird, and with a slight movement of her head touched him with hot, dry lips. Without changing the position of their bodies, they drifted smoothly into intercourse.

"Bird, can you hold out while I make it?" Himiko's voice was still asleep. She must have prepared against the danger of pregnancy, for now she had taken the first irreversible step toward her own pleasure.

"Certainly I can hold out," Bird replied manfully, tensing, a navigator just informed that a storm was on its way. He performed warily, determined that restraint should not be swept away from the movements of his own body. He hoped to make amends now for his pitiful performance in the lumberyard.

"Bird!" Himiko raised a piteous scream that suited the childish face straining upward through the darkness. Like a soldier accompanying a comrade in arms to private battle, Bird stood by in stoic self-restraint while Himiko wrested from their coition the *genuine* something that was all her own. For a very long time after the sexual moment, Himiko's whole body trembled. Then she grew delicate, helpless, soft in an infinitely feminine way, and finally, releasing a muffled sigh like a baby animal with a full belly, fell fast asleep just where she lay. Bird felt like a rooster watching over a chick. Smelling the healthy odor of sweat that rose from the head half-hidden beneath his chest, he lay perfectly still, supporting his weight on his elbows lest he oppress the girl beneath him. He was still terrifically aroused, but he didn't want to interrupt Himiko's natural sleep. Bird had banished the curse on everything feminine that had occupied his brain a few hours ago, and, though she was more womanly than ever, he was able to accept Himiko completely. His astute sexual partner sensed this: soon Bird heard her breathing grow regular and knew that she was fast asleep. But when he tried carefully to withdraw from the girl, he felt something on his penis like the grip of a warm, gentle hand. Himiko was experimenting with a slight retaining action while she slept. Bird tasted mild but wholly sexual satisfaction. He smiled happily and immediately fell asleep.

Once again sleep was like a funnel. Bird entered the sea of sleep with a smile, but on his way back to the shores of reality he was seized by a stifling, claustrophobic dream. He fled from the dream crying. When he opened his eyes, Himiko was awake, too, peering anxiously at his tears.

8

A S Bird started up the stairs toward his wife's hospital room, his
shoes in one hand and a bag of grapefruit under his arm, the
young doctor with the glass eye started down. They met halfway. The
one-eyed doctor halted several steps above Bird and launched his voice
downward in what felt to Bird like high imperiousness. In fact, he said
merely, "How is everything?"

"He's alive," Bird said.

"And, what about surgery?"

"They're afraid the baby will weaken and die before they can
operate," Bird said, feeling his upturned face blush.

"Well, that's probably for the best!"

Bird's color deepened noticeably and a twitch appeared at the corners
of his mouth. His reaction made the doctor blush, too.

"Your wife hasn't been told about the baby's brain," he said,
speaking into the air above Bird's head. "She thinks there's a defective
organ. Of course, the brain *is* an organ, there's no getting around that,
so it's not a lie. You try lying your way out of a tight spot and you only
have to lie all over again when the truth gets out. You know what I
mean?"

"Yes," Bird said.

"Well then, don't hesitate to let me know if there's anything I can
do." Bird and the doctor bowed decorously and passed each other on the
stairs with faces averted. Well, that's probably for the best! the doctor
had said. To weaken and die before they could operate. That meant
escaping the burden of a vegetable baby, and without fouling your own
hands with its murder. All you had to do was wait for the baby to
weaken and die hygienically in a modern hospital ward. Nor was it
impossible to forget about it while you waited: that would be Bird's job.

91

Well, that's probably for the best! The sensation of deep and dark shame renewed itself in Bird and he could feel his body stiffen. Like the expectant mothers and the women who had just given birth who passed him in their many-colored rayon nightgowns, like those who carried in their bodies a large, squirming mass, and those who had not quite escaped the memory and habit of it, Bird took short, careful steps. He was pregnant himself, in the womb of his brain, with a large squirming mass that was the sensation of shame. For no real reason, the women in the corridor eyed him haughtily as they passed, and under each glance Bird meekly lowered his head. These were the women who had watched him leave the hospital in an ambulance with his grotesque baby, that same host of pregnant angels. For a minute he was certain they knew what had happened to his son since then. And perhaps, like ventriloquists, they were murmuring at the back of their throats Ah! if it's that baby you mean, he's been installed on an efficient conveyer system in an infant slaughterhouse and is weakening to death this very minute —well, that's probably for the best!

A squalling of many infants beset Bird like a whirlwind. His eye wildly wheeling fell on the rows of cradles in the infant ward. Bird fled down the corridor at a near run: he had a feeling several of the infants had stared back.

In front of the door to his wife's room, Bird carefully sniffed his hands and arms and shoulders, even his chest. There was no telling how it might complicate his predicament if his wife, waiting for him in her sickbed with her sense of smell honed to keenness, should scent out Himiko's fragrance on his body. Bird turned around, as if to make certain of an escape route: paused all along the dim corridor, young women in their nightgowns were peering at him through the dimness. Bird considered scowling back but he merely shook his head weakly and turned his back, then gave a timid knock at the door. He was performing the role of the young husband who has been visited by sudden misfortune.

When Bird stepped into the room his mother-in-law was standing with her back to the lush greenery in the window, and his wife was staring in his direction, lifting her head like a weasel beyond the mound of blanket that covered her spread thighs. Both wore startled looks in the greenly tinged, fecund light. In moments of surprise and sadness,

Bird observed, the blood bond between these two women was manifest in all their features and even the slightest gesture.

"I didn't mean to startle you, I knocked, but lightly—"

"Ah, Bird," his wife sighed, fixing him with wasted eyes that now were filling rapidly with tears. With her face clean of make-up and the pigment darkly evident on the surface of her skin, she had the firm, boyish look of the tennis player she had been when Bird had met her several years ago. Exposed to her gaze as he was, Bird felt horribly vulnerable; when he had put the bag of grapefruit down on the blanket, he stooped as if to conceal himself and deposited his shoes beneath the bed. If only, he wished ruefully, he could talk from the floor, crawling around like a crab. Out of the question: Bird straightened up, forcing himself to smile.

"Hey," he sang, working to keep his voice light, "is the pain all gone now?"

"It still hurts periodically. And every so often there's a contraction like a spasm. Even when I'm not in pain somehow I don't feel right, and the minute I laugh it hurts."

"That's miserable."

"It is. Bird, what's wrong with the baby?"

"What's wrong? That doctor with the glass eye must have explained, didn't he?" As he spoke, trying to keep the song in his voice, Bird looked quickly in his mother-in-law's direction, like a boxer with no confidence darting a glance behind him at his trainer. Beyond his wife's head in the narrow space between the bed and the window, his mother-in-law was transmitting secret signals frantically. Bird couldn't catch the nuances, only that he was being commanded to say nothing to his wife, that much was clear.

"If they would just tell me what was wrong," his wife said in a voice as lonely as it was withdrawn. Bird knew that the dark demons of doubt had driven her a hundred times to whisper these same words in this same helpless tone.

"There's a defective organ somewhere, the doctor won't talk about the details. They're probably still testing. Another thing, those university hospitals are bureaucratic as hell!" Bird could smell the stench of his lie even as he told it.

"I just know it must be his heart if they have to make so many tests. But why should my baby have a bad heart?" The dismay in his wife's voice made Bird feel again like scuttling around on the floor. Instead, he spoke harshly, affecting the tone of voice of a peevish teen-ager: "Since there are experts on the case why don't we leave the diagnosing to them! All the speculation in the world isn't going to do us one damn bit of good!"

An unconfident Bird turned a guilty eye back to the bed and saw that his wife had tightly shut her eyes. He looked down at her face and wondered uneasily if a sense of everyday balance would be restored to it; the flesh of the eyelids was wasted, the wings of the nose were swollen, and the lips seemed large out of all proportion. His wife lay motionless, with her eyes closed; she seemed to be falling asleep. All of a sudden a whole river of tears spilled from beneath her closed lids. "Just as the baby was born I heard the nurse cry 'Oh!' So I suspected that something must have been wrong. But then I heard the Director laughing happily, or I thought I did, it got so I couldn't tell what was real and what was a dream—when I came to, the baby had already been taken away in an ambulance." She spoke with her eyes closed.

That hairy Director son of a bitch! Anger clogged Bird's throat. He had made such an uproar with his giggling that a patient under anesthesia had heard him; if he has a habit of doing that when he's astonished, I'll lie for him in the dark with a lead pipe and make the cocksucker laugh his head off! But Bird's rage was that of a child's, limited to a moment. He knew he would never grip a club of any kind, never lie in wait in any darkness. He had to acknowledge that he had lost the self-esteem essential to rebuking someone else.

"I brought you some grapefruit," Bird said in a voice that asked forgiveness.

"Grapefruit! Why?" his wife challenged. Bird realized his mistake immediately.

"Damn! I forgot you always hated the smell of grapefruit," he said, stumbling into self-disgust. "But why would I have gone out of my way to buy grapefruit of all things?"

"Probably because you weren't really thinking of me or the baby, either. Bird, do you ever think seriously of anyone but yourself? Didn't we even argue about grapefruit when we were planning the menu at the wedding dinner? Really, Bird, how could you have forgotten?"

Bird shook his head in impotence. Then he fled from the hysteria that was gradually tightening his wife's eyes and turned to stare at his mother-in-law, still transmitting signals from the cramped niche between the bed and the wall. His eyes implored her for help.

"I was trying to buy some fruit and I had this feeling that grapefruit meant something special to us. So I bought some, without even thinking what it was that made them special. What shall I do with them?"

Bird had gone to the fruit store with Himiko, and there was no doubting that her presence had cast its shadow on the something special he had felt. From now on, Bird thought, Himiko's shadow would be falling heavily on the details of his life.

"You must have known I can't be in the same room with even one grapefruit; the smell irritates me terribly," Bird's wife gave chase. Bird wondered apprehensively if she hadn't detected Himiko's shadow already.

"Why don't you take the whole bag down to the nurses' office?" As his mother-in-law spoke, she flashed Bird a new signal. The light filtering through the lush greenery in the window at her back ringed her deeply sunken eyes and the spatulate sides of her soaring nose with a quivering, greenish halo. Bird finally understood: this radium spook of a mother-in-law was trying to tell him that she would be waiting in the corridor when he returned from the nurses' office.

"I'll be right back," he said. "Is the office downstairs?"

"Next to the clinic waiting room," she said with a long look at Bird.

Bird stepped into the dusky corridor with the bag of grapefruit under his arm. Even as he walked along, the fruit began discharging its bouquet; it seemed to infuse his face and chest with particles of fragrance. Bird reflected that the smell of grapefruit could actually provoke an attack in some asthmatics. Bird thought about his wife lying peevishly abed and that woman with green halos in the hollows of her eyes, flagging signals like the poses in a Kabuki dance. And what about himself, toying with the relationship between asthma and grapefruit! It was all an act, a bad play, only the baby with the lump on its head was for real: only the baby gradually wasting away on a diet of sugar-water instead of milk. But why sugar the water? It was one thing to deprive the baby of milk, but to flavor the substitute in any way, didn't that make the whole nasty business more like a contemptible trick?

Bird presented the bag of grapefruit to some off-duty nurses and started to introduce himself; suddenly, as if the stuttering that had afflicted him as a schoolboy had returned, he found himself unable to get out a single word. Rattled, he bowed in silence and hurried away. Behind him the nurses' bright laughter rose. It's all an act, phony, why did everything have to be so unreal? Scowling, his breath coming hard, Bird climbed the steps three at a time and passed the infants' ward warily, afraid he might carelessly glance inside.

In front of a service kitchen for the use of relatives and companions of the patients, a kettle in one hand, Bird's mother-in-law was standing proudly erect. Bird, approaching, saw around the woman's eyes instead of a halo of light sifted through green leaves an emptiness so wretched it made him shudder. Then he noticed that her erectness had nothing to do with pride: exhaustion and despair had robbed her body of its natural suppleness.

They kept the conversation simple, one eye on the door to Bird's wife's room fifteen feet away. When Bird's mother-in-law confirmed that the baby was not dead, she said, reproachfully, "Can't you arrange for things to be taken care of right away? If that child ever sees the baby, she'll go mad!"

Bird, threatened, was silent.

"If only there was a doctor in the family," the woman said with a lonely sigh.

We're a pack of vermin, Bird thought, a loathsome league of self-defenders. Nonetheless he delivered his report, his voice hushed, wary of the patients who might be crouching like mute crickets behind the closed doors that lined the corridor, their ears aflame with curiosity: "The baby's milk is being decreased and he's getting a sugar-water substitute. The doctor in charge said we should be seeing results in a few days."

As he finished, Bird saw the miasma that had enveloped his mother-in-law vanish utterly. Already the kettle of water seemed a weight too heavy for her arm. She nodded slowly and, in a thin, helpless voice, as if she wanted badly to go to sleep, "Oh, I see. Yes, I see. When this is all over, we'll keep the baby's sickness a secret between us."

"Yes," Bird promised, without mentioning that he had spoken to his father-in-law already.

"Otherwise, my little girl will never agree to have another child, Bird."

Bird nodded; but his almost physical revulsion for the woman merely heightened. His mother-in-law went into the kitchen now, and Bird returned to his wife's room alone. But wouldn't she see through a ruse this simple? It was all playacting, and every character in this particular play was a dissembler.

Bird knew by the face his wife turned to him as he stepped into the room that the hysteria about the grapefruit was forgotten. He sat down on the edge of the bed. "You're all worn down," his wife said, extending abruptly an affectionate hand and touching Bird's cheek.

"I am—"

"You've begun to look like a sewer rat that wants to scurry into a hole." The slap caught him unawares. "Is that so?" he said with a bitterness on his tongue, "like a sewer rat?"

"Mother is afraid you'll start drinking again, that special way you have, no limits, night and day—"

Bird recalled the sensations of protracted drunkenness, the flushed head and the parched throat, belly aching, body of lead, the fingers numb and the brain whisky-logged and slack. Weeks of life as a cave dweller enclosed in whisky walls.

"If you did start drinking again you'd end up dead drunk and no good to anybody just when our baby really needed you. You would, Bird."

"I'll never drink that way again," Bird said. It was true that the tiger of a ferocious hangover had sunk its teeth in him, but he had torn himself away without recourse to more liquor. But how would it have been if Himiko hadn't helped? Would he have begun once again to drift on that dark and agonizing sea tens of hours wide? He wasn't sure, and not being able to mention Himiko made it difficult to convince his wife of his power to resist the whisky lure.

"I very much want you to be all right, Bird. I think sometimes that, when a really crucial moment comes, you'll either be drunk or in the grip of some crazy dream and just float up into the sky like a real bird."

"Married all this time and you still have doubts like that about your own husband?" Bird spoke playfully, but his wife did not fall into his saccharine trap; far from it, she rocked him on his heels with this:

"You know, you often dream about leaving for Africa and shout things in Swahili! I've kept quiet about it all this time, but I've known you have no real desire to lead a quiet, respectable life with your wife and child. Bird?"

Bird stared in silence at the soiled, wasted hand his wife was resting on his knee. Then, like a child weakly protesting a scolding though he recognizes that he has misbehaved, "You say I shout in Swahili; what do I say?"

"I don't remember, Bird. I've always been half-asleep myself; besides, I don't know Swahili."

"Then what makes you so sure it was Swahili?"

"Words that sound that much like the screaming of beasts couldn't come from a civilized language."

In silence, Bird reflected sadly on his wife's misconception of the nature of Swahili.

"When mother told me two days ago and then again last night that you were staying at the other hospital, I suspected you'd gotten drunk or run away somewhere. I really had my doubts, Bird."

"I was much too upset to think about anything like that."

"But look how you're blushing!"

"Because I'm mad," Bird said roughly. "Why would I run away? With the baby just born and everything—"

"But, when I told you I was pregnant, didn't the ants of paranoia swarm all over you? Did you really want a child, Bird?"

"Anyway, all that can wait until after the baby has recovered—that's all that matters now," Bird said, breaking for easier ground.

"It *is* all that matters, Bird. And whether or not the baby recovers depends on the hospital you chose and on your efforts. I can't get out of bed, I haven't even been told where the sickness is nesting in my baby's body. I can only depend on you, Bird."

"That's fine; depend on me."

"I was trying to decide whether I could rely on you to take care of the baby and I began to think I didn't know you all that well. Bird, are you the kind of person who'll take the responsibility for the baby even at a sacrifice to yourself?" his wife asked. "Are you the responsible, brave type?"

If he had ever been to war, Bird had thought often, he would have been able to say definitely whether he was a brave type. This had occurred to him before fights and before his entrance examinations, even before his marriage. And always he had regretted not having a definite answer. Even his longing to test himself in the wilds of Africa which opposed the ordinary was excited by his feeling that he might discover in the process his own private war. But at the moment Bird had a feeling he knew without having to consider war or travel to Africa that he was not to be relied on: a craven type.

Irritated by his silence, Bird's wife clenched into a fist the hand she was resting on his leg. Bird started to cover her hand with his own and hesitated: it appeared to simmer with such hostility that it would be hot to the touch.

"Bird, I wonder if you're not the type of person who abandons someone weak when that person needs you most—the way you abandoned that friend of yours," Bird's wife opened her timid eyes wide as if to study Bird's reaction, ". . . Kikuhiko?"

Kikuhiko! Bird thought. A friend from his days as a tough kid in a provincial city, younger than himself, Kikuhiko had tagged along wherever Bird had gone. One day, in a neighboring town, they had had a bizarre experience together. Accepting a job hunting down a madman who had escaped from a mental hospital, they had roamed the city on bicycles all night long. Whereas Kikuhiko soon grew bored with the job, began to clown, and finally lost the bicycle he had borrowed from the hospital, Bird's fascination only increased as he listened to the townspeople discussing the madman, and he kept up his ardent search all through the night. The lunatic was convinced that the real world was Hell, and he was terrified of dogs, which he took to be devils in disguise. At dawn, the hospital's German shepherd pack was to be loosed on the man's trail, and everyone agreed that he would die of fright if the animals brought him to bay. Bird therefore searched until dawn without a moment's rest. When Kikuhiko began to insist that they give up the hunt and return to their own city, Bird, in his anger, shamed the younger boy. He told Kikuhiko he knew of his affair with an American homosexual in the CIA. On his way home on the last train of the night Kikuhiko sighted Bird, still bicycling through the night in his eager search for the madman. Leaning out of the train window, he shouted, in a voice that had begun to cry, "—Bird, I was afraid!"

But Bird abandoned his poor friend and continued the search. In the end he succeeded only in discovering the madman hanging by the neck on a hill in the middle of the town, but the experience marked a transition in his life. That morning, riding next to the driver in the three-wheel truck that was carrying the madman's body, Bird had a premonition that he was soon to say good-by to the life of a delinquent; the following spring, he entered a university in Tokyo. The Korean war was on, and Bird had been frightened by rumors that young men on the loose in provincial cities were being conscripted into the police corps and shipped off to Korea. But what had happened to Kikuhiko after Bird had abandoned him that night? It was as if the puny ghost of an old friend had floated up from the darkness of his past and said hello to him.

"But what made you feel like attacking me with past history like Kikuhiko? I'd forgotten I'd even told you that story."

"If we had a boy, I was thinking of naming him Kikuhiko," his wife said.

Naming him! If that grotesque baby ever got hold of a thing like a name! Bird winced.

"If you abandoned our baby, I think I'd probably divorce you, Bird," his wife said, unmistakably a line she had rehearsed in bed, her legs raised in front of her, gazing at the greenery that filled the window.

"Divorce? We wouldn't get divorced."

"Maybe not, but we'd argue about it for a long time, Bird." And in the end, Bird thought, when it had been determined that he was a craven type not to be relied on, he would be turned out to live the rest of his melancholy life as a man unfit to be a husband. Right now, in that overbright hospital ward, that baby is weakening and about to die. And I'm just waiting for it to happen. But my wife is staking the future of our married life on whether I take sufficient responsibility for the baby's recovery—I'm playing a game I've already lost. Still, for the present, Bird could only perform his duty. "The baby's just not going to die," he said with many-faceted chagrin.

Just then his mother-in-law came in with the tea. Since she was trying not to telegraph their grim exchange in the corridor, and since Bird's wife was determined to conceal from her mother the enmity between herself and Bird, their little conversation over tea was comprised, for the first time, of ordinary talk. Bird even attempted some dry humor with an account of the baby without a liver and the little man who was its father.

Just to make certain, Bird looked back at the hospital windows and verified that all of them were masked behind trees in lush leaf before he approached the scarlet sports car. Himiko was fast asleep, wedged under the steering wheel as if she were bundled into a sleeping bag, her head on the low seat. As Bird bent forward to shake her awake, he began to feel as if he had escaped encirclement by strangers and had returned to his true family. Guiltily, he looked back at the branches rustling high at the top of the ginkgo trees. "Hi, Bird!" Himiko greeted him from the MG like an American co-ed, then wiggled out from under the steering wheel and opened the door for him. Bird got in quickly.

"Would you mind going to my apartment first? We can stop at the bank on the way to the other hospital."

Himiko pulled out of the driveway and immediately accelerated with a roar of exhaust. Bird, thrown off balance, told Himiko the way to the house with his back still pinned against the seat.

"You sure you're awake? Or do you think you're flying down a highway in a dream?"

"Of course I'm awake, Bird! I dreamed I was making it with you."

"Is that all you ever think about?" Bird asked in simple surprise.

"Yes, after a trip like last night. It doesn't happen that way often, and even with you that same tension isn't going to last forever. Bird, wouldn't it be great to know just what you had to do to make the days of marvelous lays go on and on! Before we know it, even you and I won't be able to stifle the yawns when we confront each other's nakedness."

But we've only just begun!—Bird started to say, but with Himiko's frantic hand on the wheel, the MG was already churning the gravel in Bird's driveway and then nosing deeply into the garden.

"I'll be down in five minutes; and try to stay awake this time. You can't dream much of a lay in five minutes!"

Upstairs in the bedroom, Bird threw together a few things he would need right away for a stay at Himiko's house. He packed with his back to the baby's bassinet: it looked like a small, white coffin. Last of all he packed a novel written in English by an African writer. Then he took down his Africa maps from the wall and, folding them carefully, thrust them into his jacket pocket.

"Are those road maps?" Himiko asked as her keen eye lighted on Bird's pocket. They were under way again, driving to the bank.

"They certainly are; maps you can really use."

"Then I'll see if I can find a shortcut to the baby's hospital while you're at the bank."

"That would be a good trick: these are maps of Africa," Bird said, "the first real road maps I've ever owned."

"May the day come when you'll be able to use them," Himiko said with a touch of mockery.

Leaving Himiko wedged beneath the steering wheel and beginning to drop off to sleep, Bird went in to arrange for the baby's hospitalization. But the baby's lack of a name created a problem. Bird answered endless questions for the girl at the reception window and finally had to protest: "My infant son is dying. For all I know he may be dead already. Now would you mind telling me why I am obliged to give him a name?" he said stiffly.

Miserably rattled, the girl yielded. It was then that Bird sensed, for no special reason, that the baby's death had been accomplished. He even inquired about making arrangements for the autopsy and crema-tion.

But the doctor who met Bird at the intensive care ward disabused him instantly: "Where do you come off waiting so impatiently for your son to die? Hospitalization here isn't that high, you know! And you must have health insurance. Anyway, it's true that your son is weakening, but he's still very much alive. So why don't you relax a little and start behaving like a father? How about it!"

Bird wrote Himiko's number on a page of his memo book and asked the doctor to phone him if anything decisive happened. Since he could feel everybody in the ward reacting to him as something loathsome, he went straight back to the car, without even pausing to peer into the incubator at his son. No less than Himiko, who had been asleep in the open car, Bird was drenched in sweat after his run through the sun and shadow of the hospital square. Trailing exhaust fumes and an animal odor of perspiration, they roared off to sprawl naked in the hot afternoon while they waited for the telephone call that would announce the baby's death.

All that afternoon, their attention was on the telephone. Bird stayed behind even when it was time to shop for dinner, afraid the phone might ring while he was out. After dinner, they listened to a popular Russian pianist on the radio, but with the volume way down, nerves screaming still for the phone to ring. Bird finally fell asleep. But he kept waking up to the ringing of a phantom bell in his dream and walking over to the phone to check. More than once the boundaries of the dream extended to lifting the receiver and hearing the doctor's voice report the baby's death. Waking yet another time in the middle of the night, Bird felt the suspense of a condemned murderer during a temporary stay of execution. And he discovered encouragement of unexpected depth and intensity in the fact that he was spending the night with Himiko and not alone. Not once since becoming an adult had he so needed another person. This was the first time.

9

NEXT morning, Bird drove Himiko's car to school. Parked in the schoolyard full of students, the scarlet MG smelled vaguely of scandal, something that didn't worry Bird until he had put the keys into his pocket. He sensed that lacunas had formed in each of the pleats of his consciousness since the trouble with the baby had begun.

Bird pushed through the crowd of students milling around the car with his face in a scowl. In the teachers' room, he was informed by his department chairman, a little man who wore his loud jacket askew in the manner of a nisei, that the Principal wanted to see him. But the report merely burrowed into the corroded portion of his consciousness and left Bird undisturbed.

"Bird, you are really *quelque-chose, toi,*" the chairman said pleasantly, as though in jest, even while he inspected Bird with keen eyes. "I don't know if you're brave or just brazen, but you're certainly plenty bold!"

Naturally, Bird couldn't help wincing as he entered the large lecture room where his students were waiting for him. But this was a group from a different class; most of them wouldn't know about yesterday's dishonorable incident. Bird encouraged himself with the thought. During the lesson he did notice a few students who evidently knew, but they were from city high schools, cosmopolitan and frivolous; to them, Bird's accident was merely ludicrous and just a bit heroic. When their eyes met his own, they even flashed teasing, affectionate smiles. Bird of course ignored them.

When Bird left the classroom, a young man was waiting for him at the top of the spiral stairs. It was his defender from the day before, the student who had protected him from the violence of that rancorous class. Not only had the student cut his own class in some other room, he

104

had been waiting for Bird directly in the sun. Beads of sweat glistened on the sides of his nose, and his blue denims were smirched with mud from the step he had been sitting on.

"Hi!"

"Hi!" Bird returned the greeting.

"I bet the Principal called you in. That horse's ass really did go to him with a story, he even had a photograph of that vomit, took it with a miniature camera!" The student smirked, exposing large, well-cared-for teeth.

Bird smiled too. Could his accuser have carried a miniature camera around with him all the time, in hopes of catching Bird in a weak moment and then taking the case to court?

"He told the Principal you came to class with a hangover, but five or six of us want to testify that you had food poisoning instead. We thought it would be a good idea to get together with you first and, you know, get our stories straight," the boy said craftily, a smug conspirator.

"I did have a hangover, so it's you fellows who are wrong. I'm guilty as accused by that puritan." Bird slipped past the student and started down the stairs.

"But sensei!" the boy persevered, climbing down the stairs after Bird, "you'll be fired if you confess to that. The Principal is the head of his local chapter of the Prohibition League, for God's sake!"

"You're joking!"

"So why not let it go as food poisoning? It's just the season for it —you could say the pay here is so bad you finally took a bite of something—old."

"A hangover isn't something I feel I have to cheat about. And I don't want you to lie for me."

"Humm!" was what the boy was brash enough to say.

"Sensei, where will you be going when you leave here?"

Bird decided to ignore the student. He didn't feel up to involving himself in any new plots. He discovered that he had become extraordinarily diffident; it had to do with those faults in his consciousness.

"You probably don't need a job at a cram-school, anyway. The Principal is going to feel pretty silly when he has to fire an instructor who drives a red MG. Hah!"

Bird walked straight away from the student's delighted laughter and went into the teachers' room. He was putting away the old chalk box and the reader in his locker when he discovered an envelope addressed to him. It was a note from the friend who sponsored the study group; the others must have decided at their special meeting what to do about Mr. Delchef. Bird had torn open the envelope and was about to read the note when he remembered from his student days a funny superstition about probability—when you were faced with two errands at the same time and didn't know what either held in store, one would always be pregnant with good fortune if the other turned out calamitously—and stuffed the letter into his pocket unread. If his meeting with the Principal went very badly, he would have a valid reason for expecting the best of the letter in his pocket.

One look at the Principal's face as he looked up from his desk told Bird that this meeting would be pregnant with disaster. He resigned himself; at least he would try to spend whatever time the interview took as pleasantly as he could.

"We have a little mess on our hands here, Bird. To tell the truth, it's awkward for me, too." The Principal sounded like the keen tycoon in a film about a business empire, at once pragmatic and austere. Still in his mid-thirties, this man had transformed an ordinary tutoring service into this full-blown preparatory school with its large and integrated curriculum, and now he was plotting to establish a junior college. His bulky head was shaved clean and he wore custom-made glasses—two oval lenses suspended from a thick, straight frame—which accented the irregularities of his face. In the guilty eyes behind the bluff and bluster of his glasses, however, was something that never failed to move Bird to mild affection for the man.

"I know what you're referring to. And I was at fault."

"The student who complained is a regular contributor to the school magazine—an unpleasant lad. It could be troublesome if he made a fuss. . . ."

"Yes, of course. I'd better resign right away," Bird quickly said, taking the lead himself in order to lighten the Principal's burden. The Principal snorted through his nose with unnecessary vigor and put on a look of mournful outrage.

"Naturally, the professor will be upset. . . ." he said, a request that Bird explain the situation to his father-in-law himself.

Bird nodded. He sensed that he would begin to get irritated if he didn't leave the office right away.

"One more thing, Bird. It seems that some of the students are insisting you had food poisoning and are threatening that tattletale. He claims that you're putting them up to it. That can't be right, can it?"

Bird lost his smile and shook his head. "Well, then, I don't want to take any more of your time," he said.

"I'm sorry about all this, Bird," the Principal said in a voice richened with sincerity. The eyes swelling behind the oval lenses darkened with feeling. "I've always liked you, you've got character! Was that really a hangover you had?"

"Yes. A hangover," Bird said, and he left the room. Instead of returning to the teachers' room, Bird decided to cut through the custodian's room and across the courtyard to the car. Now he felt melancholy defiance rising darkly in himself, as if he had been unjustly humiliated.

"Sensei, are you leaving us? Be awful sorry to see you go," the janitor volunteered. So news of the incident had spread. Bird was popular in the custodian's room.

"I'll be around to bother you for the rest of this term," he said, thinking dismally that he was not worthy of the expression on the old man's wrinkled face.

Bird's irrepressible ally was sitting on the door of the MG, scowling like an adult in the heat and glare of the sun. Bird's unexpected exit from the back door of the custodian's room took him by surprise and he scrambled to his feet. Bird climbed into the car.

"How did it go? Did you tell him it was food poisoning and stick up for your rights?"

"I told you, I had a hangover."

"Great! That's just great!" the boy jeered as though in disgust. "You know you're fired!"

Bird put the key in the switch and started the motor. Instantly his legs were bathed in sweat; it was like stepping into a steam bath. Even the steering wheel was so baking hot that Bird's fingers recoiled with a snap.

"Son of a bitch!" he swore.

The student laughed, delighted. "What are you going to do when they fire you? Sensei!"

What do I intend to do when they fire me? And bills still to be paid at two hospitals! Bird thought. But his head was frying in the sun and would not give birth to a single viable plan, only ooze rivers of perspiration. With vague uneasiness, Bird discovered he was once again in the grip of diffidence.

"Why don't you become a guide? Then you wouldn't have to worry about making a few lousy yen at a flunk-out school; you could squeeze those dollars out of foreign tourists!"

"You know where there's a guide service?" Bird asked with interest.

"I'll find out—where can I reach you?"

"Maybe we could get together after class next week."

"Leave it to me!" the student shouted with excitement.

Cautiously, Bird drove the sports car out into the street. He had wanted to get rid of the student so he could read the letter in his pocket. But he discovered as he accelerated that he was feeling grateful to the boy. If the student hadn't put him in a joking mood as he drove away in a grimy sports car from a job he had just lost—how wretched he would have felt! It was certain; he was destined to be helped out of impossible situations by a band of younger brothers. Bird remembered that he needed gas and drove into a station. After a minute's thought he asked for high test, then from his pocket took the letter which, according to that student superstition, was guaranteed to be entirely captivating news.

Mr. Delchef had ignored an appeal from the legation and was still living in Shinjuku with a young delinquent. He was not disillusioned politically with his own country, not planning spy activity or hoping to defect. He was simply unable to take leave of this particular Japanese girl. Naturally, the legation was most afraid that the Delchef incident might be used politically. If certain Western governments used their influence to launch a propaganda campaign based on Mr. Delchef's life as a recluse, the repercussions were certain to be widely felt. Accordingly, Mr. Delchef's government was anxious to get him back to the legation as quickly as possible so that he could be sent home, but enlisting the cooperation of the Japanese police would only publicize the incident. If, on the other hand, the legation itself attempted to use force, Mr. Delchef, who had fought with the resistance during the war, was certain to put up a terrific fight and the police would become involved after all. With nowhere else to turn, the legation finally had requested the members of the Slavic languages study group to try as quietly as possible to persuade Mr. Delchef of his folly. On Saturday afternoon, at one o'clock, there was to be another meeting in the restaurant across the street from the university Bird and the others had graduated from. Since Bird was closest to Mr. Delchef, his friend wrote, everyone was particularly anxious that he attend.

Saturday, the day after tomorrow: yes, he would go! The pump jockey, like a bee suffusing the air around its body with the fragrance of honey, was wrapped in a caustic gasoline haze. Bird paid him and pulled away from the gas stand with a roar of exhaust. Assuming the telephone call announcing the baby's death wouldn't come today, or tomorrow, or even the day after tomorrow, acquiring an outside errand to occupy the irritating hours of the reprieve was certainly a stroke of good luck. It had been a good letter after all.

Bird stopped at a grocery store on the way home and bought some beer and canned salmon. Parking in front of the house, he walked up to the front door and found it locked. Could Himiko have gone out? An arbitrary rage seized Bird, he could almost hear the telephone jangling for long, unheeded minutes. But when he walked around to the side of the house and called up at the bedroom window just to make sure, Himiko's eye peeped reassuringly from between the curtains. Bird sighed and, sweating heavily, walked back to the front door.

"Any word from the hospital?" he asked, his face still taut.

"Nothing, Bird."

It felt to Bird as if he had squandered energy along a huge perimeter by climbing into a scarlet sports car and circling Tokyo on a summer day. He found himself caught in the claws of a formidable lobster of fatigue, as if word of the baby's death would have invested the day's activity with meaning and fixed it in its proper place. Bird said gruffly: "Why do you keep the door locked even in the daytime?"

"I guess I'm scared. I have this feeling a disgusting goblin of misfortune is waiting for me just outside."

"A goblin after you?" Bird sounded puzzled. "It doesn't look to me as if you're in the least danger of any misfortune right now."

"It hasn't been that long since my husband killed himself. Bird, aren't you trying to say in your amazing arrogance that you're the only one around who has to watch out for goblins of misfortune?"

It was a terrific wallop. And Bird escaped the knock-down only because Himiko turned her back on him and hurried back into the bedroom without following through with a second punch.

With his eye on Himiko's naked shoulders glistening with fat in front of him, Bird struggled through the heavy, tepid air in the dim living room, and was stepping into the bedroom when dismay brought him to a halt. A large girl about Himiko's age, no longer young, was lounging on the bed beneath the haze of tobacco smoke that hung over the room like a gaseous cloud, her arms and shoulders bared.

"It's been a hell of a long time, Bird," the girl drawled a hoarse greeting.

"Hey!" Bird said, not yet the master of his confusion.

"I didn't want to wait for the phone call all alone so I asked her over, Bird."

"You didn't have to work at the station today?" Bird asked. This was another of Bird's classmates, from the English department. For two years after she had graduated, the girl had done nothing but amuse herself; like most of the girls from Bird's college, she had turned down every offer of a job because she considered them all beneath her talent. Finally, after two years of idleness, she had become a producer at a third-rate radio station with only a local broadcasting range.

"All my shows are after midnight, Bird. You must have heard that vomity whispering that sounds as if the girls are screwing the whole radio audience with their throat," the producer said with syrup in her voice. Bird recalled the assorted scandals in which she had involved the radio station that had so gallantly employed her. And he could remember perfectly well the disgust he had for her in their student days, when she had been not only a big girl but fat as well, with something he could never quite put his finger on around her eyes and nose that reminded him of a badger. "Can we do something about all this smoke?" Bird said with reserve, depositing the beer and canned salmon on the TV set.

Himiko went to open the ventilator in the kitchen. But her friend, without troubling herself about Bird's smarting eyes, lit a new cigarette with unsightly fingers with silver-polished nails. In the light of the silver Dunhill's orange flame, Bird saw, despite her hair hanging over her face, the sharp creases in the girl's brow and the tiny spasms rippling her darkly veined eyelids. Something was gnawing at the girl: Bird grew wary.

"Don't either of you girls mind the heat?"

"God, I do, I'm just about to faint," Himiko's friend said gloomily. "But it is unpleasant if the air is swirling around in a room when you're having a good talk with a close friend."

While Himiko moved briskly around the kitchen, wedging the beer into spaces between the ice trays, dusting the tins of canned food, and inspecting the labels, her producer friend watched disapprovingly from the bed. This dog will probably spread the hot news about us with terrific zest, Bird thought; I wouldn't be surprised if it got on the air late one night.

Himiko had thumbtacked Bird's map to the bedroom wall. Even the African novel he had concealed in his bag was sprawled on the floor like a dead rat. Himiko must have been reading it in bed when her girlfriend arrived. So she had thrown the book on the floor, gone out to unlock the door, and then left it lying there. Bird was peeved: his African treasures were being treated so carelessly, it had to be a bad sign. I suppose I won't see the sky over Africa as long as I live. And no more talk about putting money away for the trip, I just lost the job I needed to keep alive from day to day.

"I got fired today," Bird said to Himiko. "The summer program, too —everything."

"No! But what happened, Bird?"

Bird was obliged to talk about the hangover, the vomiting, the indefatigable puritan's assault, and gradually the story turned into a dank, unpleasant thing. Bird sickened, wound up quickly.

"And you could have defended yourself in front of the Principal! If some of the students were willing to say it was food poisoning, there wouldn't have been a thing wrong with letting them back you up! Bird, how could you have consented so easily to being fired!"

That's a point, why did I accept being fired so easily? For the first time, Bird felt an attachment to the instructor's chair he had just lost. That wasn't the kind of job you just threw away half-jokingly. And what kind of report could he make to his father-in-law? Would he be able to confess that he had drunk himself unconscious on the day his abnormal baby had been born, and then behaved so miserably the next morning because of his hangover that he had lost his job? And on the Johnnie Walker the professor had made him a present of . . .

"There wasn't a single thing left in the world that I could justifiably

assert my right to, it was that kind of feeling. Besides, I was so anxious
to cut short that interview with the Principal, I just agreed to everything;
it was reckless as hell."

"Bird," the girl producer broke in, "are you saying that you feel as if
you've lost all your rights in the world because you're just sitting
around waiting for your own baby to die?"

So Himiko had told her girlfriend the whole nasty story!

"Something like that," Bird said, annoyed at both Himiko's indiscre-
tion and the girl producer's forwardness. It was easy even now to
imagine himself in the middle of a scandal widely known.

"It's the people who have begun to feel they have no more rights in
the real world who commit suicide. Bird, please don't commit suicide,"
Himiko said.

"What's all this about suicide!" said Bird, at heart threatened.

"It was right after he began feeling that way that my husband killed
himself. If you hung yourself in this same bedroom—Bird, I'd be sure I
was a witch."

"I've never even considered suicide," Bird declared.

"But your father was a suicide, wasn't he?"

"How did you know that?"

"You told me about it the night my husband killed himself, trying to
console me. You wanted me to believe that suicide was the kind of
ordinary thing that happens every day."

"I must have been all upset myself," Bird said limply.

"You even told me that story about your father beating you before he
killed himself."

"What story is that?" the girl producer asked, her curiosity igniting.

But Bird remained morosely silent, so Himiko told the story as she
had heard it.

One day Bird had approached his father with this question; he was six
years old: *Father, where was I a hundred years before I was born?
Where will I be a hundred years after I'm dead? Father, what will
happen to me when I die?* Without a word, his young father had
punched him in the mouth, broke two of his teeth and bloodied his face,
and Bird forgot his fear of death. Three months later, his father had put
a bullet through his head with a German army pistol from World War I.

"If my baby dies of undernourishment," Bird said, remembering his
father, "at least I'll have one thing less to be afraid of. Because I

wouldn't know what to do if my child asked me that same question when he got to be six. I couldn't punch my own child in the mouth hard enough to make him forget his fear of death. Not even temporarily."

"Just don't commit suicide, Bird, all right?"

"Don't worry about it," Bird said, turning away from Himiko's swollen, bloodshot eyes his own eyes that felt as if they were beginning to show disorder.

The girl producer turned to Bird as if she had been waiting for Himiko's silence, "Bird, isn't this waiting around for your baby to weaken on sugar-water in a distant hospital the worst state you could be in? Full of self-deception, uncertain, anxious! And isn't that why you're so run down? It's not just you, either, even Himiko has lost weight."

"But I can't just yank him home and kill him," Bird protested.

"At least that way you wouldn't be deceiving yourself, you'd have to admit that you were dirtying your own hands. Bird, it's too late now to escape the villain in yourself, but you had to become a villain because you wanted to protect your little scene at home from an abnormal baby, so there's even an egotistical logic to it. But what you're doing is leaving the bloody work to some doctor in a hospital while you mope around playing the gentle victim of sudden misfortune, as if you were really a very good man, and that's what's bad for your mental health! You must know as well as I do, Bird, that you're deceiving yourself!"

"Deceiving myself? Sure, if I were trying to convince myself that my hands were clean while I wait impatiently for my baby to die when I'm not around, certainly that would be dishonest," Bird said in denial. "But I know perfectly well that I'll be responsible for the baby's death."

"I wonder about that, Bird," the woman producer said in utter disbelief. "I'm afraid you'll find yourself in all kinds of trouble the minute the baby dies, that's the penalty you'll pay for having deceived yourself. And it's then that Himiko will really have to keep a sharp eye on Bird to see he doesn't kill himself. Of course, by then he'll probably be back with his long-suffering wife."

"My wife says she'd want to think about a divorce if I neglected the baby and it died."

"Once a person has been poisoned by self-deception, he can't make decisions about himself as neatly as all that," Himiko said, elaborating her friend's terrific prophecy. "You won't get a divorce, Bird. You'll justify yourself like crazy, and try to salvage your married life by confusing the real issues. A decision like divorce is way beyond you now, Bird, the poison has gone to work. And you know how the story ends? Not even your own wife will trust you absolutely, and one day you'll discover for yourself that your entire private life is in the shadow of deception and in the end you'll destroy yourself. Bird, the first signs of self-destruction have appeared already!"

"But that's a blind alley! Leave it to you to paint the most hopeless future you can think of." Bird lunged at jocularity but his large, heavy classmate was perverse enough to parry him: "Right now, it's too clear that you *are* up a blind alley, Bird."

"But the fact that an abnormal baby was born to my wife was a simple accident; neither of us is responsible. And I'm neither such a tough villain that I can wring the baby's neck nor a tough enough angel to mobilize all the doctors and try to keep him alive somehow no matter how hopeless a baby he may be. So all I can do is leave him at a university hospital and make certain that he'll weaken and die naturally. When it's all over if I get sick on self-deception like a sewer rat that scurries down a blind alley after swallowing rat poison, well, there's nothing I can do about it."

"That's where you're wrong, Bird. You should have become either a tough villain or a tough angel, one or the other."

Bird caught just a whiff of alcohol stealing into the sweet sourness of the air. He looked at the girl producer's large face and even in the dimness saw that it was flushed and twitching, as though from facial neuritis.

"You're drunk, aren't you; I just realized—"

"That doesn't mean you escape unscathed from everything I've said up to now," the girl declared triumphantly, and, publicly expelling her hot, whisky breath, "however you may deny it, Bird, the problem of the dregs of self-deception after the baby's death just isn't apparent to you now. Can you deny that your biggest worry at the moment is that your freaky baby may grow like a weed and not die at all?"

Bird's heart constricted: the sweat began to pour. For a long time he sat in silence, feeling like a beaten dog. Then he stood up without a word and went to get some beer from the refrigerator. A frosty part where it had lain against the ice tray and the rest of the bottle warm —Bird instantly lost his thirst for beer. Still, he took the bottle and three glasses back to the bedroom with him. Himiko's friend was in the living room, with the light on, fixing her hair and make-up and putting on her dress. Bird turned his back on the living room and filled a glass for himself and one for Himiko with beer that clouded to a dirty brown.

"We're having a beer," Himiko called in to her friend.

"None for me; I have to go to the station."

"But it's still so early," Himiko said coquettishly.

"I'm sure you don't need me now that Bird is here," the girl said, as if to trap Bird in a net of suggestion. Then, directly to Bird: "I'm fairy godmother to all the girls who graduated with me. They all need a fairy godmother, need me, because they don't know what they want yet. And whenever it looks as if someone is about to have some difficulty I turn up and lend her strength. Bird, try not to drag Himiko too deeply into your private family problems? Not that I don't sympathize personally—"

When Himiko had left with her friend to see her to a cab, Bird dumped the rest of the tepid beer into the sink and took a cold shower. He recalled as the water pelted him an elementary school excursion when he had been caught in an icy downpour after having dropped behind and lost his way. The overwhelming loneliness, and the mortifying sense of helplessness. At the moment, like a soft-shell crab that had just shed its shell, he yielded instantly under attack by even the puniest enemy. He was in the worst condition ever, Bird thought. That he had managed to offer considerable resistance in his fight with the teen-age gang that night now seemed like such an impossible miracle that he was afraid all over again.

Vaguely aroused after his shower, Bird lay down naked on the bed. The smell of the outsider had disappeared; once again the house gave off its distinctive odor of oldness. This was Himiko's lair. She had to rub the odor of her body into all its corners and thereby certify her territory or she could not escape anxiety, like a small, timid animal. Bird was already so used to the odor of the house that he mistook it sometimes for the odor of his own body. What could be keeping Himiko? Bird had washed the old sweat away in the shower and now his skin was beading again. He moved sluggishly to the kitchen and tried another bottle of the slightly chilled beer.

When Himiko finally returned an hour later she found Bird disgruntled.

"She was jealous," she said in defense of her friend.

"Jealous?"

"Would you believe, she's the most pathetic member of our little group. Every so often one of us girls will go to bed with her to make her feel a little better. And she's convinced herself that that makes her our fairy godmother."

Bird's moral mechanism had been broken since he had abandoned his baby in the hospital; Himiko's relationship with her producer friend didn't shock him particularly.

"Maybe she was speaking out of jealousy," he said, "but that doesn't mean I got away from everything she said unscathed."

10

THEY were watching the midnight news, Bird in bed on his stomach, lifting only his head like a baby sea urchin, Himiko hugging her knees on the floor. The heat of day had departed and like primeval cave dwellers they were enjoying the cool air in nakedness. Since they had turned the volume way down with the telephone bell in mind, the only sound in the room was a voice as faint as the buzzing of a bee's wings. But what Bird heard was not a human voice endowed with meaning and mood, nor was he distinguishing meaningful shapes in the flickering shadows on the screen. From the external world he was letting in nothing to project its image on the screen of his consciousness. He was simply waiting, like a radio set equipped with a receiver only, for a signal from the distance which he wasn't even certain would be transmitted. Unitl now the signal had not arrived and the waiting receiver, Bird, was temporarily out of order. Himiko abruptly put down the book on her lap, *My Life in the Bush of Ghosts*, by the African writer Amos Tutuola, and, leaning forward, turned up the volume on the television set. Even then, Bird received no clear impression of the picture his eyes were watching or the voice his ears heard. He merely continued to wait, gazing vacantly at the screen. A minute later Himiko extended one arm, her knees and the other hand on the floor, and turned the set off. The mercury dot blazed, receded instantly, extinguished itself—a pure abstraction of the shape of death. Bird gasped, my baby may have died just now! he had felt. From morning until this late hour of the night he had been waiting for word by phone; save for lunching on some bread and ham and beer and entering Himiko repeatedly, he had done nothing, not even looked at his maps or read his African novel (Himiko, as though Bird's African fever had infected her, was en-

117

thralled by the maps and the book), thought about nothing but the baby's death. Clearly, Bird was in the midst of a regression.

Himiko turned around on the floor and spoke to Bird, a fervid glitter in her eye.

"What?" he frowned, unable to read her meaning.

"I say this may be the beginning of the atomic war that will mean the end of the world!"

"What makes you say that?" Bird said, surprised. "You have a way of saying things out of the blue sometimes."

"Out of the blue?" It was Himiko's turn to be surprised. "But wasn't the news just now a shock to you, too?"

"What news was that? I wasn't paying attention, it was something else that startled me."

Himiko stared at Bird reproachfully, but she seemed to realize at once that he was neither having fun with her nor aghast at what he had heard. The glitter of excitement in her eyes dulled.

"Get a hold of yourself, Bird!"

"What news?"

"Khrushchev resumed nuclear testing; apparently they exploded a bomb that makes the hydrogen bombs up to now look like firecrackers."

"Oh, is that it," Bird said.

"You don't seem impressed."

"I guess I'm not—"

"How strange!"

It *was* strange, Bird felt now for the first time, that the Soviet resumption of nuclear testing had not in the least impressed him. But he didn't think he could be surprised even by word that a third World War had erupted with a nuclear bang. . . .

"I don't know why, I honestly didn't feel anything," Bird said.

"Are you completely indifferent to politics these days?"

Bird had to think in silence a minute. "I'm not as sensitive to the international situation as I was when we were students; remember I used to go with you and your husband to all those protest rallies? But the one thing I have been concerned about all along is atomic weapons. Like the only political action our study group ever took was to demonstrate against nuclear warfare. So I should have been shocked by the news about Khrushchev, and yet I was watching all the time and didn't feel a thing."

"Bird—" Himiko faltered.

"It feels as if my nervous system is only sensitive to the problem of the baby and can't be stimulated by anything else," a vague anxiety impelled Bird to say.

"That's just it, Bird. All day today, for fifteen hours, you've talked of nothing but whether or not the baby is dead yet."

"It's true his phantom is in control of my head; it's like being submerged in a pool of the baby's image."

"Bird, that's not normal. If the baby should take a long time weakening and it went on this way for, say, one hundred days, you'd go mad. You would, Bird!"

Bird glowered at Himiko. As if the echo of her words might bestow on the baby weakening on sugar-water and thinned milk the same energy that Popeye found in a can of spinach. Ah, one hundred days! Twenty-four hundred hours!"

"Bird! If you let the baby's phantom possess you this way, I don't think you'll be able to escape from it even after the baby is dead." Himiko quoted in English from Macbeth: " 'These deeds must not be thought after these ways,' Bird, 'so it will make us mad.' "

"But I can't help thinking about the baby now, and it may be the same after he's dead. There's nothing I can do about that. And you may be right, for all I know the worst part will come after the baby's death."

"But it's not too late to call the hospital and arrange for him to get whole milk—"

"That's no good," Bird interrupted in a voice as plaintive and agitated as a scream. "And you'd know it was no good if you saw that lump on its head!"

Himiko peered at Bird and shook her head gloomily at what she saw. They avoided each other's eyes. Presently Himiko turned off the light and burrowed into the bed alongside Bird. It was cool enough now for two people to lie together on one cramped bed without oppressing each other. For a time they lay in silence, perfectly still. Then Himiko wrapped herself around Bird's body, moving with a clumsiness that was surprising in one ordinarily so expert. Bird felt a dry tuft of pubic hair against his outer thigh. Loathing grazed him unexpectedly, and passed. He wished that Himiko would stop moving her limbs and slip away into her own feminine sleep. At the same time he was poignantly hopeful that she would remain awake until he was asleep himself. Minutes passed. Each sensed and tried not to show he knew that the other was wide awake. At last Himiko said, as abruptly as a badger who could endure playing dead no longer, "You dreamed about the baby last night, didn't you?" Her voice was curiously shrill.

"Yes, I did. Why?"

"What kind of dream?"

"It was a missile base on the moon, and the baby's bassinet was all alone on those fantastically desolate rocks. That's all. A simple dream."

"You curled up like an infant and clenched your fists and started bawling in your sleep. Waagh! Waagh! Your face was all mouth."

"That's a horror story, it's not normal!" Bird said as though in rage, drowning in the hot springs of his shame.

"I was afraid. I thought you might go on that way and not come back to normal."

Bird was silent, his cheeks flaming in the darkness. And Himiko lay as still as stone.

"Bird—if this weren't a problem limited just to you personally, I mean if it was something that concerned me, too, that I could share with you, then I'd be able to encourage you so much better—" Himiko's tone was subdued, as if she regretted having mentioned Bird's moaning in his sleep.

"You're right about this being limited to me, it's entirely a persoanl matter. But with some personal experiences that lead you way into a cave all by yourself, you must eventually come to a side tunnel or something that opens on a truth that concerns not just yourself but everyone. And with that kind of experience at least the individual is rewarded for his suffering. Like Tom Sawyer! He had to suffer in a pitch-black cave, but at the same time he found his way out into the light he also found a bag of gold! But what I'm experiencing personally now is like digging a vertical mine shaft in isolation; it goes straight down to a hopeless depth and never opens on anybody else's world. So I can sweat and suffer in that same dark cave and my personal experience won't result in so much as a fragment of significance for anybody else. Hole-digging is all I'm doing, futile, shameful hole-digging; my Tom Sawyer is at the bottom of a desperately deep mine shaft and I wouldn't be surprised if he went mad!"

"In my experience there is no such thing as absolutely futile suffering. Bird, right after my husband killed himself I went to bed, unprotected, with a man who might have been sick and I developed a syphilis phobia. I suffered with that fear for an awfully long time, and while I was suffering it seemed to me that no neurosis could be as barren and unproductive as mine. But you know, after I recovered, I had gained something after all. Ever since then, I can make it with almost anything, no matter how lethal it might be, and I never worry about syphilis for very long!"

Himiko related her story as if it were a droll confession; she even finished with a titter of laughter. What did it matter that her own gaiety was counterfeit, Bird sensed the girl making an effort to cheer him up. Still, he permitted himself a cynical flourish: "In other words, the next time my wife has an abnormal child I won't have to suffer for very long."

"That isn't what I meant at all," Himiko said dejectedly. "Bird, if only you could convert this experience from a vertical shaft type to a cave experience with an exit tunnel—"

"I don't think that's possible."

The conversation was at an end. "I'm going to get a beer and some sleeping pills," Himiko said at last. "I guess you'll need some too?"

Of course Bird needed some too, but it wouldn't do to miss the telephone when it rang. "None for me," he said in a voice that sharpened with an excess of longing. "I hate waking up in the morning with the taste of sleeping pills in my mouth." *None for me* would have sufficed. But the extra words were necessary to extinguish the demand for beer and sleeping pills that was flaming in his throat.

"Really?" Himiko said callously as she washed the tablets down with half a glass of beer. "Now that you mention it, it's like the taste of a broken tooth."

Long after Himiko had fallen asleep Bird lay awake at her side, his body rigid from shoulders to belly as though he had been stricken with elephantiasis. Having to lie in bed with another felt like a sacrifice of his own body so great as to be unjust. Bird tried to recall what it had been like during the first year of his marriage, when he and his wife had slept in the same bed, but with so little success it might have been a mistake of memory. Bird finally resolved to sleep on the floor, but as he tried to sit up Himiko moaned savagely in her sleep and twined herself around his body, gnashing her teeth. Bird felt again a scratchy tuft of pubic hair against his outer thigh. From the darkness beyond Himiko's partly opened lips blew a rusty metallic odor.

With no room to move, despairing at the pain mounting in his body, Bird lay hopelessly awake. Before long, a suffocating suspicion took hold of him. Might not the doctor and those nurses be feeding the baby ten quarts of rich milk an hour? Bird could see the baby gulping condensed milk, two red mouths open in two red heads. The millet seeds of fever were sowed in every furrow of his body. Bird's shame lightened, and weight was added to the pan on the other side of the scales, his victimized sense of being harmed by a grotesque baby: the psychological balance weighing Bird's reprieve tipped. Bird sweated, tormented by an egotistical anxiety. He no longer saw anything, not even the furniture rising out of the darkness, nor heard any sound, not even the rumble of passing trucks; he was now a life form aware only of the prickliness of the heat on its skin and the sweat welling from within its own body. Lying perfectly still, Bird continued to ooze the green-smelling liquid, like a garden slug dusted with a grub killer.

I know the doctor and those nurses are feeding my baby ten quarts of rich milk an hour. . . .

It would be morning soon, but even then Bird wouldn't be able to tell Himiko about this disgraceful paranoia: it was the very paranoia the girl producer had predicted in belittling him. He might not speak to Himiko, but very likely he would go over to the ward and reconnoiter when the agony of waiting for the call became too great to bear. The sky dawned and the telephone had not rung. Then dawn passed, morning light began to creep between the curtains, and Bird was still immersed to his neck in a tar vat of anxiety, sleepless, sweating, none but a phantom bell ringing in his ears.

In disgruntled silence, their shoulders rubbing, Bird and the doctor peered through the glass partition as if to examine an octopus in a water tank. Bird's baby had come out of the incubator and was lying alone on a regular bed. He might just have come from surgery to correct a harelip, there was nothing covert to suggest that special measures were being taken. Bright red as a boiled shrimp, he didn't look to Bird like a creature weakened to the point of death. He was even somewhat bigger than before. And the lump on his head seemed to have developed. His head tipped sharply back in order to balance the weight of the lump, the baby was rubbing furiously behind its ears with the undersides of its thumbs, trying to scratch the lump perhaps, with shriveled hands that wouldn't reach. Its eyes were closed so tightly that half its face was wrinkled.

"Do you suppose the lump itches?"

"What's that?" the doctor said, and, comprehending, "I don't really know. But the skin on the underside of the lump is so inflamed it's ready to split; it could very well be itching. We injected some antibiotic in there once, but now that we've stopped all that the lump is liable to split any time. If it does burst, the baby will probably develop breathing difficulty."

Bird stared at the doctor and started to open his mouth but swallowed in silence instead. He wanted to verify that the doctor had not forgotten that he, the father, desired this baby's death. Otherwise, he would be trampled once again beneath the hoofs of a suspicion like last night's. But all he could do was swallow.

"The crisis should come today or tomorrow," the doctor said. Bird peered at the baby rubbing its head as before with its large, red hands held up above its ears. The baby's ears were identical to Bird's, rolled in against its head. "I appreciate all you're doing," Bird said in a whisper, as if he were afraid the baby would hear. Then he quickly bowed to the doctor, his cheeks on fire, and hurried out of the ward.

The minute the door closed Bird regretted not having made clear his desire to the doctor once again. He put his hands behind his ears as he walked along the corridor and began to rub his head just below the hairline with the fleshy pads of his thumbs. Gradually he arched backward, as if a heavy weight were attached to his head. He stopped short a minute later when he realized he was imitating the baby's gestures, and glanced around him nervously. At the corner of the corridor, standing in front of a drinking fountain, two women from the maternity ward were staring blankly in his direction. Feeling his stomach heave, Bird turned toward the main wing and broke into a run.

Bird's friend spotted him from the restaurant as he slowly drove by looking for a parking place, and he came out into the street. When Bird finally managed to park, he looked at his watch. Thirty minutes late. His friend's face as he approached was moldy with impatience.

"The car belongs to a friend," Bird said in embarrassed justification of the MG. "Sorry I'm late. Is everybody here?"

"Just you and me. The others went to that protest rally at Hibiya Park."

"Oh, that," Bird said. He remembered knowing at breakfast that Himiko was reading about the Soviet bomb in the paper and not feeling the least involved himself. Right now my primary worry is personal, a grotesque baby, I've turned my back on the real world. It's all right for those others to participate in global destiny with their protest rallies: a baby with a lump on its head doesn't have its teeth in them.

"None of the others want to get involved with Mr. Delchef, that's why they went down to the park." His friend glanced at Bird irritably, as if he disapproved of Bird's simple acceptance of the others' absence. "A few thousand people protesting on the mall in Hibiya Park isn't going to get anyone in trouble with Mr. Khrushchev personally!"

Bird considered each member of the study group. There was no denying that deep involvement with Mr. Delchef now could lead to trouble for all of them. Several were employed by first-rate export houses, others were with the Foreign Office or taught at universities. In the event that the newspapers picked up the Delchef incident and treated it as a scandal, their situation was certain to be awkward if their superiors should discover that they were associated with the man in any way. Not one of them was as free as Bird, instructor at a cram-school and soon to be fired.

"What are we going to do?" Bird prompted his friend.

"There's nothing we can do. It seems to me our only choice is to refuse the legation's request for help."

"You've decided you don't want to get involved with Mr. Delchef either?" Bird asked merely out of interest with no ulterior motives, yet his friend's eyes reddened suddenly and he glowered at Bird, as if he had been insulted. Bird realized with surprise that he had been expected to approve at once of turning down the legation's request.

"But look at this from Mr. Delchef's point of view," Bird objected quietly. His friend submerged in peevish silence. "Allowing us to persuade him to come back may be his last chance. Didn't they say they'd have to go to the police if we failed? Knowing that, I don't see how we can refuse with a clear conscience!"

"If Mr. Delchef let himself be persuaded by us, fine, great! But if it didn't go well and this developed into a scandal, we'd find ourselves in the middle of an international incident!" Avoiding Bird's face, the friend spoke with his eyes on the gutted sheep's belly that was the driver's seat of the MG. "It just doesn't seem wise to me to mess with Mr. Delchef while all this is going on."

Bird could feel his friend imploring him to agree without further argument; the plea was so naked it was sad. But awesome words like *scandal* and *international incident* failed entirely to impress him. Even now he was over his head in the scandal of the bizarre baby, and the domestic incident created by the baby had a firmer and more poignant hold on the scruff of his neck than any international incident could ever have. Bird was free of the fear of all the pitfalls he supposed must be concealed around Mr. Delchef's person. And he noticed now for the first time since the trouble with the baby had begun that the breadth of his life from day to day permitted him a far larger than ordinary margin of action. He was even amused by the irony.

"If you decide to turn down the legation appeal as a group, I'd like to meet Mr. Delchef on my own. I was close to him, and even if the incident does come out in the open and I get involved in a scandal, well, it isn't going to bother me particularly."

Bird was looking for something that would occupy him today and tomorrow, the new period of reprieve the doctor's words had granted him. Besides, he honestly wanted a look at Mr. Delchef's life as a recluse.

The instant Bird accepted, his friend turned to gold, so swift was the alchemy that Bird on his part was a little embarrassed: "If you feel that's what you want to do, go ahead! I can't think of anything better," the friend said with feverish conviction. "To tell the truth, I was hoping you'd agree to take the job on. The others got cold feet the minute they heard the news about Mr. Delchef, but you were as composed and detached as could be. Bird, I admired you for that!"

Bird smiled blandly, not wishing to offend his suddenly loquacious friend. At the moment, as long as the baby was not involved, his capacity for calm detachment was infinite. But that was no reason, he thought bitterly, for the rest of Tokyo's millions without the shackles of a grotesque baby around their necks to feel envious of him.

"I'll tell you what, I'll treat you to lunch," the friend proposed eagerly. "Let's have a beer first."

Bird nodded, and they walked back to the restaurant together. They were seated across a table and had called for beer when Bird's elated friend said: "Bird, did you have that habit of rubbing behind your ears with your thumbs when we were in school together?"

As he edged into the narrow alley that opened like a crack between a Korean restaurant and a bar, Bird wondered if there wasn't another exit hidden in this labyrinth. According to the map his friend had drawn for him, he had just entered a blind alley by the only entrance. The cul-de-sac was shaped like a stomach, a stomach with an obstruction in the duodenum. How could a man leading a fugitive life bury himself in a place as closed in as this and not feel anxious about it? Had Mr. Delchef felt so hounded that no other spot would have done as a hideaway? Chances were, he wasn't hiding in this alley anymore. Bird cheered himself with the thought, and then he had come to the tenement house at the end of the alley. He stopped at the entrance to what might have been a secret trail to a mountain fortress, and wiped the sweat off his face. The alley itself seemed shady enough, but Bird saw when he looked up at the sky that the fierce sunlight of summer noon covered it like a white-hot platinum net. His face still uplifted to the glitter of the sky, Bird closed his eyes and rubbed his itching head with his thumbs. Suddenly he let his arms fall as if they had been struck down, and snapped his head upright; in the distance, a girl had raised her voice in a lunatic scream.

With his shoes in one hand, Bird climbed a few stairs that were gritty with dirt and went into the building. The left side of the hallway was lined with prison-like doors. The right side was a blank wall, heavily scrawled on. Bird moved toward the back, checking the numbers on the doors. He could sense people behind each of the doors, yet all of them were closed. Then what did the tenants in this building do about escaping the heat? Was Himiko the forerunner of a tribe propagating wildly all over the city which shut itself up in locked rooms even in the middle of the day? Bird got all the way to the end of the hall and discovered a flight of steep, narrow stairs hidden away like an inside pocket. Then he happened to look behind him: a large woman was planted in the entranceway, peering in his direction. She was in heavy shadow and so was the hall, for her back shut out the light from the street.

"What do you want back there?" the woman called, moving as though to shoo a dog away.

"I've just come to visit a foreign friend of mine," Bird replied in a quaking voice.

"American?"

"He's living with a young Japanese girl."

"Ah, why didn't you say so! The American is the first room on the second floor." With that, the large woman nimbly vanished. Assuming "the American" was Mr. Delchef, it was clear that he had won a place in the giantess's affections. Bird was still doubtful as he climbed the unfinished wooden stairs. But then he executed a turn on the particularly narrow landing and there in front of him, his arms extended in welcome though his eyes were puzzled, Mr. Delchef stood. Bird felt a surge of joy: Mr. Delchef was the only tenant in the building with the wholesome good sense to leave his door open as a measure against the heat.

Bird propped his shoes against the wall in the hallway and then shook hands with Mr. Delchef, who was beaming at him from just inside the door. Like a marathon runner, he wore only a pair of blue shorts and an undershirt; his red hair was cropped short but he sported a bushy and expectably reddish mustache. Bird could find nothing to indicate that the man in front of him was a fugitive—except his stupendous body odor, worthy of a hulking bear of a man though Mr. Delchef was slight of build. Probably he hadn't found the opportunity to take a bath since secluding himself here.

When they had exchanged greetings in mutually meager English, Mr. Delchef explained that his girlfriend had just left to have her hair set. Then he invited Bird inside, but Bird pointed to the tatami mat floor and declined with the excuse that his feet were dirty. He wanted to say what he had to say standing in the hall. He was afraid of being stuck in Mr. Delchef's room.

Bird could see that the apartment was empty of furniture. A single window was open in the back, but it was obstructed by a severe wooden fence less than a foot away. It was probable that other private lives were being unfurled on the far side of the fence, better not observed from Mr. Delchef's window.

"Mr. Delchef, your legation wants you to go back quickly," Bird said, plunging headlong into his mission.

"I will not go back; my girlfriend wants me to stay with her," Mr. Delchef smiled. The poverty and crudeness of their English made the dialogue seem a game. It also permitted them a harsh frankness.

"I shall be the last messenger. After me someone from the legation will come, or maybe the Japanese police even."

"I think the police will not do anything. Please remember, I am still a diplomat."

"Perhaps not. But if the people from the legation come and take you away you must be sent back to your own country."

"Yes, I am prepared. Since I have caused trouble, I must be assigned to a less important post or I must lose my job as a diplomat."

"Therefore, Mr. Delchef, before it becomes a scandal it would be better to return to the legation."

"I will not return. My girlfriend wants me to stay," Mr. Delchef said with a broad smile.

"Then it is not for political reasons? You are hiding away here simply because of sentimental attachment to your girlfriend?"

"Yes, precisely."

"Mr. Delchef, you are a strange man."

"Strange, why?"

"But your friend cannot speak English, can she?"

"We understand each other always in silence."

A bulb of intolerable sadness was gradually sprouting in Bird.

"Well, I shall make my report now and the people from the legation will come right away to take you back."

"Since I will be taken against my will there is nothing I can do. I think my friend will understand."

Bird weakly shook his head in admission of defeat. Sweat sparkled in the fine copper hair around Mr. Delchef's mustache. Then Bird noticed that brilliant beads of sweat were trembling in the hair all over Mr. Delchef's body.

"I shall tell them how you feel," Bird said, and stopped to pick up his shoes.

"Bird, was your baby born?"

"Yes, but the baby is not normal and now I am waiting for it to die." Bird couldn't have explained the impulse to confess. "The baby has a brain hernia, the condition is so terrible that the baby appears to have two heads."

"Why do you wait for the baby to die when it needs an operation?" Mr. Delchef's smile vanished and a look of manly courage fiercened the lines of his face.

"There is not one chance in one hundred that the baby would grow up normally even after surgery," Bird said in consternation.

"Kafka, you know, wrote in a letter to his father, the only thing a parent can do for a child is to welcome it when it arrives. And are you rejecting your baby instead? Can we excuse the egotism that rejects another life because a man is a father?"

Bird was silent, his cheeks and eyes feverish with the violent blushing that had become a new habit. No longer was Mr. Delchef an eccentric foreigner with a red mustache who maintained a humorous presence of mind though his predicament was severe. Bird felt as if he had been downed by a bullet of criticism from an unexpected sniper. He gathered himself to protest at whatever the cost and suddenly hung his head, sensing he had nothing to say to Mr. Delchef.

"Ah, the poor little thing!" Mr. Delchef said in a whisper. Bird looked up, shuddering, and realized the foreigner was talking not about his baby but about him. Silently he waited for the moment when Mr. Delchef would set him free.

When Bird was finally able to say good-by, Mr. Delchef presented him with a small English dictionary of his native language. Bird asked his friend to autograph the book. Mr. Delchef wrote a single word in a Balkan language, signed his name beneath it and then explained: "In my country, this means *hope*."

At the narrowest part of the alley, Bird awkwardly crossed paths with a small Japanese girl. Smelling the scent of freshly set hair and seeing the unhealthy whiteness of her neck as the girl squeezed past him with her head lowered, Bird stopped himself from speaking to her. Bird emerged in the dizzying light and ran for the car like a fugitive, sweat cascading down his body. At this hottest hour of the day, he was the only man in the city on the run.

11

S UNDAY morning, Bird woke up to find the bedroom brimming with unexpected light and fresh air: the window was wide open, a breeze was making a lightful sweep of the room and blowing into the hall. From the living room came the drone of a vacuum cleaner. Accustomed to the dimness of the house, Bird was embarrassed in all this light by his own body beneath the covers. Hastily, before Himiko could storm in and tease him in his nakedness, he put on his pants and shirt and went out to the living room.

"Good morning, Bird!" Himiko said brightly. Her head turbaned in a towel, she was wielding the vacuum cleaner as though it were a pole with which she wanted to crush a scampering mouse. The flushed face she turned to Bird had regained its look of youth. "My father-in-law came over; he's taking a walk while I finish cleaning."

"I'd better leave."

"Why must you run away, Bird?" Himiko said resentfully.

"I feel like a recluse these days; it just seems queer to meet someone new when you're living in a hideaway."

"My father-in-law knows that men often stay the night here and it's never bothered him specially. But I think he would be disturbed if one of my friends seemed to rush away like a fugitive the minute he got here." Himiko's face was still hard.

"O.K. Then I'd better shave." Bird went back to the bedroom. Himiko's show of resentment had been a shock. Bird reflected that he had been clinging doggedly to himself from the minute he had moved into his friend's house, aware of Himiko as a single cell only in the organism of his consciousness. How could he have been so certain of such absolute rights! He had become a chrysalis of personal misfortune,

130

seeing only the inner walls of the cocoon, never doubting for an instant the chrysalis's prerogatives. . . .

Bird finished shaving and glanced into the fogged mirror at the pale, grave face of a chrysalis of personal misfortune. He noticed that his own face looked wizened, not, he had a feeling, simply because he had lost weight.

"Ever since I barged in on you I've been acting mostly like an egomaniac," Bird volunteered when he returned to the living room. "I'd even started to feel as if that was the only way to behave."

"Are you apologizing?" Himiko teased. Her face again was utter softness.

"I've been sleeping in your bed and eating the food you cooked for me, even making you wear my own tether. I have no right to any of this, and yet I've felt perfectly at home here."

"Bird, are you going to leave?" Himiko said uneasily.

Bird stared at the girl and was stricken by something like a sense of destiny: never again would he cross paths with a person suited so perfectly to himself. The taste of regret was harsh on his tongue.

"Even if you do leave eventually, stay for a while, will you, Bird?"

In the bedroom again, Bird lay down on his back and closed his eyes, clasping his hands behind his head. He wanted a minute alone with his gratitude.

Later the three of them sat around the table in the restored living room discusssing the leaders of the new African states and the grammar of Swahili. Himiko took down the map of Africa from the bedroom wall and spread it on the table to show her father-in-law.

"Why don't you and Himi take a trip to Africa?" the older man proposed abruptly. "If you sold this house and property you'd have all the money you needed."

"That's not such a bad idea—" Himiko glanced at Bird as if to test him. "You could forget your unhappiness about the baby, Bird. And I could forget my husband's suicide."

"Exactly, and that's so important!" Himiko's father-in-law declared. "Why don't the two of you just pack up and leave for Africa?"

So rudely was he rocked by this proposal that Bird submitted to panic unprotestingly. "I couldn't do that, I just couldn't," he said with a feckless sigh.

"Why not?" Himiko challenged.

"It's too slick, that's why, just happening to forget in the course of traveling around Africa that your baby's life has ebbed away. I . . . ," Bird stuttered, blushing, ". . . I just couldn't do it!"

"Bird is an extremely moral young man," Himiko said derisively.

Bird's blush deepened and he arranged his face in a look of reproach. In fact he was thinking he would have melted like a cube of bouillon under boiling water if her father-in-law had suggested undertaking a trip to Africa with the moral objective of rescuing Himiko from the phantom of her husband, how eagerly would he then have released himself to that journey into sweet deception! Bird was terrified the older man might make the suggestion in just such a way, at the same time he longed to hear the words: in his loathsome needfulness he felt like concealing himself in a dark hole. An instant later Bird saw in Himiko's eyes the white flicker of awakening.

"Bird will be going back to his wife in a week or so."

"Oh, I didn't realize—" her father-in-law said. "I only suggested the trip because this is the first time I've seen Himi so alive since my son died. I hope you're not angry."

Bird looked at Himiko's father-in-law in puzzlement. His head was short, and utterly bald, and it wasn't clear where it stopped, because the sunburned skin on the back of his skull grew in a piece to his neck and from there to his shoulders. A head that recalled a sea lion, and two slightly clouded, tranquil eyes. Bird looked for some clue to the man's nature and came up with nothing at all. So he maintained his wary silence and smiled a vague smile, laboring to conceal the disgraceful disappointment gradually climbling from his chest to clog his throat.

Late that night, in slothful positions that minimized the burden on their bodies, Bird and Himiko fucked in the humid darkness for an uninterrupted hour. Like copulating animals, they were silent to the end. Again and again Himiko soared into orgasm, with brief intervals at the beginning and then after increasingly languorous pauses; Bird each time recalled the sensation of flying a model airplane on the evening playground at his elementary school. Himiko swooped around the axis of his body in ever widening circles, trembling and groaning her way through the sky of her orgasms like a model airplane laboring under the burden of a heavy motor. Then she would descend yet again to the landing ground where Bird waited, and the period of silent, dogged repetition would revive. Sex for them was rooted now in sensations of daily quietude and order; Bird felt as if he had been fucking the girl for more than a hundred years. Her genitals were simple now, and certain, lurking there were not the buds of even the most insubstantial fears. No longer a somehow inscrutable thing, Himiko's vagina was simplicity itself, a pouch of soft, synthetic resin from which no ghostly hag could possibly emerge to harry Bird. He felt profoundly at peace, because Himiko explicitly and without qualification limited the object of their sex to pleasure. Bird remembered how it was with his wife, their timidity and the unflagging sense of peril. Even now, after years of marriage, they foundered on the same gloomy psychological shoals every time they made love. Bird's long, clumsy arms and legs would prod his wife's body, withered and rigid in its battle to overcome disgust, and she invariably would receive the impression that he had meant to strike her. Angry then, she would rail at Bird, even try to strike him back. Ultimately, the alternatives were always the same: he could become involved in a piddling quarrel, withdraw from his wife's body and continue far into the night the sparring that made the antlers of aroused desire glitter, or he could finish in agitated haste with a wretched feeling of receiving charity. Bird had pinned his hopes for a revolution in their sex life on the birth of the child and what would follow. . . .

Since Himiko repeatedly compressed Bird's penis like a milking hand as she circled her private skies, Bird might have chosen her most ardent orgasm as the moment for his own. But fear of the long night that would follow coitus continually drove him back. Dumbly Bird dreamed of the most saccharine sleep of all, achieved midway on the gentle slope toward orgasm.

But Himiko continued to fly, dropping groundward in smooth descent and suddenly dancing back into the sky like a kite caught in an upward draft. It was on yet another of these false landings that Bird, carefully restraining himself, heard the telephone ring. He tried to rise, but Himiko clasped her soaking arms around his back. "Go ahead, Bird," she said a minute later, relaxing her grip. Bird leaped for the phone still ringing in the living room. A young man's voice asked for the father of the infant in the intensive care ward at the university hospital. Bird, stiffening, answered in a voice like the whine of a mosquito. It was an intern calling with a message from the doctor in charge of the case.

"I'm sorry it's so late but we've had our hands full over here," the voice from the distance said. "I'm to ask you to come to brain surgery at eleven o'clock tomorrow morning, it's the Assistant Director's office. The doctor would have called you himself but he was exhausted. We had our hands full over here until late!"

Bird took a deep breath and thought: *the baby died, the Assistant Director is going to do the autopsy.*

"I understand. I'll be there at eleven. Thank you."

The baby weakened and died! Bird told himself again as he put the receiver back. But what kind of visit had death paid the baby that the doctor had worn himself out? Bird tasted the bitterness of bile rising from his belly. Something colossal and terrific was glaring at him out of the darkness right in front of his eyes. Like an entomologist trapped in a cave alive with scorpions, Bird gingerfooted back to the bed, trembling from head to toe. The bed, a safe lair: in silence Bird continued to shiver. Then, as if to burrow more satisfactorily into the depths of the lair, he tried to enter Himiko's body. Impetuously repeating failure and only partially erected, Bird was guided by Himiko's fingers and, eventually, secured. Quickly his agitation coaxed from her the frenzied motion of the moment when partners share a climax and desist—Bird awkwardly recoiled and, abruptly, emptied in masturbative isolation. Aware of the hammering at the back of his chest as pain, Bird collapsed at Himiko's side and believed for no reason he could name that he would die one day of a heart attack.

"Bird, you really can be horrid," Himiko said, not so much reproachfully as in lament, peering at Bird's face through the darkness quizzically.

"Ah, I'm sorry."

"The baby?"

"Yes, but apparently not before he gave them a hell of a time," Bird said, terrified all over again.

"What was that about the Assistant Director's office?"

"They want me there in the morning."

"You should take some sleeping pills with whisky and go to sleep, you don't have to wait for a telephone call anymore." Himiko's voice was infinitely gentle.

When Himiko had turned on the bedside lamp and gone into the kitchen, Bird shut his eyes against the light, covered them furthermore with one hand on top of the other, and tried to consider the single, sharply pointed kernel that was lodged in his vacant brain—why had the dying baby kept the doctor moving until so late at night? But Bird immediatly encountered a notion that roiled the fear in him and he drew back with arrow swiftness. Opening his eyes just a crack, he took from Himiko's hand a glass one-third full of whisky and far more than the prescribed number of sleeping tablets, choked them down in a single breath, and closed his eyes again.

"That was my share too," Himiko said.

"Ah, I'm sorry," Bird repeated stupidly.

"Bird?" Himiko lay down on the bed at a somehow formal distance from Bird's side.

"Yes?"

"I'll tell you a story until the whisky and pills take effect—an episoae from that African novel. Did you read the chapter about the pirate demons?"

Bird shook his head in the dark.

"When a woman conceives, the pirate demons elect one of their own kind to sneak into the woman's house. During the night, this demon representative chases out the real fetus and climbs into the womb himself. And then on the day of the birth the demon is born in the guise of the innocent fetus. . . ."

Bird listened in silence. Before long, such a baby invariably fell ill. When the mother made offerings in hopes of curing her child, the pirate demons secretly deposited them in a secret cache. Never were these babies known to recover. When the baby died and it was time for the burial, the demon resumed its true form, and, escaping from the graveyard, returned to the lair of the pirate demons with all the offerings from the secret cache.

". . . apparently the bewitched fetus is born as a beautiful baby so it can capture the mother's heart and she won't hesitate to offer everything she has. The Africans call these babies 'children born into the world to die,' but isn't it wonderful to imagine how beautiful they must be, even pigmy babies!"

Probably Bird would tell the story to his wife. And since our baby was born to die if any baby was, she'll imagine him as a terrifically

beautiful baby; I may even correct my own memory. And that will be
the hugest deception of my whole life. My grotesque baby died with no
correction of his ugly double head, my baby is a grotesque baby with
two heads for all of infinite time after death. And if there is a giant
presence which imposes order on that infinite time, the baby with the
double head must be visible to him, and the baby's father, too. His
stomach churning, Bird plummeted into sleep like a plane falling out of
the sky, sleep in a can hermetically sealed against the light of any
dream. Still, in the final glinting reflection of consciousness, Bird heard
his fairy godmother whisper once again: "Bird, you really can be
horrid!" Bird arched backward as if a weight were hanging from his
head and, trying to rub behind his ears with the pads of his thumbs,
rammed his elbow into Himiko's mouth. Her eyes tearing from the
pain, Himiko peered through the darkness at the unnaturally contracted
figure of her sleeping friend. Himiko wondered if Bird hadn't misinter-
preted the phone call from the hospital. The baby hadn't died at all;
wasn't it that he had been returned to regular milk feedings and the road
to recovery? And didn't they want Bird at the hospital to discuss the
baby's operation? The friend sleeping at her side with his body doubled
up uncomfortably like an orangutan in a cage and the stink of whisky
flaming on his breath seemed to Himiko at once ridiculous and pitiful.
But this sleep would serve as a brief respite before tomorrow morning's
furor. Himiko got out of bed and tugged at Bird's arms and legs; he was
as heavy as a giant under a magic spell, yet his body offered no
resistance. When Bird lay stretched full length on the bed so that he
could sleep more comfortably, Himiko wrapped herself in a sheet in the
manner of a Greek sage and went into the living room. She intended to
study the maps of Africa until the sun came up.

Suddenly aware of his mistake, Bird flushed angrily as though he had
been cruelly ridiculed. He had just entered the Assistant Director's
office and had found them waiting for him there, several young doctors
including the pediatrician in charge of his baby's case and an elderly
professor with an air of benign authority—realizing his mistake, Bird
had come to a dumb halt just inside the door. Now he sat down in a
yellow leather chair in the center of the doctor's circle. He felt like a
convict who had been dragged back to the guards' quarters after

bungling a clumsily planned escape from the prison of the grotesque baby. And what about these guards! Hadn't they conspired to lay a trap for him with that ambiguous phone call the night before in order to enjoy his flight and failure from the height of their lookout tower?

When Bird remained silent, the pediatrician introduced him: "This gentleman is the infant's father." Then he smiled as though in embarrassment and withdrew to an observer's corner. The professor of brain surgery must have said something on his rounds about the baby's undernourishment, and the young doctor had probably betrayed him. Damn him to hell! Bird thought, glaring at the young doctor.

"I examined your child yesterday and again today; I think we'll be able to operate if he gets a little stronger," the brain surgeon said.

Stand your ground! Bird commanded his brain before panic could overwhelm him; you must resist these bastards, protect yourself from that monstrosity. Bird had been on the run from the moment he had realized his sanguine mistake and now he could think of nothing but turning back from time to time to defend himself in flight. I must forbid them to operate, otherwise the baby will march into my world like an occupying army.

"Is there any chance the baby will grow up normally if you operate?" Bird asked mechanically.

"I can't say anything definite yet."

Bird fiercely narrowed his eyes, as if to say he was not the man to be made a fool of. In the field of his brain there appeared a flaming circle of shame's hottest fire. Like a circus tiger, Bird steeled himself for the leap that would carry him through the ring.

"Which is the stronger possibility, that the baby will grow up normally or not?"

"I can't give you a definite answer to that either, not until we operate."

Without even blushing, Bird cleared the fiery ring of shame: "Then I think I'd rather you didn't operate."

All of the doctors stared at Bird and seemed to catch their breath. Bird felt capable of even the most shameless assertions at the top of his voice. A good thing he didn't exercise this audacious freedom, for the brain surgeon was quick to indicate that Bird had made himself clear.

"Will you take the infant with you, then?" he said brusquely, his anger evident.

"Yes, I will." Bird spoke quickly, too.

"Don't let me keep you waiting." The most appealing doctor Bird had encountered in this hospital laid bare the disgust he felt for him.

Bird stood up and the doctors rose with him. The bell at the end of the match, he thought, I've fended the monster baby off.

"Are you really going to take the baby away?" the young pediatrician asked hesitantly as they stepped into the hall.

"I'll come back for him this afternoon."

"Don't forget to bring something for the infant to wear." The doctor flicked his eyes off Bird's face and moved off down the corridor.

Bird hurried out to the square in front of the hospital. It was probably the overcast sky; both Himiko in her sunglasses and the scarlet sports car had an ugly, faded look. "It was all a mistake, the laugh's on me," Bird sneered, his face contorting.

"I was afraid of that."

"Why?" Bird's voice was savage.

"No special reason, Bird . . ." Himiko meekly faltered.

"I decided to take the baby home."

"Where, to the other hospital? Back to your apartment?"

Instantly Bird submerged in consternation. He hadn't even considered what he might do later, he had merely desperately resisted the doctors in this hospital who wanted to try their hand at surgery and then saddle him for the rest of his life with a baby whose head was mostly cave. The other hospital would never accept again "the goods" it had managed to get rid of once; and if he took the baby back to his apartment he would have to contend with the landlady's benevolent curiosity. Suppose he continued in his own bedroom the lethal diet therapy which the hospital had administered until a day ago, the baby with the double head would scream its hunger to the whole neighborhood and have the local dogpack howling with it. And suppose the baby died after a few days of that clamor, what doctor in the world would make out a death certificate? Bird pictured himself being arrested on charges of infanticide and the gruesome stories in the press.

"You're right, I can't take the baby anywhere." Bird slumped, expelling sour breath.

"If you have no plan at all in mind, Bird—"

"Well?"

"I was wondering how it would be to leave things up to a doctor I know. I'm sure he'd lend a hand to someone who didn't want his baby —I met him when I needed an abortion."

Once again Bird knew the panic of a craven foot soldier intent on defending himself after his platoon had been decimated by the monster baby's attack; paling, he cleared another ring of fire: "I'm willing if the doctor will agree."

"Naturally—asking the doctor to help us—will mean that we . . ." there was an abnormal lassitude in Himiko's voice, ". . . are dirtying our own hands with the baby's murder—"

"Not *our hands*. Mine! I'll be dirtying *my* hands with the baby's murder." At least he had liberated himself from one deception, Bird thought. Not that it brought him any joy, it was like descending a stairway into a dungeon, just one step.

"*Our hands*, Bird—you'll see—would you mind—driving?"

Bird realized that the drawl in Himiko's speech was a result of her extreme tension. Walking around the front of the car, he climbed into the driver's seat. He saw in the rear-view mirror that Himiko's face was ashen and splotched, as if a whitish powder had been dabbed around her lips. His own face must have looked equally abject. Bird tried to spit out of the car but his mouth was bone dry and he achieved only a futile little noise like the tisking of a tongue. He catapulted the car into the street with a rudeness learned from Himiko.

"Bird, the doctor I have in mind, he's that middle-aged man with a head like an egg who was calling outside the window the first night you stayed at the house. You remember him?"

"I remember," Bird said, thinking it had seemed possible at one time that he might live out his entire life without any contact with such a man.

"When we've phoned him we can figure out what we'll need to pick up the baby."

"The doctor told me not to forget to bring clothes."

"We can stop off at your apartment; you must know where the clothes are put away."

"I think we'd better not!" With a vividness that overwhelmed him, Bird recalled scenes of daily zealous preparation for the baby. Now he felt rejected by all the baby paraphernalia, the white bassinet, the ivory-white baby dresser with handles shaped to look like apples, everything.

"I can't take clothes for the baby out of there—"

"No, I guess not, your wife would never forgive you if she knew you were using the baby's things for this purpose."

There's that, too, Bird thought. But he wouldn't have to take anything out of the apartment; all his wife would have to know never to forgive him was that the baby died shortly after being moved from this hospital to another. Now that this decision had been made it would no longer be possible to prolong their married life by enveloping his wife in vague doubts. That was beyond his power now, no matter what kind of anguished battle he waged against the internal itchiness of deception. Bird hit into another reality coated with the sugars of fraud.

As the car approached a broad intersection—one of the large freeways that circled the giant city—they were stopped by a traffic light. Bird glanced impatiently in the direction he wanted to turn. The cloud-heavy sky hovered just above the ground. A wind blew up, pregnant with rain, and hissed high through the branches of the dusty trees along the street. Changing to green, the light stood out sharply against the cloudy sky; it made Bird feel he was being drawn into it bodily. That he was being protected by the same traffic signal as people who had never considered murder in their entire lives, pestered his sense of justice.

"Where do you want to phone from?" he said, feeling like a criminal on the run.

"From the nearest grocery store. Then we can get some sausage and have a little lunch."

"All right," Bird said submissively, despite the unpleasant resistance he could feel originating in his stomach. "But do you think this friend of yours will agree to help?"

"That humpty-dumpty head of his makes him look benign, but he's done some really awful things. For example . . ." Himiko lapsed unnaturally into silence and licked her lips with the snaking tip of her tongue. So the little man had perpetrated such horrors that Himiko lacked the courage to report them! Bird felt nauseous again, a lunch of sausages was out of the question. Truly.

"When we've phoned," Bird said, "we should buy something for the baby to wear instead of worrying about sausage, and a bassinet, too. I guess a department store would be quickest. Not that I'm crazy about having to shop for baby clothes."

"I'll get what we need, Bird, you can wait in the car."

"Just after she got pregnant I went shopping with my wife, it was lousy with mothers-to-be and screaming babies, there was something animal about the atmosphere in there."

Bird glanced at Himiko and saw the color draining from her face; she must have felt nauseated, too. The two of them drove on, pale and silent. When Bird finally spoke, it was out of a need to abuse himself:

"When the baby is dead and my wife has recovered I imagine we'll get a divorce. Then I'll really be a free man now that I've been fired and all, and that's surely what I've been dreaming about for years. Funny, I'm not particularly happy about it."

The wind was stronger now and blowing from Bird toward Himiko, so that she had to raise her voice above it. When she spoke it was nearly a shout: "Bird, when you do become a free man, can't we sell the house the way my father-in-law suggested and go to Africa together?"

Africa actually in sight! But it was only a desolate, insipid Africa that Bird was able to picture now. This was the first time since he had conceived his passion for it as a boy that Africa had lost its radiance inside him. A free man halted desolately in the gray Sahara. He had murdered an infant on the island hovering like a dragonfly at one hundred forty degrees east longitude. Then he had fled here, wandered all of Africa and failed to trap a single shrewmouse let alone a savage wart hog. Now he stood dumbly in the Sahara.

"Africa?" Bird said woodenly.

"You're just a little withdrawn now, Bird, like a snail inside its shell. But you'll get back your passion the minute you set foot on African soil."

Bird was silent.

"Bird, I've become fascinated with your maps. I want you to get divorced so we can travel to Africa together and use them as real road maps. Last night I studied them for hours after you went to sleep and I guess I caught the fever, too. And now your freedom has become essential to me, Bird, I need you as a free man. You wouldn't agree when I said we'd be dirtying *our hands* but you were wrong, Bird, really you were. *Our hands.* Bird, we'll go to Africa together, won't we!"

As if he were bringing up painful phlegm, "If that's what you want," Bird said.

"At first our relationship was only sexual, I was a sexual refuge from your anxiety and from your shame. But last night I realized that a passion for Africa was developing in me, too. And that means a new bond between us, Bird, now we have a map of Africa for a go-between. We've leaped from a merely sexual lowland to much higher ground, something I'd hoped would happen all along, and now I honestly feel it, Bird, the same passion! That's why I'm introducing you to my doctor friend and dirtying my own hands along with yours!"

A web of cracks seemed to open in the low windshield as a white rain as fine as mist spattered the glass. The same instant, Bird and Himiko felt rain on their brows and in their eyes. The sky darkened in all directions as if dusk had suddenly arrived and a waspish whirlwind rose. "Is there a roof you can put on this car?" Bird said like a mournful idiot. "Otherwise, the baby will get all wet."

12

B Y the time Bird had finished putting up the convertible's black hood the wind careening around the alley like a frightened chicken was smelling of sausage and burned garlic. Fry thinly sliced garlic in butter, add sausage and just enough water to steam: it was a dish Mr. Delchef had taught him. Bird wondered what had happened to Mr. Delchef. By now he had probably been taken away from that small, pallid Japanese girl and returned to his legation. Had he attempted violent resistance in their lair at the end of the blind alley? Had his girlfriend screamed in Japanese as incomprehensible to Mr. Delchef himself as to the legation people who had come to take him back? Finally, their only choice must have been to submit.

Bird gazed at the sports car. With the black hood on top of its scarlet body, the car looked like the torn flesh of a wound and scabs around it. Disgust stirred in Bird. The sky was dark, the air damp and swollen; a wind was clamoring. Rain would suffuse the air like mist and then a gust of wind would whirl it away into the distance and as suddenly it would return. Bird looked up at the trees billowing above the rooftops in their opulence of leaf and saw that the squalling rain had washed them to a somber yet truly vivid green. It was a green that transported him, as the traffic light had done at the highway intersection. Perhaps, he mused, he would see this kind of vibrant green when he lay on his deathbed. Bird felt as if he were about to be led to his own death at the hands of a shady abortionist. Not the baby.

The basket and baby clothes waited on the steps in front of the house. Bird gathered them up and stuffed them into the space behind the driver's seat. Underwear and socks, a woolen top and pants, even a tiny cap: these were the things Himiko had taken so much time to select. Bird had been kept waiting a full hour; he had even begun to wonder if

Himiko hadn't deserted him. He couldn't understand why she had lavished such care on choosing clothes for a baby soon to die: a woman's sensibilities were always queer.

"Bird, lunch is ready," Himiko called from the bedroom window.

Bird found Himiko standing in the kitchen eating sausage. He peered into the frying pan and then pulled back, repulsed by the odor of garlic. Turning to Himiko, who was watching him curiously, he weakly shook his head. "If you have no appetite why don't you take a shower?" The suggestion reeked of garlic.

"I think I will," Bird said with relief: sweat had caked the dust on his body.

Bird circumspectly bunched his shoulders as he showered. A hot shower aroused him ordinarily, but now he experienced only a painful hammering of his heart. Bird shut his eyes tight in the warm rain of the shower, arched his head backward, consciously this time, and tried rubbing behind his ears with the undersides of his thumbs. A minute later, Himiko leaped to his side in the shower with her hair in a vinyl shower cap patterned with something like watermelons and began to scratch at her body with a bar of soap, so Bird stopped playing the game and left the bathroom. It was as he was drying himself, he heard the thud of something large and heavy hitting the ground outside. When he went to the bedroom window, he saw the scarlet sports car listing critically, like a ship about to sink. The right front tire was missing! Bird hurried into his clothes without bothering to dry his back and went out to inspect the car. He was aware of footsteps retreating down the alley, but he stopped to examine the damage instead of giving a chase. There was no trace of the tire, and the right headlight was shattered: someone had jacked up the MG, removed the tire, then stood on the fender and tilted the car so roughly to the ground that the shock had shattered the headlight. Under the car the jack lay like a broken arm.

"Somebody stole a tire," Bird shouted to Himiko, still in the shower. "And one of the headlights is busted. I hope you have a spare!"

"In the back of the shed."

"But who would steal one tire?"

"Remember the boy at the window that night, hardly more than a child? Well, that's him being mean. He's hiding somewhere near with the tire and I bet he's watching us," Himiko shouted back as if nothing had happened. "If we pretend not to be the least bit upset and make a grand exit out of here, I bet we can make him cry in his hiding place, he'll be so mortified. Let's try it."

"That's fine if the car will run. I'll see if I can get that spare on."

Bird changed the tire, getting mud and grease all over his hands. The work made him sweatier than he had been before his shower. When he had finished he started the engine cautiously: nothing in particular seemed wrong. They might be a little late but certainly it would all be over before dusk, they wouldn't need the headlights. Bird felt like another shower but Himiko was ready to leave; besides, he was so exasperated now that even the briefest delay would have been intolerable. They left as they were. As they drove out of the alley, someone behind them threw pebbles at the car.

"You come too!" Bird entreated when Himiko made no move to get out of the car. Together they hurried down the long corridor toward the intensive care ward, Bird clasping the basket, Himiko the baby's clothes. Bird was aware of a special tension today, an aloofness in all the patients who passed them in the corridor. It was the influence of the rain whipping in on the rude wind and abruptly withdrawing as though pursued, and of the dull thunder in the distance. As Bird walked down the corridor with the basket in his arms, he searched for words with which to broach safely to the nurses the matter of the baby's withdrawal from the hospital; gradually his consternation grew. But when he reached the ward it was known that he would take the baby with him. Bird was relieved. Even so, he maintained a wooden face and kept his eyes on the floor, responding as briefly as possible to procedural questions only. Bird was afraid of leaving the curious young nurses an opening to ask why he was taking the baby away without an operation or just where he intended to take him.

"If you'll just take this card to the office and make the necessary payments," the nurse said. "Meanwhile I'll call the doctor in charge."

Bird took the large card; it was a lewd pink.

"I brought some clothes for the baby—"

"We'll need them, of course; I'll take them now." As she spoke, the nurse's eyes unveiled her sharp disapproval. Bird handed over all the baby's clothes at once; the nurse inspected them one by one and thrust back at him only the cap. Bird rolled it up sheepishly and stuffed it into his pocket. Then he peevishly turned to Himiko, who hadn't noticed.

"What?"

"Nothing. I have to go to the office for a minute."

"I'll come too," Himiko said hurriedly, as though afraid of being abandoned. Throughout the negotiations with the nurses, the two of them had been standing with their bodies wrenched around in such a way that the infants on the other side of the glass partition could not possibly enter their field of vision.

When the girl at the reception window had taken the pink card, she asked for Bird's seal and said: "I see you're leaving us—congratulations!"

Bird, neither affirming nor denying, nodded.

"And what name have you given your child?" the girl continued.

"We . . . haven't decided yet."

"At present the baby is registered simply as your first-born son, it would be a big help if we could have a name for our records."

A name! thought Bird. Now, as in his wife's hospital room, the idea was profoundly disturbing. Provide the monster with a name and from that instant it would seem more human, probably it would begin asserting itself in a human way. The difference between death while the monster was nameless and death after Bird had given it a name would mean a difference to Bird in the nature of the creature's very existence.

"Even a temporary name you're not certain about will do," the girl said pleasantly, though her voice betrayed her stubbornness.

"It can't hurt to name him, Bird," Himiko broke in impatiently.

"I'll call him Kikuhiko," Bird said, remembering his wife's words, then he showed the girl the characters to use.

The account settled, Bird got back nearly all the money he had left as security. The baby had consumed only diluted milk and sugar-water, and since even antibiotics had been withheld, its stay at the hospital had been economical beyond compare.

Bird and Himiko walked back down the corridor toward the intensive care ward.

"This is money I took out of savings for a trip to Africa in the first place. And the minute I decide to murder the baby and go to Africa with you, it's back in my pocket again—" Bird spoke out of a tangle of feelings, not certain what he really wanted to say.

"Then we should actually use the money in Africa," Himiko said easily. Then: "Bird, that name, Kikuhiko—I know a gay bar called

Kikuhiko, written with those same characters. The mama's name is Kikuhiko."

"How old a guy is he?"

"It's hard to tell with faggots like that, four, maybe five years younger than you."

"I bet he's the same Kikuhiko I knew years ago. During the Occupation he had an affair with an American cultural officer and then he ran away to Tokyo."

"What a coincidence! Bird, why don't we go over there after!"

After, Bird thought, *after* abandoning the baby with a shady abortionist!

Bird recalled abandoning his young friend Kikuhiko late one night in a provincial city. And now the baby he was about to abandon was also to be called Kikuhiko. So devious traps surrounded even the act of naming. For an instant Bird considered going back and correcting the name, but this intention was corroded instantly in the acid of enervation. Bird was left only with a need to inflict pain upon himself. "Let's drink away the night at the gay bar Kikuhiko," he said. "It will be a wake."

Bird's baby—Kikuhiko had been carried around to this side of the glass partition and he was lying in his basket in the wooly baby clothes Himiko had chosen for him. Next to the basket the pediatrician in charge was waiting self-consciously for Bird. Bird and Himiko faced the doctor across the basket. Bird could feel the shock Himiko received when she looked down and saw the baby. It was a size larger now, its eyes open like deep creases in its crimson skin and staring at them, sidelong. Even the lump on the baby's head seemed to have grown considerably. It was redder than its face, lustrous, tumescent. Now that its eyes were open, the baby had the shriveled, ancient look of the hermits in the Southern Scrolls, but it definitely lacked a human quality, probably because the frontal portion of its head that ought to have counterpoised the lump was still severely pinched. The baby was oscillating its tightly clenched fists, as if it wanted to flee its basket.

"It doesn't look like you, Bird," Himiko whispered in a rasping, ugly voice.

"It doesn't look like anybody; it doesn't even look human!"

"I wouldn't say that—" the pediatrician offered in feeble reproof.

Bird glanced quickly at the babies beyond the glass partition. At the moment all of them were writhing in their beds, uniformly agitated. Bird suspected they were gossiping about their comrades who had been taken away. Whatever happened to that piddling pocket-monkey of an incubator baby with the meditative eyes? And the fighting father of the baby without a liver, was he here to start another argument in his brown knickers and wide leather belt?

"Are you all checked out at the office?" the nurse asked.

"All finished."

"Then you may do as you like!"

"You're sure you won't reconsider?" The pediatrician sounded troubled.

"Quite sure," Bird adamantly said. "Thanks for everything."

"Don't thank me—I've done nothing."

"Well then, good-by."

The doctor flushed around his eyes and, as if he regretted having raised his voice just now, said in a voice as soft as Bird's: "Good-by, take care of yourself."

As Bird stepped out of the ward, the patients loitering in the corridor turned as if at a signal and advanced toward the baby. Bird, glowering, marched straight down the corridor with his elbows cocked, hunching protectively over the basket. Himiko hurried after him. Dismayed by the fury in Bird's face, the convalescents moved to the sides of the dim corridor, suspicious still, but, probably on the baby's account, smiling.

"Bird," said Himiko, turning to look behind her, "that doctor or one of the nurses might notify the police."

"Like hell they will," Bird said savagely. "Don't forget they nad a crack at killing the baby themselves, with watered milk and sugar-water!"

They were approaching the main entrance and what looked to Bird like a seething crowd of out-patients; to defend the baby from their mammoth curiosity with nothing but his own two elbows this time, seemed a pure impossibility. Bird felt like a lone player running with a rugby ball at a goal defended by the entire enemy team. He hesitated, and, remembering, "There's a cap in my pants pocket. Would you get it out and cover the back of his head?"

Bird watched Himiko's arm tremble as she did his bidding. Together then they hurled themselves at the strangers who sidled toward them with brash smiles. "What a darling baby, like an angel!" one middle-aged lady crooned, and though Bird felt like the butt of a horrid joke he didn't falter or even lift his head until he had broken free of the crowd.

Outside it was raining again, yet another of the day's downpours. Himiko's car backed through the rain with the fleetness of a water skimmer to where Bird waited with the basket. Bird handed the basket to Himiko, then climbed into the car himself and took it back. In order to secure it on his lap, Bird had to hold himself rigidly erect, statue of an Egyptian king.

"All set?"

"Ah."

The car leaped forward as at the start of a race. Bird struck his ear against the metal brace of the roof and caught his breath in pain.

"What time is it, Bird?"

Bird, supporting the basket with his right arm only, looked at his wristwatch. The hands stood at a nonsensical hour; the watch had stopped. Bird had been wearing the watch out of habit but he hadn't looked at the time in days, much less set or wound the watch. He felt as if he had been living outside the zone of time which regulated the placid lives of those who were not afflicted with a grotesque baby.

"My watch has stopped," he said.

Himiko pushed a button on the car radio. A news broadcast: the announcer was commenting on the repercussions of the Soviet resumption of nuclear testing. The Japan Anti-Nuclear Warfare League had come out in support of the Soviet test. There was factional strife within the League, however, and a strong possibility that the next world conference on the abolishment of nuclear weapons would founder in a hopeless bog of disagreement. A tape was played, Hiroshima victims challenging the League's proclamation. Could there really be such a thing as a *clean* atomic weapon? What if the tests *were* being conducted by Soviet scientists in the wastelands of Siberia, could there really be such a thing as a hydrogen bomb that was not harmful to man or beast?

Himiko changed the station. Popular music, a tango—not that Bird could distinguish between one tango and another. This one was interminable: Himiko finally switched the radio off. They had failed to come up with a time signal.

"Bird, it looks like the ANWL has copped out on the issue of Soviet tests," Himiko said with no particular interest in her voice.

"It seems that way," Bird said.

In a world shared by all those others, time was passing, mankind's one and only time, and a destiny apprehended the world over as one and the same destiny was taking evil shape. Bird, on the other hand, was answerable only to the baby in the basket on his lap, to the monster who governed his personal destiny.

"Bird, do you suppose there are people who want an atomic war, not because they stand to benefit from the manufacture of nuclear weapons economically, say, or politically, but simply because that's what they want? I mean, just as most people believe for no particular reason that this planet should be perpetuated and hope that it will be, there must be black-hearted people who believe, for no reason *they* could name, that mankind should be annihilated. In northern Europe there's a little animal like a rat, it's called a lemming, and sometimes these lemmings commit mass suicide. I just wonder if somewhere on this earth there aren't lemming-people. Bird?"

"Lemming-people with black hearts? The UN would have to get right to work on a program for tracking them down."

Bird, though he played along, felt no desire to march in the crusade against the lemming-people with black hearts. In fact, he was aware of a black-hearted lemming presence whispering through himself.

"Hot, isn't it," Himiko said, as if to suggest by her brusque changing of the subject that their conversation so far had not much interested her.

"Yes, it's hot all right."

Heat from the engine continued to vibrate upward from the thin metal plate of the floor, and since the canvas hood sealed the car shut they began gradually to feel as if they were trapped inside a hothouse. But clearly the wind would blow in the rain if they detached a corner of the hood. Bird examined the latches wistfully; it was a particularly old-fashioned hood.

"There's nothing you can do, Bird." Himiko had detected his despair. "Let's stop every once in a while and open the door."

Bird saw a rain-soaked sparrow lying dead in the road just ahead of the car. Himiko saw it, too. The car bore down on the dead bird, and, as it sank out of sight, sharply swerved and dropped one tire into a pothole which lay hidden under muddy yellow water. Bird rapped both hands against the dashboard, but he didn't loosen his grip on the baby's basket. Sadly Bird thought: by the time we get to the abortionist's clinic I'll be covered with bruises.

"Sorry, Bird," Himiko said. She must have taken a blow, too, it was a voice set against pain. They both avoided mentioning the dead sparrow.

"It's nothing serious." Settling the basket on his lap again, Bird looked down at the baby for the first time since he had climbed into the car. The baby's face was burning a steadily angrier red, but whether it was breathing wasn't clear. Suffocation! Bird was driven by panic to shake the basket. Abruptly, opening its mouth wide as if to sink its teeth into Bird's fingers, the baby began to cry in a voice too loud to be believed.

Waaaaaaaaaagh-uh. . . . waaaaaaaaaagh-uh. . . . waaaa-aaaaaagh-uh. . . . on and on the baby screamed and delicately convulsed while tear after large, transparent tear seeped from tightly closed eyes like inch-long shreds of thread. As Bird recovered from his panic, he moved to cover with his palm the screaming baby's rosy lips and barely checked himself in time as a new panic welled. Iiiiiiiiiigh-uh. . . . iiiiiiiiiigh-uh . . . the baby continued to bawl. . . . Yaaaaaaaaa-uh. . . . yaaaaaaaaagh-uh. . . . fluttering the cap with the pattern of baby goats that covered the lump on its head.

"You always feel that a baby's cry is full of meaning," Himiko said, raising her voice above the baby's. "For all we know, it may contain all the meaning of all of man's words."

Still the baby wailed: waaaaaaaaaagh-uh. . . . yaaaaaaaaaaaagh-uh. . . . aaaaaaaaaaaagh-uh. . . . waagh . . . waagh . . . waagh . . . waagh. . . . yaiiiiiiiiigh-uh. . . .

"It's a lucky thing we don't have the ability to understand," Bird said uneasily.

The car sped on, carrying with it the baby's screams. It was like a load of five thousand shrilling crickets, or again as if Bird and Himiko had burrowed into the body of a single cricket and were stridulating with it. Soon the heat trapped in the car and the baby's crying became unbearable; Himiko pulled over and they opened both doors. The damp, hot air inside the car roared out like a feverish invalid's belch; cold, wet air gushed in and with it, the rain. Bird and Himiko had been bathed in sweat, now they shivered with a chill. A little rain even stole into the basket on Bird's lap, the water clinging to the baby's flaming cheeks in drops much smaller than tears. Now the baby's crying was fitful——aagh-uh—aagh-uh—aagh-uh——and every so often a spasm of coughing would shake its body. The coughing was clearly abnormal: Bird wondered if the baby hadn't developed a respiratory disease. By tilting the basket away from the door he finally managed to shield it from the rain.

"Bird, it's dangerous to expose a baby suddenly to cold air like this when he's been living in an incubator—he could even catch pneumonia!"

"I know," Bird said, his fatigue heavy and deep-rooted.

"I can't think what to do."

"What the hell are you supposed to do to make a baby stop crying at a time like this?" Never before had Bird felt so utterly inexperienced.

"I've seen them given a breast to suck lots of times—" Himiko paused as though in horror, then she quickly added, "We should have brought some milk along, Bird."

"Watered milk? Or maybe sugar-water?" It was the fatigue that dredged up the cynic in him.

"Let me just run into a drugstore. They might have one of those toys, what do you call them? you know, they're shaped like nipples?"

And Himiko dashed out into the rain. Bird, rocking the baby's basket uncertainly, watched his lover hurry away in her flat shoes. No Japanese woman her age was better educated than Himiko, but that education was rotting on the pantry shelf; nor was she as knowledgeable about daily life as even the most ordinary of women. Probably she would never have children of her own. Bird remembered Himiko as she had been in their first year at college, the liveliest of a group of freshman girls, and he felt pity for the Himiko who was now flopping through a mud puddle like a clumsy dog. Who in the whole world would have foreseen this future for that co-ed so full of youth and pedantry and confidence? Several long-distance moving vans rumbled by like a herd of rhinoceros, shaking the car and Bird and the baby with it. Bird thought he could hear a call in the rumbling of the trucks, urgent though its meaning was unclear. It had to be an illusion, but for a futile minute he listened hard.

Himiko leaned into the rainy gusts of wind as she labored back to the car, her face so publicly in a scowl that she might have been fuming alone in the dark. She wasn't running anymore: Bird read in all of her ample body an ugly fatigue to match his own. But when Himiko reached the car she said happily, raising her voice above the baby's, who was crying as before, "They call these sucking toys pacifiers, it just slipped my mind for a minute—here, I bought two kinds."

Rummaging the word "pacifier" out of the storeroom of distant memory seemed to have given Himiko back her confidence. But the yellow rubber objects resting in her open hand like enlarged, winged maple seeds looked like troublesome implements for a newborn baby to manage.

"The one with the blue stuff inside is for teething, that's for older infants. But this squooshy one should be just what the doctor ordered." As she spoke, Himiko placed the pacifier in the screaming baby's pink mouth.

Why did you have to buy one for teething? Bird started to ask. Then he saw that the baby wasn't even responding to the pacifier intended for infants. The only indication it was aware of the gadget inserted in its mouth was a slight working of its face, as if the baby was trying to expel the pacifier with its tongue.

"It doesn't seem to work; I guess he's too young," Himiko said miserably after experimenting for a minute. Her confidence again was gone.

Bird withheld criticism.

"But I don't know any other way to quiet a baby down."

"Then we'll have to go on this way—let's get started." Bird closed the door on his side.

"The clock in the drugstore just now said four o'clock. I think we can get to the clinic by five." Himiko started the engine, an ugly look on her face. She too was heading for the north pole of disgruntlement.

"He can't possibly cry for a whole hour," Bird said.

Five-thirty: the baby had cried itself to sleep but they had not yet reached their destination. For a full fifty minutes now they had been making a grand tour around the same hollow. They had driven up and down hills, crossed a winding, muddy river any number of times, blundered down blind alleys, emerged again and again on the wrong side of one of the steep slopes that rose out of the valley to the north and south. Himiko remembered having driven right to the entrance of the clinic, and when the car climbed to the top of a rise she was even able to locate its general vicinity. But then they would descend into the crowded hollow with its maze of narrow streets and it would become impossible to say with certainty even which direction they were heading. When they finally turned into a street Himiko thought she remembered, it was only to encounter a small truck which refused absolutely to yield the way. They had to back up a hundred yards, and when they had let the truck pass and tried to go back, they found that they had turned a different corner. The street at the next corner was one way: return was impossible.

Bird was silent throughout, and so was Himiko. They were both so irritated that they lacked the confidence to say anything for fear of hurting each other. Even a remark as innocent as *I'm sure we've already passed this corner twice* seemed dangerously likely to open a jagged crack between them. And there was the police box they kept driving by. An officer was certain to be sitting just inside the entrance to the ramshackle wooden structure, and each time they whispered by they grew a little more afraid of attracting his attention. Asking the policeman directions to the clinic was out of the question; they were unwilling even to check the address with any of the local delivery boys. A sports car carrying a baby with a lump on its head was looking for a clinic with a questionable reputation—such a rumor was certain to cause trouble. In fact, the doctor had gone as far as to caution Himiko on the phone not to make any stops in the neighborhood, not even for cigarettes. And so they continued what began to seem like an endless tour of the vicinity. And gradually, paranoia took hold of Bird: probably they would drive around all night and never reach the clinic they were looking for; probably a clinic for murdering babies never existed in the first place. Nor was paranoia Bird's only problem, there was a tenacious sleepiness. What if he fell asleep and the baby's basket slid off his lap? If the skin on the baby's lump were really the dura mater that enclosed the brain, it would rupture instantly. The baby would submerge in the muddy water seeping through the floorboards between the gear shift and the brake, then he would develop breathing difficulty and gasp his life away—but that was much too horrible a death. Bird labored to stay awake. Even so he sank for an instant into the shadows of unconsciousness and was called back by Himiko's tense voice pleading: "For God's sake, Bird, stay awake!"

The basket was slipping off Bird's lap. Shuddering, he gripped it with both hands.

"Bird, I'm sleepy too. I have this scary feeling I might run into something."

Even now the dusky aura of evening was dancing down into the hollow. The wind had died, but the rain had continued here and changed at some point to mist which narrowly closed the field of vision. Himiko switched on the headlights and only one lamp lighted: her childish lover's spite had begun to take effect. As the car again approached the twin ginkgo trees in front of the police box, an officer who might have been a young farmer ambled into the street and waved them to a stop.

It was a pale, bedraggled, and thoroughly suspicious state that Bird and Himiko were exposed to the policeman's gaze, as, stooping, he peered into the car.

"Driver's license please!" The cop sounded like the world's most jaded policeman. In fact he was about the age of Bird's students at the cram-school, but he knew perfectly well that he was intimidating them and he was enjoying it. "I could see you had only one good light, you know, the first time you drove by. And I looked the other way. But when you keep coming around the way you have, well, you're just begging to get stopped. And now you cruise up as big as life with just that one light on—you can't get away with that. It reflects on our authority."

"Naturally," Himiko said, with no inflection whatsoever.

"That a baby in there or what?" Himiko's attitude appeared to have offended the officer. "Maybe I better ask you to leave the car here and carry the baby."

The baby's face was now grotesquely red, its breath coming in ragged rasps through its open mouth and both its nostrils. For an instant Bird forgot the police officer peering into the car to wonder if the baby had come down with pneumonia. Fearfully he pressed his hand against the baby's brow. The sensation of heat was piercing, of an entirely different quality from that of human body temperature. Bird involuntarily cried out.

"What?" said the startled cop in a voice appropriate to his age.

"The baby is sick," Himiko said. "So we decided to bring him in the car even though we noticed the headlight was broken." Whatever Himiko was plotting involved taking advantage of the policeman's consternation. "But then we lost the way and now we don't know what to do."

"Where do you want to go? What's the doctor's name?"

Hesitating, Himiko finally told the policeman the name of the clinic. The officer informed her that she would find it at the end of the little street just to the left of where they were parked. Then he said, anxious to demonstrate that he was no soft-hearted pushover of a cop: "But since it's so close it won't hurt you to get out and walk, maybe I'd better ask you to do that."

Himiko hysterically extended one long arm and plucked the woolen cap from the baby's head. It was the decisive blow to the young policeman.

"If he's moved at all he must be shaken as little as possible."

Himiko had pursued the enemy and overwhelmed him. Glumly, as though he regretted having taken it, the policeman returned her driver's license. "See that you take the car in to be repaired as soon as you drop the baby off," he said stupidly, his eyes still fixed to the lump on the baby's head. "But—that's really awful! Is that what you call brain fever?"

Bird and Himiko turned down the street the officer had indicated. By the time they had parked in front of the clinic, Himiko was composed enough to say: "He didn't take down my license number or name or anything—what a dumb-ass cop!"

The clinic seemed to be built of plasterboard; they carried the baby's basket into the vestibule. There was no sign of nurses, or patients either; it was the man with the egg-shaped head who appeared the minute Himiko called. And this time he wasn't wearing a linen tuxedo but a stained, terrifying smock.

Ignoring Bird completely, he chided Himiko in a gentle voice, peering all the while into the baby's basket as though he were buying mackerel from a fish peddler:

"You're late, Himi. I was beginning to think you were having a little joke with me."

It was Bird's overwhelming impression that the clinic vestibule was ruinous: he felt menaced to the quick.

"We had some trouble getting here," Himiko said coolly.

"I was afraid you might have done something dreadful on the way. There are radicals, you know, once they've decided to take the step they don't see any distinction between letting a baby weaken and die and strangling it to death—oh, dear," the doctor exclaimed, lifting the baby's basket, "as if he wasn't in enough trouble already, this poor little fella is coming down with pneumonia." As before, the doctor's voice was gentle.

13

LEAVING the sports car at a garage, they set out in a cab for the gay bar Himiko knew. They were exhausted, anguished with a need to sleep, but their mouths were dry with an occult excitement that made them uneasy about returning all by themselves to that gloomy house.

They stopped the cab in front of a clumsy imitation of a gas lantern with the word KIKUHIKO in blue paint written on the glass globe. Bird pushed open a door held together tenuously with a few boards of unequal length and stepped into a room as crude and narrow as a shed for livestock; there was only a short counter and, against the opposite wall, two sets of outlandishly high-backed chairs. The bar was empty except for the smallish man standing in a far corner behind the counter who now confronted the two intruders. He was of a curious rotundity, with lips like a young girl's and misted sheep-eyes which were warily inspecting but by no means rejecting them. Bird stood where he was, just inside the door, and returned his gaze. Gradually, a memento of his young friend Kikuhiko permeated the membrane of the ambiguous smile on the man's face.

"Would you believe, it's Himi, and looking a sight!" The man spoke through pursed lips, his eyes still on Bird. "I know this one; it's been ages now, but didn't they used to call him Bird?"

"We might as well sit down," Himiko said. She appeared to be discovering only an atmosphere of anticlimax in the drama of this reunion. Not that Kikuhiko was exciting any very poignant emotion in Bird. He was fatigued utterly, he was sleepy: he felt certain nothing in the world remained that could interest him vitally. Bird found himself sitting down a little apart from Himiko.

"What do they call this one now, Himi?"

"Bird."

"You can't mean it. Still? It's been seven years." Kikuhiko moved over to Bird. "What are you drinking, Bird?"

"Whisky, please. Straight."

"And Himi?"

"The same for me."

"You both have that tired look and it's still so early in the night!"

"Well, it has nothing to do with sex—we spent half the day driving around in circles."

Bird reached for the glass of whisky that had been poured for him and, feeling something tighten in his chest, hesitated. Kikuhiko—he can't be more than twenty-two yet he looks like a more formidable adult than I; on the other hand, he seems to have retained a lot of what he was at fifteen—Kikuhiko, like an amphibian at home in two ages.

Kikuhiko was drinking straight whisky, too. He poured himself another drink, and one for Himiko, who had emptied her first glass in a swallow. Bird found himself watching Kikuhiko and Kikuhiko glanced repeatedly at Bird, the nerves of his body arching like the back of a threatened cat. At last he turned directly to Bird and said: "Bird, do you remember me?"

"Of course," said Bird. Strange, he was more conscious of talking to the proprietor of a gay bar (this was his first time) than to a sometime friend whom he hadn't seen in years.

"It's been ages, hasn't it, Bird. Ever since that day we went over to the next town and saw a G.I. looking out of a train window with the bottom half of his face shot off."

"What's all this about a G.I.?" Himiko said. Kikuhiko told her, his eyes impudently roaming Bird.

"It was during the Korean war and these gorgeous soldier boys who'd been all wounded in the field were being shipped back to bases in Japan. Whole trainloads of them and we saw one of those trains one day. Bird, do you suppose they were passing through our district all the time?"

"Not all the time, no."

"You used to hear stories about slave dealers catching Japanese high-school boys and selling them as soldiers, there were even rumors that the government was going to ship us off to Korea—I was terrified in those days."

Of course! Kikuhiko had been horribly afraid. The night they had quarreled and separated, he had shouted "Bird, I was afraid!" Bird thought about his baby and decided it was still incapable of fear. He felt relieved, a suspect, brittle relief. "Those rumors were certainly meaningless," he said, trying to veer his consciousness from the baby.

"You say, but I did all kinds of nasty things on account of rumors like that. Which reminds me, Bird. Did you have any trouble catching that madman we were chasing?"

"He was dead when I found him, he'd hung himself on Castle Hill—I knocked myself out for nothing." The taste of an old regret returned sourly to the tip of Bird's tongue. "We found him at dawn, the dogs and I. Talk about something being meaningless!"

"I wouldn't say that. You kept up the chase until dawn and I dropped out and ran in the middle of the night and our lives have been completely different ever since. You stopped mixing with me and my kind and went to a college in Tokyo, didn't you? But I've been like falling steadily ever since that night and look at me now—tucked away nice and comfy in this nelly little bar. Bird, if you hadn't . . . gone on alone that night, I might be in a very different groove now."

"If Bird hadn't abandoned you that night, you wouldn't have become a homosexual?" Himiko audaciously asked.

Rattled, Bird had to look away.

"A homosexual is someone who has chosen to let himself love a person of the same sex: and I made that decision myself. So the responsibility is all my own." Kikuhiko's voice was quiet.

"I can see you've read the existentialists," Himiko said.

"When you run a bar for faggots, you have to know where all kinds of things are at!" As though it were part of the song of his profession, Kikuhiko sang the line. Then he turned to Bird and said, in his normal voice, "I'm sure you've been on the rise all the time I've been falling. What are you doing now, Bird?"

"I've been teaching at a cram-school, but it turns out that I'm fired as of the summer vacation—'on the rise' isn't quite how I'd put it," Bird said. "And that isn't all; it's been one weird hassle after another."

"Now that you mention it, the Bird I knew at twenty was never this droopy-woopy. It's as if something has got you awfully scared and you're trying to run away from it—" This was a shrewd and observant Kikuhiko, no longer the simple fairy Bird had known: his friend's life of apostasy and descent could not have been easy or uninvolved.

"You're right," Bird admitted. "I'm all used up. I'm afraid. I'm trying to run away."

"When he was twenty this one was immune to fear, I never saw him frightened of anything," Kikuhiko said to Himiko. Then he turned back to Bird, and, provokingly: "But tonight you seem extra sensitive to fear; it's like you're so afraid you don't have the foggiest notion where your head is at!"

"I'm not twenty anymore," Bird said.

Kikuhiko's face froze over with icy indifference. "The old gray mare just ain't what she used to be," he said, and moved abruptly to Himiko's side.

A minute later two of them began a game of dice and Bird was given his freedom. Relieved, he lifted his glass of whisky. After a blank of seven years it had taken him and his friend just seven minutes of conversation to eliminate everything worthy of their mutual curiosity. *I'm not twenty anymore! And of all my possessions at the age of twenty, the only thing I've managed not to lose is my childish nickname* —Bird gulped down his first whisky of what had been a long day. Seconds later, something substantial and giant stirred sluggishly inside him. The whisky he had just poured into his stomach Bird effortlessly puked. Kikuhiko swiftly wiped the counter clean and set up a glass of water; Bird only stared dumbly into space. *What was he trying to protect from that monster of a baby that he must run so hard and so shamelessly? What was it in himself he was so frantic to defend? The answer was horrifying—nothing! Zero!*

Bird eased out of the bucket chair and slowly lowered his feet to the floor. To Himiko, questioning him with eyes slackened by fatigue and sudden drunkenness, he said: "I've decided to take the baby back to the university hospital and let them operate. I've stopped rushing at every exit door."

"What are you talking about?" Himiko said suspiciously. "Bird! What's happened to you! What kind of a time is this to start talking about an operation!"

"Ever since the morning my baby was born I've been running away," Bird said with certainty.

"But you're having that baby murdered right this minute, dirtying your hands and mine. How can you call that running away? Besides, we're leaving for Africa together!"

"I left the baby with that abortionist and then I ran away, I fled here," Bird said obstinately. "I've been running the whole time, running and running, and I pictured Africa as the land at the end of all flight, the final spot, the terminal—you know, you're running away, too. You're just another cabaret girl running off with an embezzler."

"I'm participating, Bird, dirtying my own hands along with yours. *Don't you say I'm running away!*" Himiko's shout echoed in the caves of her hysteria.

"Have you forgotten that you drove the car into a pothole today rather than run over a dead sparrow? Is that what a person does just before he cuts a baby's throat?"

Himiko's large face flushed, swelling, then darkened with fury and a presentiment of despair. She glared at Bird, shuddering in vexation: she was trying to fault him and couldn't find her voice.

"If I want to confront this monster honestly instead of running away from it, I have only two alternatives: I can strangle the baby to death with my own hands or I can accept him and bring him up. I've understood that from the beginning but I haven't had the courage to accept it—"

"But Bird," Himiko interrupted, waving her fingers threateningly, "that baby is coming down with pneumonia! If you tried to take him back to the hospital he'd die in the car on the way. Then where would you be? They'd arrest you, that's where!"

"If that happened, it would mean that I'd killed the baby with my own two hands. And I'd deserve whatever I got. I guess I'd be able to take the responsibility."

Bird spoke clamly. He felt that he was now evading deception's final trap, and he was restoring his faith in himself.

Himiko glowered at Bird with tears collecting in her eyes; she appeared to be groping frantically for a new psychological attack, and when at last a strategy occurred, she leaped at it: "Let's say you let them operate and saved the baby's life, what would you have then, Bird? You told me yourself that your son would never be more than a vegetable! Don't you see, it's not only that you'd be creating misery for yourself, you'd be nurturing a life that meant absolutely nothing to this world! Do you suppose that would be for the baby's good? Do you, Bird?"

"It's for my own good. It's so I can stop being a man who's always running away," Bird said.

But Himiko still refused to understand. She stared distrustfully at Bird, challenging him still, and then she labored to smile despite the tears welling in her eyes and mockingly said: "So you're going to manhandle a baby with the faculties of a vegetable into staying alive —Bird! is that part of your new *humanism?*"

"All I want is to stop being a man who continually runs away from responsibility."

"But . . . Bird . . ." Himiko sobbed, ". . . what about our promise to go to Africa together? *What about our promise?*"

"For God's sake Himi, get ahold of yourself! Once Bird here begins worrying about himself, he won't hear you no matter how loud you cry."

Bird saw something akin to raw hatred glitter in Kikuhiko's clouded eyes. But his former friend's command to Himiko was the cue she had been waiting for: once again she became the Himiko who had welcomed Bird several days before when he had arrived so forlornly at her door with his bottle of Johnnie Walker, a girl no longer young, infinitely generous: tender, placid Himiko.

"That's all right, Bird. You don't have to come. I'll sell the house and property and go to Africa anyway. I'll take that boy who stole the tire along for company. Now that I think about it, I've been pretty horrid to him." The tearfulness remained, but there was no mistaking that Himiko had ridden the storm of her hysteria.

"Miss Himi will be all right now," Kikuhiko prompted.

"Thank you," Bird said simply, meaning it, no more to one than to the other.

"Bird, you are going to have to endure all kinds of pain," Himiko said. It was meant as encouragement. "So long, Bird. Take care of yourself!"

Bird nodded, and left the bar.

The taxi raced down the wet streets at horrendous speed. If I die in an accident now before I save the baby, my whole twenty-seven years of life will have meant exactly nothing. Bird was stricken with a sense of fear more profound than any he had ever known.

It was the end of autumn. When Bird came downstairs after saying good-by to the surgeon, his parents-in-law greeted him with a smile in front of the intensive care ward; his wife stood between them with the baby in her arms.

"Congratulations, Bird," his father-in-law called. "He looks like you, you know."

"In a way," Bird said with reserve. A week after the operation the baby had looked almost human; the following week it had begun to resemble Bird. "That fault in the baby's skull was only a few millimeters across and it seems to be closing now. I can show you when we get home, I borrowed the X rays. It turns out the brain wasn't protruding from the skull; so it wasn't a brain hernia after all, just a benign tumor. There were apparently two hard kernels as white as ping-pong balls in that lump they cut away."

"This is one family that has a lot to be grateful for." The professor had been waiting for a lull in the rush of Bird's talk.

"Bird gave so much of his own blood for all those transfusions during the operation, he came out looking as pale as a princess after a date with Dracula." A rare attempt at humor from Bird's exuberant mother-in-law. "Seriously, Bird, you were as courageous and untiring as a young lion."

Frightened by the sudden change in environment, the baby lay in shriveled and unmoving silence, observing the adults out of eyes which must still have been nearly sightless. Since the women stopped repeatedly to cluck and coo over the baby, Bird and the professor gradually drew ahead as they talked. "This time you really met your problem head on," the professor said.

"As a matter of fact, I kept trying to run away. And I almost did. But it seems that reality compels you to live properly when you live in the real world. I mean, even if you intend to get yourself caught in a trap of deception, you find somewhere along the line that your only choice is to avoid it." Bird was surprised at the muted resentment in his voice. "That's what I've found, anyway."

"But it is possible to live in the real world in quite a different way, Bird. There are people who leap-frog from one deception to another until the day they die."

Through half-closed eyes Bird saw again the freighter bound for Zanzibar that had sailed a few days before with Himiko on board. He pictured himself, having killed the baby, standing at her side in place of that boyish man—a sufficiently enticing prospect of Hell. And perhaps just such a reality was being played out in one of Himiko's universes. Bird opened his eyes, turning back to the problems in the universe in which he had chosen to remain. "There is a possibility that the baby's development will be normal," he said, "but there's an equal danger that he'll grow up with an extremely low I.Q. That means I'm going to have to put away as much as I can for his future as well as our own. Naturally, I'm not going to ask you to help me find another job, not after the mess I made of the one I had. I've decided to forget about a career in college teaching—I'm thinking of becoming a guide for foreign tourists. A dream of mine has always been to go to Africa and hire a native guide, so I'll just be reversing the fantasy: I'll be the native guide, for the foreigners who come to Japan."

The professor started to say something in reply when they both had to step aside for a youth with his arm in an exaggerated sling who was being hurried down the corridor by a gang of his friends. The boys swept by, ignoring Bird and his father-in-law. They all wore soiled, shabby jackets which already looked too light for the chilliness of the season. Bird saw the dragons emblazoned on their backs and realized that this was the gang he had battled that night in early summer when his baby was being born.

"I know those boys, but for some reason they didn't pay any attention to me," he said.

"In a few weeks' time you've become almost another person; that probably explains it."

"Do you suppose?"

"You've changed." The professor's voice was warm with a relative's affection. "A childish nickname like Bird doesn't suit you anymore."

Bird waited for the women to catch up and peered down at his son in the cradle of his wife's arms. He wanted to try reflecting his face in the baby's pupils. The mirror of the baby's eyes was a deep, lucid gray and it did begin to reflect an image, but one so excessively fine that Bird couldn't confirm his new face. As soon as he got home he would take a look in the mirror. Then he would try the Balkan dictionary that Mr. Delchef had presented him before his legation had shipped him home. On the inside cover, Mr. Delchef had written the word for *hope*. Bird intended to look up *forbearance*.

Selected Grove Press Paperbacks

E732   ALLEN, DONALD M. & BUTTERICK, GEORGE F., eds. / The Postmoderns: The New American Poetry Revised 1945–1960 / $9.95

E609   ALLEN, DONALD M. and TALLMAN, WARREN, eds. / Poetics of the New American Poetry / $3.95

B445   ANONYMOUS / The Boudoir / $2.95

B334   ANONYMOUS / My Secret Life / $3.95

B415   ARDEN, JOHN / Plays: One (Serjeant Musgrave's Dance, The Workhouse Donkey, Armstrong's Last Goodnight) / $4.95

E711   ARENDT, HANNAH / The Jew As Pariah: Jewish Identity and Politics in the Modern Age, ed. by Ron Feldman / $6.95

E611   ARRABAL, FERNANDO / Garden of Delights / $2.95

B439   ARSAN, EMMANUELLE / Emmanuelle / $2.95

E127   ARTAUD, ANTONIN / The Theater and Its Double / $3.95

E425   BARAKA, IMAMU AMIRI (Leroi Jones) / The Baptism and The Toilet: Two Plays / $3.95

E670   BARAKA, IMAMU AMIRI (LeRoi Jones) / The System of Dante's Hell, The Dead Lecturer and Tales / $4.95

E96   BECKETT, SAMUEL / Endgame / $2.45

E692   BECKETT, SAMUEL / I Can't Go On, I'll Go On: A Selection from Samuel Beckett's Work, ed. by Richard Seaver / $6.95

E777   BECKETT, SAMUEL / Rockaby and Other Short Pieces / $3.95

B78   BECKETT, SAMUEL / Three Novels: Molloy, Malone Dies and The Unnamable / $3.95

E33   BECKETT, SAMUEL / Waiting for Godot / $2.95

E152   BECKETT, SAMUEL / Watt / $6.95

B411   BEHAN, BRENDAN / The Complete Plays (The Hostage, The Quare Fellow, Richard's Cork Leg, Three One Act Plays for Radio) / $4.95

E531   BERGMAN, INGMAR / Three Films by Ingmar Bergman (Through a Glass Darkly, Winter Light, The Silence) / $4.95

E331   BIELY, ANDREY / St. Petersburg / $6.95

E417   BIRCH, CYRIL and KEENE, DONALD, eds. / Anthology of Chinese Literature, Vol. I: From Early Times to the 14th Century / $8.95

E584   BIRCH, CYRIL, ed. / Anthology of Chinese Literature, Vol. II: From the 14th Century to the Present / $4.95

E368   BORGES, JORGE LUIS / Ficciones / $3.95

E9	KEENE, DONALD / Japanese Literature: An Introduction for Western Readers / $2.25
E216	KEENE, DONALD, ed. / Anthology of Japanese Literature: Earliest Era to Mid-19th Century / $7.95
E573	KEENE, DONALD, ed. / Modern Japanese Literature: An Anthology / $7.95
B253	KEROUAC, JACK / Lonesome Traveler / $2.95
B135	KEROUAC, JACK / Satori in Paris / $2.25
B454	KEROUAC, JACK / The Subterraneans / $3.50
E705	KERR, CARMEN / Sex For Women Who Want To Have Fun and Loving Relationships With Equals / $4.95
B413	LAVERTY, FRANK / The Q.K. Way To Slim / $2.95
B9	LAWRENCE, D. H. / Lady Chatterley's Lover / $1.95
E748	LESSER, MICHAEL, M.D. / Nutrition and Vitamin Therapy / $7.95
B262	LESTER, JULIUS / Black Folktales / $2.95
E163	LEWIS, MATTHEW / The Monk / $5.95
E578	LINSSEN, ROBERT / Living Zen / $3.95
E54	LORCA, FEDERICO / Poet in New York. Bilingual ed. / $4.95
B373	LUCAS, GEORGE / American Graffiti / $1.75
E701	MALRAUX, ANDRE / The Conquerors / $3.95
E719	MALRAUX, ANDRE / Lazarus / $2.95
E697	MAMET, DAVID / American Buffalo / $3.95
E778	MAMET, DAVID / Lakeboat / $4.95
E709	MAMET, DAVID / A Life in the Theatre / $3.95
E716	MAMET, DAVID / The Water Engine and Mr. Happiness / $3.95
B61	MILLER, HENRY / Black Spring / $3.95
B326	MILLER, HENRY / Nexus / $3.95
B100	MILLER, HENRY / Plexus / $3.95
B325	MILLER, HENRY / Sexus / $4.95
B10	MILLER, HENRY / Tropic of Cancer / $2.50
B59	MILLER, HENRY / Tropic of Capricorn / $3.50
E583	MISHIMA, YUKIO / Sun and Steel / $4.95
E433	MROZEK, SLAWOMIR / Tango / $3.95
E568	MROZEK, SLAWOMIR / Vatzlav / $1.95
E636	NERUDA, PABLO / Five Decades: Poems 1925–1970. Bilingual ed. / $5.95
E364	NERUDA, PABLO / Selected Poems. Bilingual ed. / $5.95
E650	NICHOLS, PETER / The National Health / $3.95
B199	OE, KENZABURO / A Personal Matter / $3.95

E672	SOPA, GESHE LHUNDUP and HOPKINS, JEFFREY / The Practice and Theory of Tibetan Buddhism / $4.95
B433	SAUNERON, SERGE / The Priests of Ancient Egypt / $3.50
E395	SHATTUCK, ROGER, and TAYLOR, SIMON WATSON, eds. / Selected Works of Alfred Jarry / $6.95
E684	STOPPARD, TOM / Dirty Linen and New-Found-Land / $2.95
E703	STOPPARD, TOM / Every Good Boy Deserves Favor and Professional Foul: Two Plays / $3.95
E489	STOPPARD, TOM / The Real Inspector Hound and After Magritte: Two Plays / $3.95
B319	STOPPARD, TOM / Rosencrantz and Guildenstern Are Dead / $2.25
E341	SUZUKI, D. T. / Introduction to Zen Buddhism / $1.95
E231	SUZUKI, D. T. / Manual of Zen Buddhism / $3.95
E749	THELWELL, MICHAEL / The Harder They Come / $7.95
B432	TROCCHI, ALEXANDER / Cain's Book / $3.50
E658	TRUFFAUT, FRANCOIS / Day for Night / $3.95
B399	TRUFFAUT, FRANCOIS / Small Change / $1.95
B395	TRUFFAUT, FRANCOIS / The Story of Adele H / $2.45
E699	TURGENEV, IVAN / Virgin Soil / $3.95
E328	TUTUOLA, AMOS / The Palm-Wine Drunkard / $2.45
E559	TUTUOLA, AMOS / My Life in the Bush of Ghosts / $4.95
E746	VITHOULKAS, GEORGE / The Science of Homeopathy / $9.50
E209	WALEY, ARTHUR, JR. / The Book of Songs / $5.95
E84	WALEY, ARTHUR / The Way and Its Power: A Study of the Tao Te Ching and its Place in Chinese Thought / $4.95
E689	WALKENSTEIN, EILEEN / Don't Shrink to Fit! A Confrontation With Dehumanization in Psychiatry and Psychology / $3.95
E579	WARNER, LANGDON / The Enduring Art of Japan / $4.95
B365	WARNER, SAMUEL J. / Self Realization and Self Defeat / $2.95
E219	WATTS, ALAN W. / The Spirit of Zen / $2.95
E112	WU, CH'ENG-EN / Monkey / $4.95
E767	WYCKOFF, HOGIE / Solving Problems Together / $7.95
B106	YU, LI / Jou Pu Tuan / $1.95

GROVE PRESS, INC., 196 West Houston St., New York, N.Y. 10014